A PAGE MARKED FOR MURDER

"When you did discover the book missing?" Detective Brookes asked. "Anything jump out at you then?"

"No, I made the assumption that Martha had second thoughts and either took it when we were packing the bag or went back for it," Addie said.

"Martha, the same person we're holding on suspicion of murder?"

Addie's gaze dropped. She knew full well that any kind of emotional appeal to this woman would be a waste of breath. Detective Ryley Brookes was all evidence-based in her investigations, and Addie couldn't argue with the evidence. Martha was seen having two public squabbles with the victim, who had a rocky history with Martha's youngest daughter, and the body was discovered behind Martha's bakery. However, Ryley's flippant attitude regarding the missing book was another thing. This was something Addie could press.

"Look, I know that you'd like nothing better than to think of this as just a misplaced children's book, and it will turn up at some point. But I'm convinced, because of the worth of this book, that something else is going on here. . . ."

Books by Lauren Elliott

MURDER BY THE BOOK

PROLOGUE TO MURDER

MURDER IN THE FIRST EDITION

PROOF OF MURDER

A PAGE MARKED FOR MURDER

Published by Kensington Publishing Corp.

A *Beyond the Page Bookstore Mystery*

A PAGE MARKED FOR MURDER

Lauren Elliott

KENSINGTON BOOKS
KENSINGTON PUBLISHING CORP.
www.kensingtonbooks.com

KENSINGTON BOOKS are published by

Kensington Publishing Corp.
119 West 40th Street
New York, NY 10018

All Kensington titles, imprints, and distributed lines are available at special quantity discounts for bulk purchases for sales promotion, premiums, fund-raising, educational, or institutional use.

Special book excerpts or customized printings can also be created to fit specific needs. For details, write or phone the office of the Kensington Sales Manager: Attn.: Sales Department. Kensington Publishing Corp., 119 West 40th Street, New York, NY 10018. Phone: 1-800-221-2647.

Kensington and the K logo Reg. U.S. Pat. & TM Off.

First Printing: November 2020
ISBN-13: 978-1-4967-2711-4
ISBN-10: 1-4967-2711-8

ISBN-13: 978-1-4967-2712-1 (eBook)
ISBN-10: 1-4967-2712-6 (eBook)

10 9 8 7 6 5 4 3 2 1

Printed in the United States of America

Chapter One

Addison Greyborne heaved her hip against the front door of Beyond the Page, her book and curio shop, to open it, and skittered through. As it began to close back on her, she clasped the box in her arms tighter to her chest and zigzagged around the wooden edge of the door. A wind gust slammed it shut behind her. She exhaled a sigh of relief—disaster avoided.

Or was it?

Another gust of wind kicked up a mini-cyclone of snow. It danced across her face, blinding her, sucking at her breath. She staggered forward and gasped. The air, heavy with the scent of wood smoke, caught in the back of her throat—a reminder of the well-stoked fireplaces residents of Greyborne Harbor used in their latest arsenal to ward off the bone-chilling cold of the past weeks. When the mini–snow twister passed, she glanced down at her cherished cargo still fully intact and smiled weakly.

Was it her imagination or did the briny tang of the wind gusts off the ocean seem warmer this morning than they'd had in weeks? She glanced at the sky. If the rays of sunshine peeking through the low-hanging clouds were any indication that the storm had finally changed course, just maybe the Fire and Ice Festival planned for the upcoming weekend would be a success after all.

Addie slid the last box of Christmas decorations from her bookstore into her Mini Cooper and closed the back hatch. Thoughts of the weekend ahead played on her mind as she eyed the now barren window displays of her bookshop.

It was already Friday, and she needed to come up with a plan fast. It was always tough for her to think up a window decoration concept to complement the Fire and Ice Festival since the event came on the heels of the Christmas season and lasted only one weekend—the one leading up to the twelfth day after Christmas.

She never really knew what to do to depict Greyborne Harbor's version of the celebration of Epiphany, or as some residents call it, the Feast of the Three Kings. A number of towns honored the twelfth day—which had been celebrated in Europe since before the Middle Ages—by holding community potluck dinners and dances, food festivals, or as Greyborne Harbor did at the end of the weekend—with a Christmas tree bonfire on the beach. However they chose to mark the day, it was their way of celebrating the old-world tradition of taking down the Christmas tree.

Greyborne Harbor had opted years ago—under the direction of Addie's great-aunt Anita, the woman whom she inherited her three-story Victorian home from—to incorporate a weekend ice carving festival along with the long-standing town tradition of the twelfth day Christmas tree burning.

Her aunt, who spent many years traveling the world and collecting books and mementos, many of which Addie still held in reverence, had made a trip to the Québec City Winter Carnival. It was said that she had been so taken by the craftsmanship and beauty of the ice sculptures she'd seen, that it didn't take her long to convince the town council to add an ice sculpture competition to the two days leading up to the bonfire.

According to Addie's friends, the event had grown over the years not only in the number of carving teams registering to participate, but also in the increased tourist traffic drawn to the spectacular display of ice sculptures. Addie knew her windows would have to appeal to both contestants and fans, and that was the tricky part—creating an all-encompassing design.

She stood in front of the window wracking her brain to come up with something new that she hadn't attempted in the previous two years. She hated the thought of letting the town or her late aunt down. So today, creating something magical would have to be her top priority.

Paige Stringer, Addie's shop assistant, poked her blond head out the door. She took one look at the patches of blue sky, giggled like a schoolgirl, and then scampered outside, dragging the small Christmas tree from the bookstore behind her. She promptly dropped it at the curb. After brushing off her hands, she stood, her pale face turned toward the intermittent shafts of light. Addie couldn't suppress her urge to laugh. Paige looked exactly like her mother Martha's cat when she sunned herself in the window of the house Paige and her young daughter, Emma, shared with Martha Stringer.

"What?" Paige shielded her eyes and squinted at Addie.

"Nothing." Addie gave a husky laugh. "I was just thinking of how much you looked like Cleo right now." Addie ruffled her hand through Paige's curly hair.

Paige scoffed at Addie, obviously not impressed with being compared to her mother's indolent cat. "But speaking of my mother," she said, lowering her voice and glancing at the bakery window, "I can't believe the nerve of her dropping her store tree at the curb in front of *your* shop."

Addie eyed the pile of trees at the curbside where volunteers would pick them up today or tomorrow to take down to the beach for the tree burning on Sunday. "I think the culprit who started it was, in fact, Serena. That one on the bottom looks suspiciously like the one she had in SerenaTEA."

"Couldn't the pile have been in front of *her* store?"

Addie shrugged. "When I figure out what goes on in that cute little red head of hers, you'll be the first to know."

"I think she has a bad case of *wedding-planning fever of the brain*."

"I know. Last week I went into her shop to buy a tea, and she was standing at the counter, looking lost in another world. When I glanced down at what she was writing on an order pad, I saw she had written 'Serena Chandler' and then crossed it out and doodled 'Mrs. Zach Ludlow' over the entire page. I'm thinking the next few months leading up to the wedding might be tough on all of us." Addie chuckled. "But we have to deal with the here and now, and right now I need your help brainstorming what we should do with these windows for the festival *this* weekend."

"Sure, what are you thinking?" Paige asked, sliding up to Addie's side as the two stared into the bleak abyss of what, not long ago, had held cheery fairy lights and an array of colorful Christmas decorations.

"Did you manage to place the order last week with our book distributor?"

"Yes," Paige said, "and the shipment should be here this morning. I think I ordered at least one copy of each book in the catalogue that had *anything* to do with the history of ice carving, sculpture design ideas, or patterns, so we're covered there."

"See?" Addie said, clapping Paige on the back. "That's exactly why I made you the assistant manager."

"I try," she said with a wide grin, her cheeks unmistakably rosier now than they had been earlier. "So, that takes care of the nonfiction. What about the fiction display?"

"As far as the books go, we might as well do what we've done the last two years and showcase any and all books with a winter theme."

"Yeah, that's what I was thinking. I already put aside Boris Pasternak's *Doctor Zhivago*, and guess what? It's the original 1957 edition."

"Excellent, we have one or two regular customers who might be fighting over that one."

"Should we call Edna or George beforehand and let them know we have it or wait and see if they discover it on their own?"

"Ooh, I like that idea. That way, we're not appearing to play favorites."

"I know." Paige snapped her fingers. "We can give them little clues each time they stop in, and then the first one to find it wins the prize—that will be hiding in plain sight—front and center in the window." Paige's petite body shook with laughter.

"We'll need to insert a couple of red herrings into the mix to tease them." Addie grinned, glancing sideways at Paige. "What about that 1931, US publisher's edition of Agatha Christie's *The Murder at Hazelmoor*? Do we still have that?"

"No, we sold that one, but a copy of it by the UK publisher came in just before Christmas. I think it's still in the back room."

"That's the one with her original title, isn't it? Before the US publisher changed the name?"

"Yeah, it's called *The Sittaford Mystery.* I'll make sure we display it, too."

"Perfect, it might even be more attractive to Edna, and that way they both win. But getting back to the display in general, I think I also saw a later edition of *The Snow Queen* by Hans Christian Andersen in the children's books that would work in the showcase, too."

"Okay, I'll start pulling any books that have a winter theme or snowy cover. What about the decorations? What are you planning for the diorama?"

"I have no idea. I'd like to have one window display the concept of ice, for the sculptor competition, especially since our little festival has recently been recognized by the National Ice Carving Association. And the other window should represent the grand finale to the weekend with the annual Christmas tree burning. But I'm at a loss."

"Ooh-ooh, I know. In the fire window we can showcase books like Dan Brown's *Inferno,* and then the winter-themed ones in the ice window."

"That sounds good." Addie hoped her disappointment

didn't show on her face or in her voice as she was hoping to come up with something a bit different this year. She glanced from one window to the other. "Yeah, I guess we'll have to stick to the tried and true. We really don't have any decorations that I can think of that would make it the magical winter wonderland I had in mind."

"Wait a minute," Paige said, looking at her. "What about that small solar garden lighthouse you picked up at the end of last summer when you and Simon went to the medical convention in Boston?"

Addie's pulse quickened. "I forgot all about that. It would be perfect in that far window." She pointed to the left of the door. "We could make a little campfire scene on a rocky shoreline to depict the tree burning on Sunday down by the lighthouse. Then some of the miniature Victorian village Christmas ornaments I just packed up, like the Christmas trees, could be stacked in piles beside it." Addie giddily clapped her hands. "We could add the Dickens village gaslight lampposts along with the ornamental wooden garden bench I bought at the same time as the lighthouse. Well, it's ideal to represent the ice carving displays in the park in this window. Plus that garden bench is the perfect size to display a few books on."

"Yeah, and we can leave the fake snow mat in place until next week when we'll have to come up with a new idea."

"Yup, but one celebration at a time," Addie said, standing back, her gaze darting from one window to the other. "I can see it now, and it'll be the ideal representation of the Fire and Ice Festival," Addie said excitedly. "I have another idea! At home I have a copy of the 1924 edition of Robert Frost's Pulitzer Prize–winning volume of poems,

New Hampshire. We could use a couple of those cute little bookmark clips we have and open the page to Frost's 'Fire and Ice' poem and display it on the garden bench. What do you think?"

"Perfect! I think we have a plan, then." Paige's face lit up in a smile that reached her sparkling blue eyes. "And I know exactly where that box with the lighthouse and the small garden bench is. I'll haul it out of the back room and get to work."

"Excellent, and make sure Kalea gives you a hand pulling the books we'll need."

"What, and risk her breaking a nail?" Paige stopped her hand on the door handle. "I think I'd rather do it all myself than have to listen to your cousin, the high and mighty Miss Hudson, complain for the rest of the day."

"Come on, Paige. You're *her* manager, remember? Just ask for her help, and I'm sure she'll get the message."

Paige raised her brow. "What message would that be?"

"That to collect a paycheck one has to actually work for it." Addie's words brought a chorus of laughter from both women as Paige headed back into the bookstore.

Addie shook her head. She knew she was going to have to speak to her cousin and soon. She had avoided having *the talk* through the holidays so as not to put a damper on the season, but if Paige was feeling frustrated enough to say *anything* to Addie about Kalea's lack of enthusiasm for work, it was clearly time for Addie to put her foot down and stop her cousin's prima donna non-sense. Addie had taken one more fleeting look at the empty window and started for her shop door when raised voices behind her brought her to a halt. She swiveled around as two men came out of the door to Martha's Bakery, vying for dominance over the narrow opening.

"I said back off." The taller, dark-haired man elbowed the shorter, gray-haired man, whose return jab indicated he had no intention of stepping aside.

"I told you to stay away," the gray-haired man shouted back at him. "But you just couldn't listen, could you? Now see what you've done."

The taller of the two staggered out onto the sidewalk, shoved his hands in his navy-blue, puffy jacket pockets, and stomped across the street to the park. The shorter man thrust his hands into his pockets with such force that Addie feared he had torn clear through the seams of his black wool peacoat. He huffed out a deep breath, turned abruptly, and marched off toward Main Street. Addie spotted Martha through the bakery window as Martha reached over the snowy landscape backdrop she had for the gingerbread castle displayed through Christmas, snatched the last gingerbread man from what once was a full display, and bit its head off. Martha spied Addie, took another bite, and grinned at her.

The look of deep satisfaction on Martha's face said it all, and Addie was unable to stop the laugh that bubbled out as she remembered her own experiences with biting the heads off gingerbread men a year ago. Still smiling, Addie reached for the door handle to Beyond the Page, but a soft whimpering sound stopped her. She glanced around and saw nothing of concern. She shrugged, grasped the handle, and then danced a step backward. Nudged against her boot was a miniature Yorkipoo. She cocked her head at book club member Gloria McBride's little dog, its tricolored body shaking violently against Addie's leg.

"Pippi, what on earth are you doing here," Addie cried, scooping her up in her arms. "Where's your mommy?" Addie glanced up and down the street and over to the park entrance, expecting to see a beaming Gloria. "Or did you come to pay me a visit without her knowing?" Addie half-heartedly scolded and then laughed as she snuggled the small dog into the crook of her arm. With one eye on the trembling dog and another peeled for Gloria, Addie paced back and forth in front of her shop—certain that at any moment, the doting woman would frantically run out of one of the stores along the street in search of her baby.

"What's wrong?" Martha called from her bakery door.

Addie wheeled around. "Pippi seems to be lost."

"Impossible." Martha harrumphed, pulled her jacket tight around the collar, and joined Addie on the sidewalk. "That woman never lets this dog out of her sight."

"I was just thinking the same thing, but I don't see Gloria anywhere, do you?"

Martha scanned the street in both directions and looked at Addie. Her eyes echoed what Addie felt in the pit of her stomach, and then they both jumped at the sound of shouting coming from the park across the road.

"Oh no," Martha cried, clutching her ample chest. "I have a bad feeling about this."

"Me too." Addie grabbed Martha's jacket sleeve. "Come on."

The two women bolted in the direction of the uproar. With Pippi clutched in her arms, Addie pushed her way through the crowd formed around the side of the gazebo. When she neared the center of the group of event decoration volunteers, her eyes filled with tears. There, lying in a heap on the snow-covered ground, was Gloria. The little basket she carried Pippi in when she worked was crushed beneath her. Beside her was a tipped-over stepladder butted up against her leg, which was severely twisted at an unnatural angle.

Chapter Two

"I know you're worried about your mom," Addie whispered into the small dog's ear, and tightened her arms around it as she resumed her pacing on the hospital sidewalk. "But she's in good hands. Doctor Emerson's taking care of her. You remember my good friend Simon, don't you? He's the one you thought was a vet because of the hospital smell." Addie chuckled and rumpled the fur on the back of Pippi's neck. "I know she's going to be okay. I just know it." Tears burned behind Addie's eyes. "Simon will make sure. He's the best doctor on the whole darn East Coast," she said, more as reassurance to herself than the small dog.

"Addie?"

"Simon," she cried, dashing toward him as he stepped through the hospital sliding-glass door.

"Hi there, both of you," he said with a chuckle as he wrapped his arms around her in a watchful hug so as not to squeeze the warm little body between them. "Martha told me you were out here somewhere with Pippi because of the no-animal policy in the emergency department, and you were gracious enough to let Martha be inside with her friend."

"Yeah." Addie reeled at the thought of being beholden to Martha and waved off his accolades. "How is Gloria?" she said, searching his blue eyes for a sign, any sign, that everything was all right. "She didn't break her hip, right? She's going to be okay?"

"I really don't know if there are any fractures at this point." His voice had a hollow ring to it, giving Addie a hint as to how busy his shift had been. When he raked his hand through his black hair, leaving small tufts in its wake, she stood on tiptoes and smoothed it for him.

"But the X-ray must show something, right?"

"It was partially dislocated for sure, and that's been reduced now and set back in place, but she's pretty groggy from the medication she had to have for the reduction, so I haven't been able to do a full post-procedural assessment yet."

"But she's okay now. You fixed it, right?"

"It's hard to say. There's always the risk of small fractures or bone chips that an X-ray won't pick up, especially in that area. So I'm going to run an MRI to check for ligament and cartilage damage, too."

"What does that mean?"

"That means given her age and medical history, I'm concerned and want to make sure there's nothing else going on."

"Like what?" Her voice teetered on panic.

"Like"—he palmed his hand down his drawn face—"we'll need to monitor the blood flow in the area and make sure the vessels are nourishing the bone properly."

Addie pulled her precious cargo closer and kissed the

top of the furry little head. "So what does that mean for, well . . . Pippi?"

Simon scratched behind the dog's perked ear. "This little girl is going to need a foster mom for a while yet." He looked at Addie, a mischievous glint in his eyes.

"Me? No, I've never owned a dog in my life. I wouldn't have a clue what to do."

A wry smile pinched at the corners of his mouth. "It's already been decided. She's to stay with you."

"What? Who decided?"

"Gloria and Martha have it all worked out, or I suppose I should say, Martha does. Since Gloria is a little blitzed on pain medication right now, she will agree to anything Martha suggests, but don't worry, it's all worked out." His eyes sparkled as if he were taking great enjoyment in tormenting Addie with the fact that Martha was making decisions for her.

She wrinkled up her nose, and he kissed it.

"I've got to get back inside. Martha should be out in a few minutes. They're just looking for Gloria's keys, so I'll let her fill you in on the details of their plan." He gave her a sly wink and disappeared back inside through the sliding door.

"So, I'm to be a dog person now, am I?" Pippi wiggled in her arms, her pink tongue lapping at the air as if she were trying to kiss Addie's face. "I just hope we both survive this." Addie flashed the dog a feeble smile. "But I'd better text Paige and Kalea and let them know what's going on." Addie shifted Pippi in her arm and fished her phone out of her handbag. She'd just finished shooting off the text when Martha's white head popped up in front of her.

"I suppose Simon told you that she's going to be here at least a few days?"

"Um, yeah, he mentioned he wants to run more tests, but that's about all he said?"

"Well, it looks like as long as those turn out clear, she'll only have to stay a couple of days, but . . . if they show any chipping or damage around the socket, then it means a hip replacement."

"Oh dear, he never told me that." Addie glanced down at Pippi, knowing this meant she could well be a foster mom for a long while yet.

"I told Gloria I'd go to her place and pack a bag for her. You might as well come with me to get what you'll need for the princess here."

"Yeah, I guess I'll need dog food, won't I?"

Martha's laugh was sudden and short but enough to engage her dimply cheeks. "Yes, among a few other things." She patted Pippi's head. "This little one is spoiled rotten. I know because I've looked after her before."

"Then here"—Addie held the little dog out—"you're probably more qualified to look after her than I am."

A look of horror filled Martha's faded-blue eyes as she scrambled backward, almost tripping when she stepped into a snow rut. "No, no, I have Cleo now, and she's not partial to dogs. Gloria and I got it all figured out. You look after Pippi because she likes you"—as if on cue, Pippi licked Addie's hand—"see, and I'll pack an overnight bag for Gloria and bring it back."

"Martha, really, I've never had a dog in my whole life. Surely she has other friends that could take her? What about Ida from the book club, they're friends, or Mildred, the owner of the Emporium on Main?"

"Nope, all her friends are cat people too, and don't

want to have to break up any dog and cat fights any more than I do. Because the problem is Pippi wants to be friends with all furry creatures, but those furry creatures . . . well . . . they're not always so obliging."

"But there must be someone who's more qualified?"

"The only person would be Gloria's cousin."

"Then let's call her."

"She lives in Arizona. If you don't take her, she's going to a boarding kennel."

Addie's chest ached at the thought. "We can't let that happen," she said, and stroked the small dog's back.

"No, we can't. Like I said, we've decided, and you're the best solution." Martha waved off Addie's look of concern. "You'll be fine."

Addie gulped. "If you think it's for the best." Addie glanced hesitantly down at her new roommate.

"I do," Martha said, whirled around, and headed off in the direction of the bakery. "I'll go get my car. You wait here," she called back over her shoulder.

Addie collapsed on the bench behind her. "I really hope we survive this, girl." She kneaded her fingers through the dog's silky soft hairs. Her text alert pinged, and Addie grabbed her phone out of her bag as Pippi made herself at home on her lap. Addie shifted on her hip as not to send her little friend plummeting to the ground and glanced down at Paige's message.

I would tell Kalea you've been delayed, but she went out to get tea over an hour ago and hasn't come back!

What! Addie's thumbs flew across the keypad. Where did she go for tea, Boston Harbor?

HarHarHar!!! I just sent a text to Serena and told her to send our wayward employee back this way. She said she hasn't been in there this morning???

"Not again," Addie groaned. Well, she is good at pulling off a disappearing act. Okay, I'll see if I can track her down. Thanks ☺ Love you! ♥

Addie shoved her phone back in her bag and absently patted the warm fur ball asleep on her lap. "Kalea, Kalea, Kalea, what are you pulling this time?"

Addie jerked at the sound of a car horn and glanced over to see Martha waving frantically at her from behind the wheel of her older-model blue Ford Taurus. She rolled down the window and called, "Hurry up. We have to make a stop at my house first."

Addie scooped up Pippi, settled her in the crook of her arm, and hopped into the front seat. "Why? What's wrong at home?"

"Nothing, but I have to pick up the key I have from Gloria's last trip to Europe. She had me take in the mail and keep an eye on the place. I always do it when she's off on one of her adventures."

"Simon said she was giving you her keys when he left to come and talk to me."

"She couldn't find them in her pockets. They must have fallen out when she fell off the ladder." Martha checked over her shoulder and pulled out onto Main Street. "I told her we would stop by the park and look for them. I'm sure they're just lying in the snow somewhere, or maybe one of the other decorating committee volunteers picked them up for her."

"Yeah, there were a lot of people milling around by

the time we got to her. I'm sure someone has them for safekeeping."

A few minutes later Martha pulled alongside the curb in front of her two-story Dutch Colonial, reminiscent of something out of a storybook, and power walked her short legs up the sidewalk. Addie cringed when Martha, legs straddled, stepped over a snowdrift across the pathway. All they needed was another hip injury, and she made a mental note to speak to Paige about taking over the chore of clearing the walkway. She needed a subtle way to remind her that in spite of her mother's seemingly good health, Martha was starting to creep up in years. However, before Addie could unfasten her seat belt and get out to assist Martha on the apparently slippery walkway for her return trip, the woman plopped back in the driver's seat, and they were off toward Gloria's house.

Addie glanced over at the white-haired woman beside her and smiled to herself. Never in a million years would she have imagined that this sense of camaraderie would ever exist between her and her onetime adversary. The change seemed to have come about not long after Paige and her little girl took Martha up on her offer to move into the family home with her. She was a lot less surly now, for the most part, and it felt good to know that her and Martha's once-turbulent relationship was in the past—like so many of Addie's darkest memories. Addie wanted to reach over and hug the woman but knew that would be pushing it a bit far, so she settled on smiling to herself and staring out the window.

Addie stomped clumps of snow off her boots on the carpet in the front entryway and smiled. Not only was the exterior of Gloria's Craftsman-style bungalow inviting with its pillared porch front, but the sense of hominess also continued through the front door and beyond. The house was a perfect reflection of the woman who lived here. A soft, subtle scent of sandalwood teased her nose as Addie hung up her jacket on the coatrack, poked her head around a square, wooden pillar, and scanned the living room. Every built-in nook and cranny was filled with treasures the travel agent had collected on her exotic adventures. It made Addie wonder if Gloria and her late aunt had shared stories of their respective travels in Aunt Anita's final days.

"Pippi probably needs to go outside," Martha called over her shoulder as she headed down the hallway to what Addie assumed was Gloria's bedroom. "The yard's fenced, so just let her out the back door while we gather up what we need."

"A fenced yard?" Horror surged through Addie, and she peered down at the wiggling bundle of fur in her arms. "Oh no, Martha. My yard isn't fenced. What am I going to do?"

The echoes of Martha's merry hoots traveled down the hallway, but Addie couldn't see the humor in what she had just confessed. "I mean it, Martha," she said, heading in the direction of the laughter. "My yard is wide open, and the back garden drops off at the edge of a cliff. I can't possibly keep Pippi at my house, can I? She wouldn't be safe. What if she got lost or . . . worse? How could I ever explain that to Gloria?"

"Relax." Martha poked her head out of a doorway. "Gloria has a portable dog run. I used to have to use it when I took care of Pippi. It's in my garage. I'll have Paige drop it off later." Her white mop of hair still shaking with her laughter disappeared back into the room. "The dog food's in the pantry cupboard in the kitchen, and I think I saw her toys and bed in the living room."

Addie heaved out a deep breath and glanced down at Pippi, who was wiggling like a worm on a hook by now. "Yup, better get you outside, hey girl." She made her way through the living room and attached dining room to the rear door and released the squirming little dog. Pippi raced over to a relatively snow-free corner of the large garden, did her business, and then dove headfirst into a bank of fresh snow, coming out the other side looking like an Abominable Snowdog.

Obviously, it was playtime, and Addie couldn't blame her. She'd spent the last few hours locked in Addie's arms and was no doubt feeling confined. Addie closed the door and set about searching through cupboards until she found the bag of dog food and a box of treats. Martha had mentioned a bed and toys, so the hunt was on for those. She really had no idea what a dog toy looked like but assumed since Gloria had no children, it would be anything not displayed on her shelves or tables. Although when Pippi whined to get in, she showed her superb tracking skills and managed to find every doggy toy and stuffed animal she had stashed away in the living area.

Addie took one more glance around the room to make sure they hadn't missed anything, and her gaze landed on a photo album lying open on the coffee table. She made her way closer and recognized the three shining schoolgirl faces of Martha, Gloria, and Ida—sitting alongside a striking blond-haired young man. There was something familiar about his eyes, but she couldn't place him. A smile tugged at Addie's lips as she gazed down at the three young women, their arms draped over each other's shoulders, grinning from ear to ear, and the man seemingly enjoying the company of three such beauties.

"What are you looking at?"

Addie jumped. She hadn't heard Martha come up behind her. "I just saw this, and I can't believe it. What were you guys in? High school?"

"Yeah, we were best friends even then." Martha's eyes glistened in the daylight streaming in through the window, and she dabbed at her nose.

"I had no idea you and Gloria have been friends all these years."

Martha shrugged. "Small towns are like that. I guess unless someone moves away or . . ."

"Or what?" Addie looked from her back to the picture.

"Or you marry the guy in that picture, and he breaks your heart and leaves you on your own with five little girls," she snapped, and turned away.

Addie stared hard at the photo, and then glanced back at Martha, who had dug a tissue out of her purse and was wiping her cheek. "Is that your ex?"

"Yeah, that's the infamous Ken Stringer," Martha said, dabbing at her eyes.

"Why does he look familiar to me?"

"He's one of the men you saw come out of my shop this morning," she choked, and blew her nose.

Ah, the reason for the decapitated gingerbread man. Now Addie understood.

"I'll be back in a minute." Martha swiveled around and bolted down the hallway.

Oh dear. A knot in Addie's stomach tightened. She had really stepped in doo-doo this time. The last thing she wanted was to upset Martha by asking about an old photograph. She bounded up the hall behind her and stopped when she found Martha sitting on the bed in Gloria's room, tears streaming down her apple cheeks. "I'm sorry, Martha. I didn't mean to say anything to upset—"

"I'm fine," Martha said, waving her tissue in the air and drawing herself up stiffly. She rose to her feet. "I think I have everything Gloria will need in the hospital. We should go."

The knot in Addie's stomach felt more like a sinking rock now. "Okay." Her gaze rested on a book lying open on the nightstand. "Should we take that? She might enjoy reading while she recovers."

"Nah, she's too doped up right now, and if she has surgery, she'll be even worse for a while. Pretty sure if that happens, she'll send me back with another list next week anyway, so I'll get it then."

"Okay, you know her best." Addie's gaze remained on the book as she moved closer to the night table. "Say, isn't that a copy of *The Secret Garden* by Frances Hodgson Burnett?"

Martha glanced at it. "Yeah, it's Paige's. She loaned it to her when Gloria told her it was the book your little club was reviewing this month."

Addie caressed the green cloth, her fingers tracing over the gilt title and illustration on the upper board of the cover. She flipped open the title page, and her breath caught in her throat. "You say this is Paige's copy?"

"Yes," Martha said, hauling a small suitcase off the bed. "Why?"

"Does Paige know it's a 1911 first edition?"

"I don't know. It's just some old book her useless father left her when he ran away from us when she was about three."

"Martha"—Addie snapped her mouth shut and stared at the woman—"this old book is worth about twenty-five thousand dollars."

"What?" Martha's hand flew to her chest.

Addie feared the older woman would keel over right then and there.

Chapter Three

"Jeez Louise!" Martha snapped off her phone and jammed the car key into the ignition. "My useless assistant, Betty, has really gone and done it this time," Martha ranted as she pulled away from the curb in front of Gloria's house. "If I had a nickel for every time—"

"Betty? I thought your assistant baker was Glenda?"

"What? No, she was three assistants ago. Keep up, girl." Martha snorted a short, harsh laugh and turned onto Main Street. "And it seems this one's going to make number four, as in past tense."

"Why? What happened?"

"She's gone and started a fire in one of the ovens. Can you believe that?"

"Oh no, is the fire department there? What about Paige and the bookstore—"

"Don't worry. Betty said she put it out, but the place is filled with smoke. I'll have to drop you off at the hospital and get back there to see what damage that fool caused this time."

"This time?"

"Yeah, it's not her first catastrophe but definitely the

last one." Martha stopped in front of the hospital entrance. "I'll take Pippi to Paige at the bookstore, and you go in and give Gloria her suitcase. You're going to have to hoof it back though, I'm afraid."

Addie, still trying to digest the flurry of information Martha had thrown at her, handed the small dog to Martha, got out, grabbed the suitcase from the back seat, and stood flabbergasted on the sidewalk as Martha pulled away. "Well then. That was interesting," she muttered, and entered through the hospital's main door. She located Gloria still in the emergency department, apparently waiting for a room upstairs, sound asleep in one of the side cubicles. Addie searched for a nurse to leave the bag with, but they all appeared to be busy with other patients, and Simon was nowhere in sight. She hesitated. Should she or shouldn't she just leave the bag unattended at Gloria's bedside?

Addie shook her head. What bizarre alternative universe had she woken up in this morning, because nothing about today resembled normal. Wherever it was, it was affecting her ability to make even the most minor decisions. How on earth had she let Martha persuade her to foster a dog? It's not that Addie disliked animals, but she had never had a pet in her entire life, not even a goldfish. Knowing she would be responsible for another life—well, frankly, it terrified her. Now here she was unable to decide what she should do or not do about a stupid suitcase.

She dropped the bag on the bedside chair and tiptoed away from Gloria's cubicle with the hope of not waking her. There was no way she could hide how overwhelmed she felt. That alone would give Gloria more cause to worry. No, Pippi and she would be fine. Somehow she'd find a way to make it work, and that was the mantra she repeated to herself as she headed to the park behind the hospital. Maybe the walk to her shop was just the thing she needed to help her regain focus and come back to earth.

Once outside under the first crystal-blue sky Greyborne Harbor had seen in weeks, her brain fog began to lift. Her jaunt through the park seemed to be the best decision she had made so far today even though it was, once again, made by Martha. However, it was exactly what she needed. Not only did it help clear her head, but it also allowed her a few minutes to search for Gloria's missing keys. No doubt finding those would help ease the poor woman's mind. She had enough other stuff to worry about.

Much to Addie's surprise, the park was buzzing with activity. The decorating committee was hard at work dismantling the Christmas displays and exchanging them for festival decorations, which included banners depicting past winning sculptures and winter carnival activities. The thirty or so teams of two sculptors were also setting up their assigned carving stations. They would guard these posts until after the final judging of the competition on Sunday evening when the winner in each category—novice, intermediate, and master sculptor—would be announced. These seasoned carvers took their craft very seriously, and none would risk vandalism or jealous sabotage of their creations. At this point, there were only blocks of ice, many of which were draped in tarps to protect them from the sun's heating rays. But soon the competition would officially begin, and that was when the magic of true artistry would take shape.

Addie sidestepped a group of volunteers deep in discussion of which lights and decorations should remain around the gazebo eaves for the ice festival. The sun's reflection off the glistening snow had Addie wondering where she had left her sunglasses as she shaded her eyes and squinted up to the top of a ladder.

"Hi, Cliff." She waved to Gloria's most diehard committee volunteer.

"Hi, Addie," he called, allowing a Christmas banner to fall through his hands and drop to the ground, sending up a flurry of snowflakes in its wake. "How's Gloria doing?" he asked as he descended to the bottom.

"She's okay and resting right now."

"What about her little doggy? Is she okay?"

"Yeah, Pippi's just fine. I have her. Say, she wasn't up on the ladder with Gloria when it happened, was she?"

"No, Gloria leaves her at the bottom in her basket when she has to go up."

"I guess that's something to be thankful for."

"Except that little basket was crushed like a pancake underneath Gloria. I've been just sick thinking about what could have happened."

"It sounds like Pippi escaped it just in time."

Cliff nodded. "Pretty sure there were only seconds between the scream and the thud."

"Wow, in all the confusion around her, the poor little thing must have panicked. At least she managed to remember that I've walked her in the park and how to get to my store from here because she came running right to me."

"That's a relief, because that little dog is Gloria's whole life, and I don't know how she'd handle it if something ever happened to her, especially if she was responsible," Cliff said, folding the ladder legs together. "Well, I guess I should see what those"—he jerked his head toward the group still in discussion—"have decided to do about the gazebo. No one has the vision Gloria has, and everyone's running around like chickens with no heads right now." He hoisted the ladder under his arm and started toward them.

"Wait, Cliff," Addie called. "Did you happen to find Gloria's keys after the accident? They seem to have dropped out of her pocket."

He shook his head. "Can't say as I did, but I wasn't the first on the scene. I was over on the other side of the gazebo when I heard the scream and the thump. By the time I got around here, there was a crowd surrounding her." He shrugged.

"Maybe someone picked them up for her?"

"Maybe. I'll ask around and keep my eyes open though."

"That'd be great, thanks."

"Heigh-ho, Heigh-ho, it's back to work I go!" he sang as he waved over his shoulder and then plunked the ladder down in front of the group of volunteers.

Addie's gaze dropped to the trampled snow piles where the indentations of the feet of the ladder were and scanned the snow. She kicked up clumps here and there, gradually enlarging her search circle until she wasn't far from the utility shed behind the library, and she still found nothing.

Not far from her was the taller man in the navy-blue jacket from Martha's Bakery talking to a dark-haired man in a trim-cut black trench coat. With the crowd of people milling around the park today, Addie normally wouldn't have thought twice about them, but she heard their raised voices over the din of chatter behind her. They definitely drew her attention. She put her money on Trench Coat Guy being one of the organizers because she was certain she had seen him before, and Bakery Man was most likely a disgruntled contestant.

She shrugged and made a mental note to ask Martha who Ken left the bakery with this morning. Their rapid-fire discussion piqued her curiosity, and she wanted to know if her instincts were right, or if she had lost those in the parallel universe she was floating through today. She shoved her hands in her pockets and headed toward the park entrance across the road from her shop.

When she got to the big maple tree by the side entrance, her heart lurched at the sight of Old Bill wearing what was obviously a charity donation navy-blue parka, at least two sizes too big for his meager frame, combing through a trash can. He was a local homeless man, and someone whom Addie had gotten to know a little as he often frequented the bin behind Martha's shop. However, the last time she had run into him, he told her not to worry anymore, that he had gotten a bed for the winter at one of the shelters. Yet, here he was, armpit deep into a trash can again. Her heart ached.

"Good afternoon, Bill." She waved. "I thought you were living at the church shelter down in the harbor area now?"

Bill stopped and stared at her over the rim of the trash can. His eyes peered out of his red-splotched, weather-etched face. "Afternoon, Miss Addie." He nervously pulled his arm out of the bin, stood upright, and shifted his weight from one foot to the other. A sheepish look crossed his face. "Yeah, it's just that, well . . ."

"I hope you understand that I was serious when I told you to come to me when you're hungry, and I'll make sure—"

"Oh, I know. You and Miss Martha have both been good to me. It's not that."

"Then what is it?"

"It's just that—" He shuffled his oversize thrift store boots in the snow. "It's that during a festival, there's always good pick'ns, and well . . ." A shy smile pulled at the corners of his winter-chapped lips. "I like festival food, too."

His weathered crinkles vanished, and Addie had a glimpse at the little boy he once was who was filled with hopes and dreams. "Tell you what. Anything you find in there today"—her eyes darted down at the trash can then back up to his—"has probably been in there since New Year's Eve. So when the food fair booths start to open up later tonight, why don't you come find me, and I'll make sure you get some fresh festival food?"

A shy smile that reached his smoky-blue eyes touched the corners of his mouth. "Sure thing, Miss Addie. See you later." He tugged his coat around his thin body and shuffled off toward the library parking lot.

Addie's heart was lighter, but she knew that wouldn't be the last trash can he would dip his arm into today. That was a sad part of life on the streets, and she hated everything about it. Since she had become more accepted in her new community, perhaps it was time she also picked up where her great-aunt Anita's legacy left off and become more involved in volunteering. She smiled and glanced back at Bill. What better way than to work with the homeless? After this weekend was through, she would go down to the shelter and offer her services. Now, this was a New Year's resolution she liked better than her original one of drinking less coffee and getting more exercise. She chuckled and dashed across the street.

She popped her head into Martha's Bakery to ask about the smoke damage. Although it wasn't too bad, Martha informed her that she would have to remain closed the next day for cleaning. Addie looked around for signs of Betty's body, because by the fiery look in Martha's eyes, it wouldn't surprise her if Martha meant cleaning up a murder scene. Once Addie was certain that no dead bodies were stashed on the premises, she headed next door to her shop, the overhead doorbells ringing out her arrival.

Paige looked up from the books she was sorting on the counter and grinned. "I take it we have a new addition to the team."

"What do you mean?" Addie wiggled out of her red wool coat and placed it on the counter.

"I mean"—Paige dropped down behind the counter and stood back up, cradling a squirming Pippi in her arms—"our new mascot."

Addie shook her head and dropped a coffee pod into the one-cup machine. "At least she'll be more dependable than the other token employee we have."

Paige let out a half-laugh, half-snorty thing and hoisted the dog over the counter to Addie. "Speaking of *her*, did you happen to run into her in the park?" Paige waved away Addie's questioning glance. "I saw you come out of the park, so I was just wondering."

Addie shook her head and secured Pippi under her one

arm as she stirred cream into her cup of fresh brew. "No, is that where she went?"

"I have no idea. She just said she was going to run out and grab us both a tea, and she never came back."

Addie walked over to the window, cuddling Pippi closer as she took a sip from her cup. When a black BMW sedan pulled up in front of the shop, her wayward cousin got out and dashed over the curb to the front door. Addie turned and glared at the tall, lanky, auburn-haired woman who rushed in to the greeting of bells.

"Hi, Cuz." Kalea waved over her shoulder as she clickity-clacked her high-heeled shoes— Addie could have sworn she was wearing flats when they drove into work together this morning—across the wooden floorboards to the back room. "I'm just going to pick something up, and then I have to go back out."

Addie's mouth gaped. She glanced over at Paige, whose mouth was as open as Addie's. A moment later, her cousin and roommate flounced back toward them. "I won't be back today and probably won't be home tonight. So don't wait up. Tootles." She waved and sauntered out the door.

"Wait, Kalea, we have to talk!" Addie dashed to the door, but she was too late. Trench Coat Man from the park held the car door open, and Kalea slipped into the passenger seat. "Paige, do you know who that guy is?"

Paige came to her side and glanced out. "I don't know who he is, but it's the same guy that's been picking her up all week."

That's why he looks familiar. "Funny, she's never mentioned him. Kind of unusual, don't you think?" She glanced sideways at Paige.

"Especially for her. She's always talking about the latest man in her life."

"Yeah, she is. I wonder what makes him so different." Addie's eyes narrowed as she watched the BMW pull out into traffic.

Chapter Four

Addie waved good-bye to Paige through the glass window of the front door and flipped the OPEN sign to CLOSED, and caught a glimpse of Cliff hurrying across the street from the park, making a beeline directly to the front door of Beyond the Page. His ruddy face brightened with an ear-to-ear grin when he spotted Addie in the door-window. "You look like a man on a mission," she said, chuckling as she opened the door.

All he could do was smile and nod as he crouched over, hands on his knees, huffing and puffing. "Yes," he finally coughed out. "I wanted to catch you before you were gone for the day." He gasped. "Sorry about this, but my emphysema and running doesn't mix well."

"Take your time."

"I'm okay now." He stood upright, patting his chest, tugged off his gloves, and fished around in his jacket pocket. "Here." He held out a key ring with a little dog charm dangling from the brass clip. "I found Gloria's keys."

Addie's eyes widened. "Where? I searched the entire

area around where she took her fall and couldn't find them."

"They were right where the foot of the ladder must have been."

"Really?" She turned them over in her hand, staring at them unbelievingly. "But I looked."

"So did I, a few times, after you mentioned it," he puffed. "But the last time, I kicked over a clump of snow, and there they were. I'm thinking they just got trampled down in all the commotion and buried deeper than I'd been looking."

"Yes, that must be it." Addie eyed the keys warily. "Well, thanks, Cliff. I know Gloria will be relieved. One less thing for her to worry about."

"I guess I better get back. We're almost done, but there are a few final touches to add on a couple of the booths." He pulled his gloves back on and headed across the street.

"Thanks again," Addie called as she closed the door. Shuddering, she watched him disappear into the park obscured in the early dusk of winter. Cliff was getting on in years, and if he had medical issues, she hoped he had the sense to know when to say enough was enough and head home. However, knowing him, he would be the last man standing when younger, healthier volunteers called it a day. He adored Gloria, their volunteer coordinator, and would never think of leaving the work half done.

"Well, my little friend," she said as she turned to the squirming fur ball at her feet, "I think you definitely know when to call it a day, don't you?" She grinned and scooped Pippi up into her arms. "Should we take you for a walk and then go meet Serena and Zach and see what's going on across the road?"

* * *

Despite the chill of a cloudless sky, the evening air felt downright balmy compared to what Greyborne Harbor had endured the last month. Still, Addie didn't decline the frothy cup of hot chocolate Zach waved under her nose. They visited the various carving stations, where contestants' eyes were fixed on the large digital clock and timer situated beside the gazebo. At precisely six p.m., carving tools were drawn, and the artists began to transform the shapeless blocks of ice into magical creations.

At this point in the process it was impossible to guess what the finished products would depict, and as Addie made her way from station to station, it was clear none of the contestants were going to give away their plans ahead of time. Even though most artists worked from a pattern or blueprint, none were left out for prying eyes to view. It was part of the magic and mystery that an ice-carving competition inspired. Bystanders and judges had to guess what the final image would represent as the ice blocks took shape over the next two days.

"I wish Simon was here." Addie's gaze landed on Serena's mitten-encased hand tucked snuggly inside Zach's gloved one, and a swell of envy swept through her. "These kinds of events bring out the diagnostician in him, and he always tries to assess the overall picture and make a determination of the end result."

"Isn't that called sleuthing?" Serena chuckled.

"I suppose it's a form if it." Addie laughed and gave her friend a shoulder nudge. "Oh, look, there's Paige . . ."

"Yeah, but what's going on? Who are those two guys with her and Martha?"

"One is her father, Ken Stringer, and the other one is a fellow he left the bakery with this morning. He was arguing with Ken, and then I saw him later, arguing with that man Kalea took off with."

"By the look on his face, I'd say whoever he is, he sure likes to argue with people."

"You're right. Whatever they're all discussing looks tense."

Serena's brows creased. "Yeah, and they're starting to attract a lot of attention from the people around them."

"Should we innocently approach them and see if we can defuse the situation?"

"But could we be subtle enough not to set Martha off even more? Knowing her, she'd think we were just sticking our noses where they don't belong."

"You're right. You never know how she's going to react at any given moment."

Paige's usually pallid complexion reddened to a crimson glow in the twinkling gazebo lights. Her eyes filled with tears, and she bolted away from the group toward the library parking lot. Martha shouted something Addie couldn't make out in the din around them, squared her round shoulders, and, huffing and puffing, pushed past Addie, Serena, and Zack toward the park entrance on Addie's shop street. Addie glanced down at the small cargo nestled under her coat to make sure Martha's brusque shoulder check hadn't harmed the little dog. By the time she glanced back up, Ken and the taller man had disappeared into the crowd.

"Wow," was all Serena could manage to say.

"Wow is right. Is Pippi okay?" Zach stroked the little dog's head as it poked out from under Addie's coat lapel.

"She seems to be, but what just happened?"

"Like I said, that guy seems to like to argue with people." Serena glared at the spot the man used to fill.

"Yeah, but poor Paige was in tears, did you see her?" Addie gazed in the direction Paige had gone. "Should I go after her? I've never seen her that upset before."

Serena shook her head. "It looked like family business, and you should stay out of it."

"You're right," Addie said, biting her lip, "but—"

"No buts. You saw the look on Martha's face. Do you want to feel her wrath when you go sticking your Miss Snoopy Nose in on their private affairs?"

Addie shook her head.

"Good, I'm sure Paige is all right, and she'll tell you everything tomorrow." Serena squeezed Addie's hand in sympathy.

"I gave her the day off because it's Emma's fourth birthday party."

"Well then, you'll just have to live in suspense a little longer, now won't you? Come on, Zach and I are going to the Ship 'n Anchor Tavern on Marine Drive for a beer. Why don't you join us? You can text Simon and tell him to meet us there."

Addie gazed down at the little black nose sticking out from under her jacket. "No, I can't. Thanks, anyway. You guys have fun. I'll go and wait for Simon at my shop, and then Pippi can run around in there for a bit."

Addie waved as her friends took off, and she shifted the cargo under her coat when her cell phone in her pocket vibrated. Wrestling with Pippi to avoid sending her into a snowbank, Addie fished her phone out and glanced down at the text from Simon.

It looks like I'll be working late, so I won't be able to meet up with you guys. Gloria's MRI came back. She's on her way to surgery. I'll call later if it's not too late. Xxx.

That's too bad on all accounts but thanks for letting me know. Addie added xxx and stuffed her phone back into her pocket.

"Well, my little friend, should we get you home for dinner and call it an early Friday night? I don't know about you, but I'm exhausted. This has been one strange day." She laughed and ruffled the top of Pippi's head.

The following day, Addie reached over the backdrop of her "Ice" window display and placed the last of her cut-crystal miniatures along the Victorian gaslight pathway. The tiny glass figurines made a perfect representation of the ice sculpture displays found in the park. It was surprising to her that they had sat in the curio cabinet by the counter for months doing nothing but collecting dust. Today, people couldn't buy enough of them right along with the books Paige had ordered specifically for the festival.

With the last miniature in place, her tummy picked that exact moment to rebel. She softly chuckled, thinking it made the perfect exclamation mark for a busier than usual Saturday morning. Many attending the carnival across the road gravitated to her windows depicting the Fire and Ice theme, and the ping of the sale key on the cash register had become as constant as the tinkling of the overhead doorbells.

Not that she was complaining, but working alone

all morning had definitely taken its toll on her and the wriggling little fur ball at her feet, who had become her shadow. "I know. You need to get out, but"—she looked around the store and spotted a few browsing customers— "we can't leave right now." Her words were met with a sad whimper, and she scooped the little dog in her arms. "Who said dogs can't understand what people say." She grinned and scratched her new little friend's ear. "Now, if Aunty Kalea had shown up by ten as she promised, we wouldn't be in this mess, would we?"

Addie couldn't help but fume over her cousin's latest antics. In spite of telling Addie not to expect her home last night, she made a grand entrance at two in the morning, waking both Addie and Pippi by banging around in the bathroom and singing up the hallway to her bedroom. Earlier in the night, Addie had placed Pippi in bed with her, so Addie could get some much-needed sleep. It was the only thing she could think of to stop the incessant whining coming from the little doggy bed on the floor at her bedside. At Kalea's late bedtime antics Addie had wanted to pull the pillow over her head to muffle the noise, but Pippi, not okay with losing her cushy sleeping place, had struggled for pillow dominance.

When Addie had gone into Kalea's room this morning to rouse her night owl cousin, Kalea had pulled her blankets over her head and moaned something about being at work by ten. She even promised. Two hours ago that window had closed. If it hadn't been for Edna popping in and laying claim to the 1957 edition of *Doctor Zhivago* and offering to take Pippi for a short walk in the park, Addie wasn't sure what she would have done. It had been a long time since she had no assistant and had forgotten how restrictive her daily activities could be. Paige had been a blessing in her life, and she really missed her. Kalea, on the other hand, not so much. Except for today, and that thought sent her blood pressure careening. Yes, it was definitely time for the talk she had been avoiding through Christmas.

The tinkling of bells snapped Addie out of her trance. A flushed-faced Martha thrust a brown paper bag in front of her. "Here," she barked, "I thought you might be hungry."

"Thank you, but I thought you were closed today."

"I was, but I got the cleanup all finished and won't be reopened now until Monday. That chicken salad was in the fridge, and it will go bad by then, so somebody should eat it up." She shrugged. "It might as well be you."

Addie glanced at the bag and back at Martha. "You have no idea how much I need this."

"I put a couple of treats in there for the princess, too." Martha scratched behind Pippi's perked little ear. "Now I have to get home to help Paige with the final setup for Emma's party."

"Right, I've been so busy I forgot that was today. I have a gift for you to take if you don't mind." Addie retrieved a small, brightly wrapped package. "Here, please give this to Emma for me. I think it's something she'll really like."

Martha shuffled over to the desk and took the gift from Addie's outstretched hand. "I'm going to hazard a guess and say it's a book." She looked ready to laugh but grinned instead.

"Yes, but not just any book. It's an early edition of

Robert McCloskey's *Make Way for Ducklings*. It's a collectors' copy."

"I'm sure she'll love it."

"I hope so. Paige told me the fascination she has for ducks and geese so . . . well, I thought it might be perfect." Addie's mind raced as Martha stuffed the present into her large Martha's Bakery shopping bag and trudged toward the door.

Should I or shouldn't I? What the heck. I might as well jump into the duck pond with both feet. "Wait," Addie called, stopping the robust woman at the door. "How is Paige this morning?"

"As good as any mother can be, hosting her first major birthday party." She chuckled as she reached for the door handle.

"I mean"—Addie dashed around the counter—"after last night? I saw her when she left the park. She looked pretty upset by something the tall man said to her." Addie felt the tetchy pricking of Martha's mind-your-own-business glare and glanced away.

"You saw all that?" Martha drew in a breath so deep it shook her ample bosom, and she noisily expelled it. "That was Brett Palmer! Emma's no-good father." She all but spat out the words.

It dawned on Addie in that moment that the tension emanating from Martha wasn't directed toward her for prying, but at this man. She locked eyes with Martha and saw the spark of fury even speaking Brett's name induced in her.

"Can you believe it? The jerk has had nothing to do with Paige or that sweet little child for nearly four years. He hasn't even paid one cent of child support since he walked out when she was a baby, and suddenly, a few days ago, he shows up and *demands* to attend Emma's fourth birthday party and *informs* Paige that from now on, *he* wants custody of that little girl and will go to court if he has to!" Martha's eyes darkened. "Don't worry. Paige is fine today because I think I've put an end to all his nonsense, and if not, I will soon. You can mark my words!" She swiveled and charged out the door.

Chapter Five

Addie couldn't usher her last customer out the door fast enough before flipping the sign to CLOSED. "Phew, we made it." She glanced down at the squirming fur ball at her feet. "Come on, let's get packed up and go meet Simon and the rest of the volunteers at the beach." She darted behind the counter, tossed all the dog toys she could see into the dog bed, scooped it and her little friend up, and headed out the back door.

When she arrived at the tourist center down on the harbor, it took her two drives around the parking lot until she spotted a space and wedged her Mini between a red fire engine and the fire chief's SUV. She couldn't believe how many people had answered the town council's plea to help with the unloading and stacking of Christmas trees. It was far more than she had expected, and between the crowds and the fading light of the day, she had no way of spotting Simon.

She pulled her phone out of her bag and typed. I'm here. Where are you?

By the stage.

Be right there.

She shoved her phone back in her bag, glanced at Pippi, and shrugged. "I think there's room in here for you, too." She laughed and placed the little dog in her oversize tote bag. Patting the black wet nose poking out the top, she headed toward the stage area. Her eyes and heart lit up when she spotted her target beside the bandstand speaking with Keith Hubert, the fire chief and husband of Martha's eldest daughter, Mellissa.

"Hi, Keith." Her head nod was returned by the tall ginger-haired man, and she slid up beside Simon and gave him a shoulder nudge.

"Addie." Simon grinned and planted a kiss on her cheek. "And good to see you, too." He placed a fleeting kiss on Pippi's head. "Is she behaving for you?" His sparkling, inquisitive blue eyes captured Addie's and sent her heart fluttering.

"Oh yeah, except she's the worst bed hog I've ever seen. Other than that, we're doing just fine."

"Say, isn't this Gloria's dog?" Keith rubbed the little head poking over the top of Addie's bag.

"Yes, it is. Do you know her?"

"Oh yeah." He clasped his large hands around Pippi's head and playfully scuffled her neck fur. "This little girl and I go way back. Martha usually takes her when Gloria goes on a trip, and there were one or two times that Mellissa and I had to dog sit when Martha was busy. How ya doing, girl?"

Pippi happily licked at his hand.

"You dog sat? Here, maybe she's better off with you." Addie started to remove Pippi from the tote bag.

"No, no, no." Keith's hand covered hers. "The bed-and-breakfast where I'm staying doesn't allow pets."

"What bed-and-breakfast?" Addie looked up at him. "Are you and Mellissa renovating the house or something?"

Simon shot Addie a warning glance, and she snapped her mouth closed.

"You might say . . . or something. Anyway, I'd better get back to work. I've got to make sure fire regulations are adhered to and all that." Keith backed away, giving Pippi one more ear scratch. "Now, you behave for the nice lady." He chuckled and joined the group of volunteers unloading trees from a flatbed truck.

Addie stared at Simon. "What was that look you gave me for, and what was all that about him living at a bed-and-breakfast?"

"Paige didn't tell you?"

"No, she rarely talks about her sisters. From what I can tell they're not that close. Age difference, I suppose. So what's up?"

"Well, Miss Snoopy, if you must know . . ." Simon placed his hand on her shoulder.

"I do. This involves Paige's family, and now I'm even more worried about her than I was before."

"Keith was just telling me that he and Mellissa are having some problems, and they have mutually agreed to live apart for a while to try to sort it out."

"Aw"—Addie's hand shot to her chest—"that breaks my heart. They have two kids, don't they?"

Simon nodded. "But why were you worried about Paige in the first place? What's going on?"

Addie proceeded to tell Simon about the incident in the park last night and repeated Martha's chilling words today. "It kind of made me shudder, you know. It wasn't so much what she said but how she said it and the look in her eye."

"I agree with Serena. Keep your nose out of it. If Paige wants to share her family drama with you, she will. After all, remember how long it took for her to even tell you that she was a single parent? Paige, like her mother, is a very private person."

"But Simon, this is Paige, and I hate to see her—"

"Shush." He placed his finger over her lips. "Let them work out whatever issues they have. It's obviously family business and none of yours."

"But—"

"No 'buts.' Now, come on. Let's get to work and help with this. Remember, it was you who signed us up in the first place."

"Yes, but—"

He flashed her one of his famous *don't-say-another-word* looks, but that wasn't enough to deter her from whining. "I signed us up when I thought that I should do more in the community like my aunt did, but look at all the trucks, Simon. How will we ever manage to unload and stack what must be over a thousand trees?" Addie eyed the seemingly endless convoy of pickups and flatbeds and decided it must be made up of every truck in the county that answered the call for volunteer drivers to collect the trees from the curbsides.

He clasped her hand in his gloved one and tugged her toward a flatbed truck. "Come on, it won't take that long. Look at all the people here to help out."

Addie groaned in protest and deposited Pippi, snug and secure in her tote bag, a safe distance from the feet of eager volunteers. Simon shot her a goofy sideways grin as he handed her a pair of insulated leather-palmed gloves, which he'd had the brilliant foresight to pick up from the hardware store on his way to meet her. She could have kissed him right then, but in a flash, he hopped onto the flatbed and handed her a tree.

It didn't take long until they matched the rhythm and pace of the two men working alongside them. Just when the bottom of the truck deck became visible, Simon was called away when an unstable stack of trees tumbled off a truck and pinned a man underneath, and he had to help transport the victim to the hospital. The two men they had been working with finished off the load, and Addie made a quick pitstop to check on Pippi. After taking her for a much-needed walk, Addie gave Pippi a few treats to hold her over until they got home for dinner.

When she returned, the two fellows were already unloading another truck with a different couple. Addie spotted Paige on the back of a three-quarter ton beside the bandstand shell and headed toward her at the same time as Martha was commandeering Paige to assist her at the volunteer snack table. Keith, took it upon himself— much to Addie's dismay—to pair her up with Elli Hollingsworth, Serena's often flaky assistant and Paige's best friend.

Addie eyed the willowy girl, the eyebrow piercing, and the unnaturally black hair. This new partnership would not work for long. Addie was aware from Serena's reports that Elli had an aversion to hard work, so Addie fully expected the girl to soon follow her friend to the less grueling job of manning the coffee table. Even though Elli was the same age as Paige, early twenties, she lacked the maturity that motherhood seemed to have brought Paige.

However, it didn't take Elli long to impress Addie and show another side of herself.

Elli proved to be a hard worker when she chose to be and didn't shirk her duties. She bore down and put her back into the task. Between the two of them, they even shared a few belly laughs over the next few hours. Laughter was good for Addie because it took her mind off the stinging of the pine needle scratches, the throbbing ache in her lower back, and the self-doubt starting to creep in about having the stamina to continue her aunt's legacy of community activism.

With the last truck unloaded, Addie took that as her cue to seek out one of the seating logs around the fire pit area. With a groan, she plopped down and pulled her tote bag, complete with the wriggling ball of fur inside, closer to her throbbing feet. She swore she would never walk again, but at the same time, a sense of pride surged through her. Without Elli's quirky sense of humor or the motivation she received from the group working around her, she would probably have packed it in long ago. Her feet certainly wished she had done what she had feared Elli would do and go off in search of less physical work. *So much for moving my community activism forward.*

Addie's partner, on the other hand, still full of energy, raced off to give Paige and Martha a hand with the coffee and sandwiches that were being distributed to the large group of exhausted and hungry volunteers. Addie snuggled Pippi, wistfully recalled what it was like to be ten years younger, and prayed that when she was ten years older than she currently was, she wouldn't be feeling the pains she endured now even more intensely. She eyed the table of food as the strong aroma of coffee wafted on the sea breezes past her nose. Could she heave her knackered body up off this log and make an effort to reach it?

She deposited Pippi back in the tote bag and managed to force herself to an upright position with minimal grunting. Bending down to retrieve the tote containing her small charge might pose another problem. *Why didn't I think about this before I stood up?*

She braced her lower back with one hand and did a deep knee bend to scoop up the bag with her other hand. Fiery pain shot up the back side of her leg to her hip, and she stumbled forward, nearly depositing poor Pippi into a snowbank. Footing secured, she gingerly took one step and then another toward the table. Her eyes focused on the lineup of Styrofoam coffee cups. She needed a caffeine fix so desperately that everything and everyone around her was only a blur.

That was until Martha bellowed from the food table. "Stop it! Both of you," she shouted and power walked her ample body in a beeline past Addie.

Addie swung around in time to see Brett—Paige's ex—pounding his fist into the jaw of Ken, Paige's father. Ken, the much smaller of the two, reeled backward against the side of the stage. Out of the corner of her eye Addie caught sight of a dark blur hurtling through the air off the stage. Before she could take another breath, Keith pulled Brett off Ken and whirled Brett toward him.

"What's gotten into you two knuckleheads?" Keith's voice boomed over the crashing of the waves on the rocky beach behind him.

"For Pete's sake, this is a family event, and look what you two morons have gone and done." Martha stomped her foot, thrust her hands on her hips, and glared at Brett and Ken. "Now knock it off or heaven help me, you'll both pay the price for your foolishness here."

As the initial shock of what just happened wore off, whispers rippled through the crowd, and Addie didn't miss the raised eyebrows and gasps from a few of the closer onlookers. Paige sobbed as she made a dash from the food table, Elli close on her heels.

Addie went after her, but by the time she got to the street, the two girls had disappeared into the crowd of people walking along the seawall. Addie glanced back at the family drama scene, and a cold chill raced up her spine.

A dark-haired woman Addie didn't recognize joined the angry pack. Given Martha's rigid body language and accusing finger pointing in the woman's face, the stranger wasn't a welcome addition to the group. Addie resigned herself to follow Simon's earlier advice and stay out of it, at least for now. Martha appeared to be on the warpath. From experience, Addie knew that despite Martha's cuddly teddy-bear look, when poked, the stuffing retracted, and claws slashed out. She was showing her fangs, too. Addie only hoped the woman saw that and backed off before Martha drew blood.

Addie's phone vibrated a text alert in her jacket pocket, and she shifted the tote on her shoulder as not to dislodge Pippi while she fished it out.

The patient from tonight needs surgery so won't be back there. I'll call after if it's not too late xxx

Addie's heart sank as her thumbs danced across the small keypad. She knew that by getting involved with Simon—a trauma surgeon, emergency department doctor, and the area coroner—that times like this would come up. But it just didn't seem fair that every time they planned on spending an evening or weekend together. He had an emergency to deal with. She reread what she'd written and deleted it, writing instead:

Sorry to hear that. I hope the guy's okay? Chat later xxx

That was better. Just because she was having an off day and feeling insecure didn't mean she should take it out on Simon. She'd made her choice. He was it. He was her person. He was who he was and did what he had to do, and she loved him even more for it. *Love?* Had she really just admitted that to herself? A soft smile crept across her lips, and she glanced down at the small wriggling parcel in her bag. "No, I haven't forgotten that you're there." She gave Pippi a head scratch. "And yes, I think I'm falling a little in love with you, too." She pulled the squirming dog out of her tote. "Well, I guess that depends on how you behave tonight, and if you leave me any pillow space." She laughed, and she set her new friend down to do her business.

Chapter Six

In Addie's mind there was nothing creepier than sensing someone watching her while she slept. She had read far too many horror books in her life, which afterward always conjured up images of some madman bending over her or of a monster that had clawed its way from under her bed while she slept. Except this time it was different.

She was painfully aware that the sensation was real, and she knew that if she opened her eyes even just a smidge, she would be forced to give up her snuggly warm cocoon in the large four-poster bed. Something she wasn't quite ready to do. It was Sunday. This was supposed to be her day to sleep in. Besides, it wasn't even seven a.m. yet, which was far too early to be traipsing around in the snow and cold so her new roommate could relieve herself. No, her little friend would have to wait at least five more minutes.

When Addie refused to budge, let alone acknowledge the probing eyes set on her, a silky, cold, wet nose nuzzled under her chin and nudged it upward. She fought to suppress the laugh bubbling up from her chest but failed, and that was it. She'd lost yet *another* battle and conceded to the wiggling ball of fur, now excitedly lapping at her cheek.

Addie threw back her comforter and seized her pink bathrobe from the foot of the bed. Even as she tied it closed around her, the chill of the morning still seeped in. She gazed longingly back at her warm, comfy nest, but Pippi was having none of it. As she excitedly danced backward toward the door, her pin-like nails clickity-clacked across the hardwood floor.

Addie stumbled along, following the skittering dog down the staircase, through the front foyer, and down the wide hallway into the kitchen at the back of her nineteenth-century Victorian. Even though the portable fencing had been a lifesaver, literally, for her furry roommate, it proved to be a genuine pain in the feet for Addie. Scampering down the steps of her rear porch to deposit the dog in the pen and race back up to the warmth of her kitchen proved painful to her poor pre-frostbitten feet. Hopping from one numbed foot to the other, she peered out the small window of her back door and waited for Pippi's signal that she was ready to come in.

Pippi performed her morning deed quickly, yapped to get in and then waited patiently while Addie filled the dog bowl with kibble. Dog fed and watered, Addie settled on one of the stools at the kitchen island and took a long, slow sip of her freshly brewed morning elixir. "Ah." She closed her eyes and took in the nutty flavors of her favorite coffee blend.

Her new friend and she had battled for pillow dominancy into the wee hours of the morning again. At this particular moment, Addie wasn't certain she'd be able to make it until midnight tonight for the fireworks display after the tree burning. Another comforting sip accompanied by a burst of energy, and she scrolled through her phone to see what she had missed due to doggy distractions.

There were two messages from Serena, who had been at a family dinner last night and missed the action on the beach. Not being the type to be left out of the loop, she demanded to know what Addie knew about the fight. Addie didn't like to spread gossip and figured that, through the town grapevine, Serena had probably heard more about it than she knew herself. She only sent back a smile emoji and a message saying they would talk this afternoon at the park. Addie giggled, knowing that would make her friend crazy, but she didn't have any inside information for her.

The next missed message was from Simon, and she grinned like a schoolgirl.

Sorry I didn't call last night. Surgery went longer than anticipated. Are we still on for today? xxxxxxxxxxxxxxxx

Ooo, so many kisses. I like that ☺. I can't wait to see you. What time?

How about noon? I'm just starting my morning rounds at the hospital.

If you see Gloria, tell her I have her keys and will drop them off later if she's up to having visitors today.

Sure, I'm heading to her room now.

Great, thanks. Also ask her what the trick is to getting Pippi to sleep in her own bed and not to cry all night? 😣

Oh dear, another bad one?

Yup, let's say you'll just have to ply me with A LOT of coffee today. 😄

No problem. 😊

I could drop the keys off just before noon and then meet when you're done so we can head right over to the festival.

Sounds good. I'll meet you in the lobby. See you then XXXXXXXX

XXXXXXXXXXXXXXXXXX

Addie sat back and sighed. Even though the kisses they exchanged were cyber ones, it was still the best way to start her day and left her with a renewed vigor. She scrolled through the local news alerts, but there was no mention of dead bodies having been found anywhere, and she took that as a good sign that Paige's family blowout had ended with the altercation she had witnessed on the beach. She drained her cup and was about to rinse it out when her text alert pinged.

Gloria says thank you for the keys, and yes, she would love the company. She wants to know if Pippi had Baxter in her doggy bed with her.

Addie's mind went blank. Who and what is Baxter?

A minute later . . . Baxter is a stuffed teddy bear Pippi can't sleep without.

Addie wracked her brain trying to picture having seen a teddy bear in the mix of toys in the doggy bed. **What color is it?**

... **Brown with a blue vest and bow tie, the right ear is droopy** **Gloria says that's because Pippi sleeps with him under her head.**

"Shoot!" Addie remembered seeing it at the store but couldn't place it upstairs in the bed. **Tell her thanks and sorry I'm such a failure as a dog sitter.** 😞

... **She says not to worry, she should have told you about Baxter before.**

Tell her I'll make sure he's in there tonight. See you soon. xxxxxxxxx

♥

Addie looked down at the ball of fur nestled up against her pink fuzzy slipper and shook her head. "Who would have thought that a teddy bear named Baxter would be what helps you sleep at night?" She grinned when the little dog's ears perked at the name, but her smile faded when Pippi laid her head on her front paws and let out a woeful whine. "Oh dear, you know exactly what I was saying, don't you?"

She scooped up her heartbroken friend and cuddled her close. "Don't worry. We'll make a stop before I return your mom's keys and we meet Simon before the festival today. I won't make you go through another night without your little buddy." Addie nestled her face into the soft fur on the back of Pippi's neck. "Tell you what, I'll spoil you rotten today to make up for it. I even have a huge straw beach bag I can turn into the perfect doggy carrier. We'll put some rolled-up towels in the bottom for comfort and to make it easier for you to see out. How does that sound?" Pippi let out a little yelp and licked Addie's cheek. "My, my, you are a smart one, aren't you? No wonder your mommy treats you like a princess." She was unable to stop the laughy snort that slipped out. "You even have me doing it, and it's only been two days."

Still chuckling, Addie carried her friend upstairs and paused at Kalea's door. With no sounds coming from inside, Addie opened the door just wide enough to glimpse sight of the empty bed and quickly closed it.

"It's a good thing it's Sunday, and I wasn't counting on her today." Addie grumbled and padded her way to her bedroom and en suite bathroom. She set her little charge on the bathmat and proceeded to get ready for her day.

Two hours later, freshly showered and loaded up on caffeine, Addie drove up the alley off Birch toward the parking space behind her shop. She glanced at the beach bag on the seat beside her and smiled at the little head poking out. She swore Pippi had an ear-to-ear grin on her face. *Can dogs actually smile?* She would have to look that up later. But somehow Pippi seemed to sense that she would be reunited with her teddy bear friend and appeared happy.

As Addie drew closer to her shop, she caught sight of a dark shape against the back wall of Martha's Bakery. She blinked, twice. It was a person wearing a navy-blue jacket and appeared to be huddled under the ovens' large ventilation duct. It looked like Bill, and her heart ached at the sight of him being so cold he'd have to seek out a warm air vent. She scowled. But hadn't he confirmed to her on Friday that he'd secured a bed for the winter at the shelter? She pressed her lips together in thought as she bounced over a tire rut in the alley. Come to think of it, she hadn't seen him all weekend, not at the festival Friday night or at the beach last night. Had something happened between when she last spoke to him and now that put him back on the street? She slid into her parking space and shifted into park.

"Bill," she called as she opened the car door. A blast of frigid sea air engulfed her. She shivered. It was no wonder he was huddled against the hot air blast. This winter was far too cold for anyone to survive without shelter. "It's me. Addie." With no reaction from him, she stepped closer. "Is everything okay?" she tentatively asked. The last thing she wanted to do was startle and scare the bejesus out of him. "Bill?" When he didn't stir, her gut tightened. She reached for his navy-blue parka collar, and he tumbled onto his side. Except it wasn't Old Bill. It was Brett Palmer.

Bile rose in the back of her throat, stifling her shrill shriek. Her stomach lurched, and she felt the blood drain from her face and pool in her toes at the sight before her. Brett Palmer's white face and gaping puncture wound at the base of his throat stared back at her.

Chapter Seven

Addie's heaving chest constricted as she bent down and pressed two fingers on Brett's neck to check for a pulse.

"I guess he wasn't sleeping."

She recoiled and whirled around toward the voice behind her. "Bill! What happened here?"

He shrugged. "I thought the guy was sleeping it off, and I was trying to be quiet, so I didn't wake him up." He stared down at the body. "Guess I didn't have to be."

Addie raked her hand over her forehead and took a deep breath to stop the erratic pounding in her chest. "Okay." She gulped. "Start at the beginning and tell me what you were doing here and what you saw."

"I didn't see nothing, Miss Addie. I swear. I was just here looking for something to eat. You know Miss Martha always leaves me a bag of food by her back door when she leaves for the day, but she didn't last night. So I came back this morning to see if it was here now."

Addie's head bobbed up and down as she tried to process the sight of the body and calm herself.

"I saw the guy huddled up over there and thought he

was sleeping." He glanced down at the ashen face. "I saw him at the beach last night real late and figured, well . . . you know."

"Yeah, he was at the beach last night with Martha and her ex-husband, Ken." Addie frowned. "But I didn't see you there."

"No, when I saw him, it was real late, like after midnight. I waited till everybody left. That's the best time to find bottles." He tugged his wool cap off his head and toyed with it in his weather-chapped hands. "Except this guy was still there. He was yelling at someone on his phone and looked real mad, kicked the logs by the fire pit and everything. So, I hightailed it out of there in case he saw me and started kicking me, too." He bit down on his lip. "I don't like to make people mad at me." He looked up at Addic. His faded eyes darkened with pain. "You're not mad at me now, are you? Cause you gotta believe me. I don't know nothing about this, Miss Addie. I really don't."

"Please . . . just call me Addie. You don't have to refer to me as 'Miss.'"

"I can't do that." He shook his head. "I was raised proper. A lady like you, I gotta show respect."

"I was raised properly, too, but that meant I should show respect to everyone, and especially my elders by referring to them as Mr. or Mrs. or Miss. So please just call me Addie because I'm not your elder, Bill."

"No, ma'am, but a fellow like me . . ." His gaze dropped.

"What do you mean 'a fellow like you'? You're a person just like I am, but, unfortunately, someone who's a bit down on his luck at the moment, right?"

"Yeah"—he shuffled his oversize booted feet—"I guess."

"Then it's settled. From now on, it's *just* Addie."

"Okay, *just* Addie." He grinned crookedly. "Whatever you say, *just* Addie."

"Oh, Bill." She tried not to smile at the childlike expression on his face and glanced down at Brett. Her stomach churned. "I'd better call the police now."

"I gotta go anyway. It should be good bottle pick'ns at the park this afternoon, and I gotta make sure I get back to the shelter early tonight. Last night, they were mad 'cause I was so late." He pulled his wool cap over his graying sandy-blond hair. "See ya around."

"You can't leave. The police are going to want to talk to you."

"No way, *just* Addie. Me and the police, well . . . we don't talk that well together."

"Bill, you don't have a choice." She grasped his jacket sleeve. "You were at the scene of a crime, and they're going to want to know everything you can tell them."

"I got nothing to say that I haven't said to you. You just tell them for me, 'kay?"

"I can't do that. They're going to want to hear it in your words."

"But—"

"I'm sorry. I know this is hard for you, but it's the way it has to be."

Less than two minutes from the time Addie placed the 911 call the first police cruiser pulled up behind her store. Jerry, an officer whom Addie was well acquainted with, got out, placed his cap on his head, adjusted his police utility belt, and sauntered toward them, his eyes focused on the mass on the ground not far from Addie's feet.

"Addie . . . Bill." He nodded, bent down, placed two fingers on Brett's neck, laid the back of his hand on his ashen cheek, stood up, and pressed a button on his shoulder-mounted police radio. "Dispatch, this is Sergeant Fowley."

"Go ahead, Sergeant."

"Yeah, you'd also better dispatch an ambulance"—he glanced at Addie—"and the coroner to the scene in the alley off Birch."

"Roger that. Ambulance and coroner dispatched."

Jerry clicked off his radio. His gaze darted between Addie and Bill. "So"—he took out a notebook and pen from the inside of his jacket pocket—"which one of you wants to be the first to tell me what you know about all this?"

Bill glanced at Addie, panic reflecting in his eyes, and his body stiffened. Addie gently laid her hand on his jacket sleeve and gave him a reassuring nod. "I'll go first," she said, taking a step forward.

Jerry's hand shot up in a *stop* motion. "Don't move until I can get impressions of both your boot soles. There are a lot of tracks here in the snow, and we have to try to figure out what's what and when they were made."

"Right." Addie dropped her gaze. "Sorry, I wasn't thinking."

Another cruiser pulled in behind Jerry's, and he ordered the young officer to bring the crime scene bag from his trunk. By the time the two officers had taken Addie's and Bill's initial statements and ink impressions of their boot soles, the laneway was filled with flashing blue and red emergency lights. Yellow crime scene tape roped around the entire perimeter, including Addie's Mini Cooper. She looked questioningly at Jerry.

"You can't leave until we take tire impressions and swab your tires for evidence."

Addie nodded in resignation. "I'll have to get Pippi out, or she's going to freeze in there."

Addie retraced her original footprints in the snow as best she could back to her car. Not being able to leave might be a good thing. It meant she would be around longer and maybe overhear some of the chitchat between officers. It never hurt to have an inside scoop. She bent into the front seat to retrieve a wiggling Pippi from the cozy basket.

"Miss Addison Greyborne," a voice boomed from directly behind her.

Startled, she jerked and smacked her head on the doorframe as she swung around to be greeted by the penetrating gaze of Marc Chandler, Greyborne Harbor chief of police.

"Imagine my surprise at discovering you at yet *another* scene that involves a dead body," Marc said, planting his hands on his hips. "Tell me, Addie, is this all part of your magnetic personality or do you go looking for bodies?"

She rubbed the top of her throbbing head but didn't know what to say. He was right, not so much about the magnetic personality bit, but about her having been at the scene of most *every* dead body discovered in Greyborne Harbor during the past two years. An uncanny coincidence, perhaps, or it could be a holdover of her run of bad luck that started three years ago when her fiancé, David, was killed during a home invasion. Six months later, her father died in a mysterious car accident.

Since then, stumbling across dead bodies had become a part of her life in Greyborne Harbor, the quaint little

New England town she had escaped to after her great-aunt Anita passed away. It was supposed to be Addie's opportunity to leave her dark past behind and start over. But since arriving . . . well . . . she glanced at the dead body in the snowbank. A cold quiver raced up her spine. She gazed back at Marc and shrugged her shoulders.

"Okay, Jerry, fill me in." He glanced at Addie, shaking his head. "Are we holding *her* on this one, or is she only the messenger here? Messenger of death is more like it," he mumbled under his breath as he took Jerry's notepad and began reading.

Addie opened her mouth to offer a quick retort, but Simon's Ford F-150 truck came into view up the alley. She remembered Simon's advice about dealing with Marc when he switched on his RoboCop mode: "Don't go poking the bear. Just count yourself lucky." She snapped her mouth closed. Since she had officially ended her and Marc's often tenuous relationship nearly a year ago, things had been strained between them. They had both moved on in their personal lives, but there was always that undertone of wanting to get a jab or two at each other when they were faced with . . . well, a dead body.

It seemed to be a pattern they had developed from the start of their relationship. Addie knew that it was only a matter of time until Marc told her, in no uncertain terms, to leave it alone and leave the investigating to the police. Then she would plead her case by telling him why she couldn't do that. In this case, it was because the victim was Paige's ex, and Addie knew things about the family history that could complicate it for everyone. She prayed Marc wouldn't jump to conclusions when he started his investigation.

Addie snuggled Pippi inside her coat, and her eyes met Simon's as he strode behind Martha's Bakery toward the body. A twitch of his lips told her that he understood what she was struggling with. He knew her history and aversion to anything related to death. She returned his half smile with a nod, indicating she was okay. He snapped on his blue rubber gloves and proceeded to examine the body.

Pippi wriggled around in her armpit for a comfortable position, and Addie fought to squelch the laugh about to bubble free.

Marc shot her a glare. "You think this is funny?"

"No, I don't." She motioned to the little head poking out the front of her coat and redirected her focus on the scene as Marc returned to Jerry's notes.

There was nothing protruding from the oven vents that could have caused a wound like the one at the base of Brett's throat. She pressed her eyes closed and opened them, forcing herself to look at Brett's body. It was just as she first thought. She wasn't an expert by any means, but in her mind, an injury like that should have produced visible evidence in the snow, but there wasn't anything other than boot marks, which could have been made any time since the last snowfall over two days ago.

Out of the corner of her eye, she saw an officer push Bill's head down and usher him into the back seat of a cruiser. Bill glanced over his shoulder at her. The hollowness in his eyes tore at her heart. "I'm sorry," she mouthed, and fought back tears as they drove away. There was no way Bill could have had anything to do with this. She needed to talk to Marc, now. She wheeled around and marched toward where he'd moved, beside Simon over by the oven vents.

"What do you have for me, Doc?"

Addie came to a stop and feigned seeing to Pippi inside her jacket, to avoid the impression that she was eavesdropping on them.

"At this point, not much."

"Is there any ID on the body to prove the victim here is, in fact, the fellow one of the witnesses named?"

"Yeah, I found this in his back pocket." Simon held out an evidence bag containing what appeared to be a man's black leather wallet. "According to his driver's licence, his name is Brett Palmer. It looks like he lives in Boston."

"Thanks." Marc retrieved the bag from his hand. "What else did you find? This guy didn't just show up behind the bakery with a hole in his throat and go to sleep, did he?"

"Honestly, Marc, I don't know what to tell you right now. The size and shape of the wound has me stumped. Until I can perform an autopsy and make a casting of the area of penetration, I have no idea what killed this man."

"So, the question is, how did he die, and if it was an accident or murder?"

"I don't think those are the only questions."

"What else you got?"

"It's also: Where did he die?"

"Yeah, the area looks pretty clean."

"Exactly, and due to the lack of blood splatter, except for this"—Simon pointed to the front of Brett's parka—"my best guess right now is that this fellow was moved or placed here after he was dead."

"Hmm." Marc's gaze narrowed in on the body. "If that's the case, it means this probably wasn't an accident."

"That's the conclusion I've come to in my initial

assessment of the body and the scene. Unless your team finds evidence to indicate otherwise, I'd say that you most likely have a murder on your hands and an entire town to comb for the original crime scene. Good luck with that."

"Any idea yet on the time of death?"

"I'll know better when I conduct the autopsy. Right now, I'd say he's been dead at least six to eight hours." Simon turned to the two paramedics and directed the loading of the body onto the gurney.

"It's going to be a long day," Marc muttered, and glanced over at Addie.

She averted her eyes, but it was too late. He had caught her listening. She fidgeted with the fluff ball, whose nose was poking out of her jacket collar, and waited for Marc to unload his infamous warning on her about staying out of a police investigation. Instead, his eyes searched her face, and he made no motion to move.

He knew her well enough to know that any information she had just gleaned would set her off on her own sleuthing adventure, and no doubt thought his words would be wasted. If so, then he was right. This was one of those cases she wouldn't be able to walk away from. There was too much at stake for Paige and her little girl, who was now left without a father, no matter how distant he'd been. *Does Marc know about Brett's connection to Paige?* The anguished look in his eyes told her he did, and like her, probably sensed that no good would come out of this regardless of who investigated.

Chapter Eight

"Are you all right?" Simon's hand on Addie's elbow startled her from her thoughts.

"Yeah, I'm fine." She forced a smile.

"Good." He gave her arm a light squeeze. "It looks like our plan for the day has changed, but I'll call you later." He kissed her cheek and started to walk away but stopped and came back. He whispered in her ear, "Remember what you told me Martha said to you yesterday?"

She nodded and swallowed hard.

"I think you'd better relay that information to Marc."

"I can't, Simon," she said, dropping her voice. "That would draw attention to Martha, and there's no way she would have had anything to do with this."

"Maybe not, but attention to Martha has already been drawn. The whole town is talking about the family squabble on the beach last night."

"Does Marc know about it?"

"Does much go on in this town he doesn't know about?"

"You're right. Okay." She bit her lip to stop the trembling and sucked in a deep breath.

"Thatta girl." His lips brushed her cheek, and he left, following the ambulance down the alley in his truck.

"Okay, little friend," she said, ruffling the top of Pippi's head, "let's hope I'm doing the right thing and not making everything worse." She walked toward Marc, where he was crouched down, examining the area where the body had lain. "Hi," she said, sliding up to his side.

"Hi." He glanced up at her.

She struggled for the words she knew she needed to say and gulped when his gaze held on hers.

"Is that it? Is all you wanted to say was 'hi'?"

"Um, no." She pressed her face into the back of Pippi's neck. Her heart and mind waged a battle inside her. "I'm surprised Detective Brookes isn't here, though. I would have thought something like this would be right up her alley."

"Is that supposed to be funny, given where we are?" He slowly rose to his feet and stared down at her.

"No, I didn't mean it like that. Just that . . . well, you know… her being former FBI and all. And with a case where there's no indication of what caused the death, and the fact that there's little to no evidence at the scene . . ." Her voice trailed off as Marc's eyes narrowed.

"Was there something else on your mind, or are you just being nosy about Ryley?"

"There's something that I should probably tell you."

He continued to fix his unblinking gaze on hers while she blinked as though she had smoke in her eyes. "If it has anything to do with what happened here, then you'd better spit it out."

"It's just that . . . well . . . um . . ."

"I'm losing patience."

"I know, but—" She nestled Pippi's head under her chin. "It's something someone said to me yesterday."

"Does it have something to do with the case?"

"That's the problem. I'm not sure if it does or not, and I don't want this person to get into trouble if it was said in innocence."

"If you don't tell me what it is, then I have no way of knowing if whatever it is you have to say is relevant or not."

She relayed to Marc what Martha had said to her at the bookstore yesterday afternoon. She ended her report with Martha's last chilling words: "'Don't worry. Paige is fine today because I think I've put an end to all his nonsense, and if not, I will soon. You can mark my words!'"

"And you're sure she was referring to Brett, Paige's ex?"

Addie nodded.

"Oh boy." Marc rubbed the back of his neck. "With what I heard about the scene at the beach last night, combined with what you just told me—Jerry!" Marc hollered.

Jerry bolted toward them, his crime scene bag in hand. "What do you need me to look at, Chief?"

Marc waved his hands erratically in the air. "Everything, just double-check everything for any traces of blood, fibers, whatever you can find." Marc swung around and stomped toward his cruiser. "Officer Collins, come here," he snapped. "I need you and Jefferies to pick up Martha, Ken, and Paige Stringer. Take the lot of them into the station."

"What! No," Addie called out. "Paige and Martha? You can't be serious?" She hugged Pippi close. "You've known them your whole life and—"

"Stop, right now. With what you just told me, I have

no choice but to bring them all in for questioning. Brett, Paige's *ex*"—he emphasized the last word—"didn't just up and impale himself and wind up behind Martha's store on his own, now did he?"

"Come on, really? Think about it. If Martha or Paige had anything to do with this, would they really have left the body in a place where it would implicate one or both of them?"

"At this point, I can't speculate until I have the facts pertaining to the cause of death and have had an opportunity to question three people who may or may not have some information about that death. Now, if you'll excuse me"—he took his cap off and tossed it on the front seat of his car—"I have some police work to do." He got in and slammed the cruiser door.

Addie heard an audible sigh and the clucking of a tongue behind her. She spun around to face Jerry. "What are you tsk-tsking about?"

"I should have warned you."

"About what?"

"The state the chief would be in today."

"Is it really any different from the one he's in most days lately?"

Jerry glanced up at her over his notes, a wry smile crossing his face.

"What?"

He shook his head and snickered.

One look at Jerry's face and she knew he was aware of and agreed with what she was talking about. From past cases they had worked on together she had no doubt he shared her thoughts about Marc's sometimes RoboCop behavior. However, she also knew that he was far too professional to ever say anything against his boss and for the most part, masked his true feelings well. "It's just that when you told me who you thought the victim was I knew it would hit him hard."

"Why? Does he know Brett?"

"Not as far as I'm aware, but he was pretty close to Martha's three oldest daughters growing up and knows how hard it was on the family when Ken, who was Marc's father's best friend, up and left them all."

"I see." Addie focused on a wriggling Pippi. "I had no idea the families were that close."

"Yeah, it's going to be a tough one on the chief. That's for sure."

Addie's gaze followed Marc's cruiser as he pulled away from where he'd been parked over by the back of his sister's tea shop, and she blinked.

"Jerry, my car's been moved outside the police barrier."

"Yup, we took tire impressions and swabbed the wheels in case you ran over any evidence when you pulled in."

"Does that mean you're done with me?"

"I guess it does. The chief never told me to hold you *this* time." He snorted out something halfway between a deep chest laugh and a comical chuckle, as though he amazed himself with his little quip.

"How big of him." Addie rolled her eyes at the still-simpering sergeant. "Does that also mean I can get into my store now?" She glanced down at Pippi nestling her head against Addie's cheek.

"Not from here. You'd better go around and use the front. We still haven't processed the area over there."

"Okay, thanks. Catch you later." She waved over her shoulder and headed to her car. "Let's go get Baxter, so we can both get some sleep tonight," she cooed into the furry top of Pippi's head.

* * *

One teddy bear named Baxter rescued from under the bookstore counter, and now safely tucked into the basket on the front seat, and one very happy little dog later, Addie pulled into a parking spot along the side of the hospital. "Now, let's see if your day can be made even better, my furry friend." Addie shouldered the basket and headed to the front information desk in the lobby.

After some explanation of why Addie felt that Pippi qualified as an emotional support dog for her owner, the clerk behind the glass-partitioned window allowed Pippi a short visit in Gloria's private room as long as Pippi stayed in her basket and did not bother any other patients. Addie happily obliged and headed to the elevator and room 207.

Gloria's bright and breezy voice drifted out into the hallway, which sent Pippi into a tailspin of excited yaps that didn't subside until Addie deposited her on Gloria's chest. The yaps turned to laps of Pippi's pink tongue over Gloria's round cheeks. Addie glanced over at the nurse Gloria had been sharing a joke with when they came in and was relieved to see that she, too, was enjoying the touching reunion of Gloria and her furry little companion. The nurse left, and Addie made herself comfortable on the chair beside the bed as the two old friends cuddled and cooed at each other.

"Addie, you have no idea how much this means to me. I've been worried sick about my baby." She snuggled Pippi under her chin. "At first, I was so terrified that I'd crushed her, I didn't even feel the pain in my hip. When I heard she ran off to find you, I was so relieved." Tears filled Gloria's big round eyes, and she kissed the little black nose inches from her face. "You, looking after her for me and bringing her here today, means so much to me."

Addie's eyes burned with tears, too, as she sat back in the chair. She could clearly see that Pippi was the best medicine Gloria could have had, and she hadn't been wrong when she'd told the clerk that Pippi was an emotional support animal.

"I can't believe I was so stupid to have fallen off that silly ladder. I play the whole thing over and over in my mind, and it doesn't make sense."

"What do you mean?" Addie shifted forward in the chair.

"I mean I've been up on that ladder hundreds of times, and never have I even come close to crashing off. I'm always so careful because of my age, and the chance of something like this"— she gingerly patted her hip— "happening."

"What was different this time? Was the ladder not level in the snow or something?"

"That's just it. I thought I had double-checked it before I went up. Everything seemed solid. I didn't even go up the last rungs to be safe. I remember that I was reaching up to unclip the Christmas banner, and out of the blue, the ladder shook and bam! It and I were going over. I think I let out a scream, but the next thing I knew, I was on the ground. There was a dark shape bending over me, but he was just a blur, so I don't even know who it was to thank him for coming to my aid so quickly."

"You don't remember who the first guy there was?"

She shook her head. "He must have been close by though because as soon as I hit the ground, he was bent over me, asking if I was okay. All I could think about was this little girl and how I must have crushed her in her basket underneath me." Gloria cradled Pippi and sobbed. "I couldn't bear the thought of that."

"Cliff told me that by the time he reached you, there was quite a crowd. Everyone must have been in shock, not just you."

"I'm sure they were, but until I saw Pippi in your arms, I could think of nothing else. That's when the pain in my hip hit me, and it gets even blurrier from there."

Addie patted Gloria's hand. In the two days she'd had the honor of fostering the little dog, she'd learned how quickly Pippi could grow on a person. She couldn't imagine the horror Gloria must have felt in that moment.

"Well, good thing Cliff found your keys in the snow." Addie fished around in the straw basket for her clutch purse. "Here." She dangled the dog charm key ring toward Gloria.

"Before you return those, I have one more favor to ask."

"Sure, what do you need?"

"There's a book on my bedside table. The one we're reading for the book club meeting at the end of the month."

"Yes, *The Secret Garden*. I remember seeing it when Martha and I went to pack up a bag and get Pippi's food."

"Right. Do you think I could bother you to bring it to me? I'm not much of a television watcher, and the days here tend to get awfully long. I can only tell the nurses about my travel adventures for so long before their eyes glaze over with my ramblings."

Addie's grin met hers. "Of course I can pick it up for you. My plans for the day have changed, so I'm free to go now, and I'm sure Pippi would love to be able to run around in her backyard for a few minutes, too."

"Perfect, thank you." Gloria snuggled her little friend to her chest.

Addie purposely neglected to explain the reason her plans changed. Since Martha was Gloria's best friend, the last thing Gloria needed as she lay helpless in a hospital bed was to hear about Martha's troubles. Her best friend was a prime suspect in a murder investigation and was no doubt being grilled in a police station interrogation room. Something Addie herself had experience in. She shivered at the memory.

Chapter Nine

"Whoa, settle down, little one." Addie laughed and released a wriggling Pippi into the wilds of Gloria's fenced backyard.

It wasn't that the garden was wild as much as the dog was, particularly when she made a beeline to a snowdrift and burrowed like a mole straight through it. Obviously, this was not going to be a quick do-your-business-and-come-back-in venture. Addie took advantage of the time and settled on the sofa, flipped open the gold-embossed cloth cover, and scanned through the pages of the old photo album she had seen the other day.

The images she glanced over made her laugh and cringe at the same time. It was hard to believe these were the same people she had come to know over the course of her two years in Greyborne Harbor. Who would have thought that Martha was once a petite beauty? By the sparkle in her eyes, the attractiveness she presented in all the photos radiated from the inside out. When Addie studied the snapshots of Ken with his suave, I'm-so-cool attitude, it broke her heart. He was no doubt the cause for Martha's change in demeanor over the years.

One picture caught her eye, and she pulled the album closer, not believing what she was seeing. It could have been a photo of Marc and Serena. The young man had the same wavy, chestnut-brown hair—albeit longer than Marc wore his—and the woman was dressed in a cream-colored peasant blouse and flowing lace skirt complete with a crown of flowers adorning her dark-red coils of braided hair. This was Marc and Serena's parents, and this photo appeared to be one from their wedding. Addie had no idea that her friend's parents, Wade and Janis Chandler, were married right after they finished high school. Addie flipped back a page to double-check the dates. The pages before were photos of graduation, and then the very next page was of the wedding party. *Well, I'll be.* Addie mirrored the smiles in the photos with one of her own. *I suppose that's life in a small town.*

Addie scanned down the page and did a double take. There was a photo depicting the happy couple beside the park's gazebo, and over Janis's right shoulder, a beaming Gloria was locked in the arms of a young Cliff. "No wonder he's so devoted to her. They were high school sweethearts," she murmured, and studied the background, noting that not a lot had changed in the park over the years.

Pippi scratched at the door, and Addie reluctantly closed the album and placed it back on the coffee table. She longed to spend the entire afternoon perusing the old photos, but it was not to be. Once she had chased down her overexcited friend and dried her wet feet, Addie headed for the bedroom to retrieve the book and paused in the doorway.

Her gaze darted from the bookless nightstand to the empty bed. Paige's first edition copy of *The Secret Garden* was gone. Except for a small Tiffany lamp and a box of tissues, there was nothing else on the bedside table. Addie scanned the room from where she stood, and then a thought struck her. "Martha!" At the name, Pippi waggled her backside and yipped. "Of course, Martha must have had second thoughts and either slipped it into your mommy's suitcase or come back for it later." Addie bent down and scooped up the excited dog.

"Let's go and ask your mommy to check *all* the compartments in her bag, and if it's not there, we'll call Aunty Martha to see where she put it."

A pink tongue lapped at her mouth. To contain her laughter, Addie pressed her lips tight as not to share too intimate of a kiss with her little furry friend.

"No, it's not in any of these side pockets," Gloria said, closing the top of the small suitcase.

"What about that zippered one inside the top? Did you check it?"

"You can take a look if you like." Gloria slid the suitcase off her tummy onto the bed beside her. "It's just my dainties"— Addie pulled back and shook her head— "but with these silly gowns they make you wear in the hospital, I can't see why Martha even bothered to bring those." She huffed. "What am I going to tell Paige? How can I ever explain to her that the book her father gave her is lost?"

"Let's not think that way right now. I'm sure Martha had second thoughts after I mentioned you might like it while you recover. Maybe she went back to get it."

"Then why hasn't she brought it yet?" Gloria stuck out her bottom lip. "She hasn't even come to visit me today. Some friend she is."

"She's probably still busy working the hot chocolate and treat table at the festival this afternoon. I'm sure she'll be by later with it." At least, Addie hoped that was the reason Martha hadn't been in yet, and it wasn't because she was still in police custody.

"I hope so." Gloria intertwined her fingers. "Here, hand me my purse. I believe the nurse put it in that bottom drawer." Gloria pointed to the nightstand beside her bed. "I'll call Martha right now and ask her about the book."

Addie hesitated. She still didn't have the heart to tell Gloria about finding Brett's body and Marc taking Martha, Paige, and Ken in for questioning. Surely everything would have been cleared up by now, and Martha would be by soon to visit. Then she could explain to Gloria what happened, and the two old friends could have a good laugh over the fact that Martha was actually a suspect in a murder investigation. Yes, it was best Addie left the telling of the tale to Martha.

"Okay, but I can call her if it's easier," Addie said, handing her the leather bag.

"It's all right. We'll get this sorted out straightaway, and then I can relax. I just couldn't face her with the news that the book is lost." Gloria held her cell to her ear and scowled, clicking it off. "Well, so much for that. She's not answering."

"If it's noisy at the park, she probably can't hear it

ringing." Addie took the purse Gloria handed back to her and tucked it in the bottom drawer. "You shouldn't worry about it being lost, though. She and I both saw it on your nightstand. The only logical explanation is she has it, or . . ."

"Or what?" Gloria asked, searching Addie's face.

"Or . . . who else has a key to your house? Maybe Cliff? Could he have gone in to get it so you'd have something to do while you recover?"

"Cliff? Why on earth would I give him a key to my house?"

"It's only that I saw a photo of the two of you in high school, and I thought—"

"Oh pish-posh." Gloria waved her hand. "That was years ago. He ended up marrying Emily Jenkins, and they had four kids."

"I had heard through Ida once that Emily passed away about ten years ago."

"So?"

"So, that means he's available, and I thought that maybe the two of you . . . well, you know, had rekindled something?" Addie glanced down at her damp hands and rubbed them over the knees of her jeans.

"Wouldn't that be something after all these years." A wistful look crossed Gloria's face as she laid her head back on the pillows, her eyes glimmering with moisture. "But no." Gloria raised her shoulders up and propped herself on her elbow. "There's way too much water under that bridge. Let's just say, no, he definitely doesn't have a key to my house."

"Does anyone else? Maybe they thought they were doing you a favor and will stop by later with it?"

Gloria shook her head. "Martha is the only person I trust with a key. Well, aside from you now. So you might as well keep mine in case you need to go back and get anything for my baby." She scratched the little dog snuggled into her chest.

"Speaking of your baby, I'd better get her home for dinner. It's almost that time."

As if on cue, a young food services attendant swept through the door, placed a tray on Gloria's bedside table, and swept back out with all the choreography of a graceful dancer. Gloria eyed the covered dishes warily. "My baby will no doubt be eating better than I will if past meals are any indication of what's under *there*." Gloria removed the largest plate cover revealing a pureed blob of something green in the center of the plate. Addie couldn't contain her snicker. "See, you'd think that after the agony of surgery, they would reward you and not kill you with this. Yuck." Gloria pushed the over-the-bed table farther away from her. "So, you'll call Martha and tell her I'm going stark raving mad without something to do, so much so that I'm even contemplating eating that goop." Gloria eyed the tray.

"Yes, I'll call her again in a little while. I'm sure she is just busy at the festival." Addie settled Pippi into the straw bag and waved good-bye, leaving Gloria to swirl her dinner around the plate with a fork.

Addie made her way past the nurses' station to the elevator and set the basket on a bench. Her stomach had plummeted when Gloria was unable to reach Martha on the phone. Surely she'd been released by now. Marc should have had plenty of time to figure out there was no way Martha or Paige could have had anything to do with

Brett's winding up dead behind the bakery. Addie tugged her phone out of her pocket and cursed. She'd forgotten she turned it off when she'd come into the hospital the first time, and now there were eight missed text messages from Serena.

"Darn it! I was so rattled by everything. I forgot to let her know Simon and I had our plans changed," she said, glancing at the little head poking over the top of the straw bag. "Serena's going to be so mad at us."

She braced herself as she read through them.

We're here. Where are you guys?

And the next ones in the stream:

Can't see you anywhere?

Are you running late?

Is everything okay? You're missing all the fun. You should see all the carvings. They're great. There's even one of a bookcase and another one of an opened book. You'd love them!!!

Addie smiled. Yes, she would love to see those. Hopefully, she'd be able to pop over to the park tomorrow and have a look. The weather was supposed to hold so the carvings would be on display for the next few weeks anyway. She read on:

OMG! I just heard that a body was found behind your store. Is that where you are? Are you okay?

I'm worried. Have you been arrested AGAIN?

Just heard, not your store but the bakery, and Martha and Paige were arrested? Call me!

And the last one:

Addie what's going on???? We're still here by the gazebo. Come and find me before I send out a search party!

Addie's thumbs clicked across the small keypad.

I'm fine. Sorry, been busy looking after a few things. Is Martha still working the refreshment booth?

No, she never showed up today. Zach and I covered her shift. Where are you?

At the hospital.

OMG! Are you okay?

Yes, fine, I was visiting Gloria.

What? Somebody got murdered, and you're off visiting? 😩 I've been worried sick! 😫

It's a long story. I'll see you at home later.

"It appears, my little friend, we have one more stop to make before I can get you that dinner I promised." Addie shouldered the straw tote, stepped into the elevator, marched outside into the dusky evening, and tramped through the snow to the police station next door.

"Hi, Carolyn," Addie said, leaning on the high countertop. "How's your day going?"

Carolyn, the desk sergeant, Simon's sister and a good friend of Addie's, glanced up from a stack of papers. "Hi, Addie. Busy is all I can say."

"I know. It's a crazy day, isn't it?"

"Yeah, and this little one"—she patted her distended baby bump—"has decided it's most comfortable with its foot either pushing on my diaphragm or kicking my kidney."

"Wowsers, I can't imagine."

"Maybe one day," Carolyn replied with an amused glint in her eyes.

Horror surged through Addie. "Oh, not for a long time, I hope. I'm just getting the hang of looking after a dog." She motioned to her straw bag. "I can't imagine four little kids." Addie shook her head adamantly. "No, no, no, I'm not sure how you and Pete do it, especially with you working full time."

"Ah, since I got put back on desk duty, it's easier." She winced, and her eyes filled with pain. "Well, most days. Anyway, what brings you in?"

"I was hoping I could speak with Martha Stringer. I believe you're holding her and Paige here." She added, muttering, "On some crazy, stupid charge."

"I didn't catch that last part." Carolyn cupped her hand around her ear. "Could you please repeat it?"

Addie shook her head.

"So what you're asking me is to allow you to speak with a suspect in an ongoing case?" Carolyn clucked her tongue. "You should know better than that."

"It was worth a try." Addie shrugged her shoulders. "But it really is important that I ask her a question."

"Ask who a question?" Detective Ryley Brookes appeared from around the door behind Carolyn.

Addie straightened her shoulders and met the detective's dark, probing gaze. "I'd like a moment to talk with Martha Stringer."

Ryley's laugh was short and humorless. Her deadpan expression was only softened by the fact that the ends of her raven, chin-length bobbed hair swayed as her shoulders shook with restrained laughter.

"Look, I know she's still here, which, by the way, is ridiculous because there is no way she had anything to do with that man's death."

"You're talking about Brett Palmer, *her* daughter's ex, who was found this afternoon behind *her* bakery, right?" Ryley's lips pressed tight as her eyes studied Addie's face. "And you know she's innocent, how?"

"Because I know Martha."

Ryley snorted out something between a laugh and a groan. "Is that it? I was hoping that all your misguided sleuthing expertise had turned up something, shall we say, concrete?"

Addie couldn't miss the sarcastic edge to the woman's tone and glanced at Carolyn, who appeared, by the glint in her eye, to be enjoying this little dance far too much. Addie snapped back the words that nearly left the tip of her tongue. She wasn't going to allow either of these women to get their evening's entertainment from her. "If you won't let me speak with her, then will you at least ask her something for me?"

Ryley leaned her hand on the desk and narrowed her gaze. "Does this have something to do with the case?"

"Um . . . no."

Ryley stood erect. "Then it can wait."

"But it is important. It's about a missing book."

"Of course it is."

"I'm serious." Addie's eyes darted between hers and Carolyn's. "It belongs to Paige and her little girl. We need to know what happened to it."

Carolyn looked up at Ryley, her eyes pleading Addie's case. "It belongs to a four-year-old, maybe you could—"

"Oh, all right! What is it you want me to ask Martha?"

"Ask her if she picked up the book Gloria had on her nightstand to take to her at the hospital."

Ryley disappeared through the door behind the desk to where the cells and interrogation rooms were located.

Carolyn shuffled the pile of papers and glanced up at Addie. "I'm guessing that by you taking the chance of upsetting *her*"—Carolyn gave a head tick in the direction Ryley had gone—"that this just isn't some run-of-the-mill children's book, is it?"

"No, it's a very valuable book."

"How much are we talking here, if you don't mind me asking?"

"I'm not certain exactly because I didn't have time to conduct a full appraisal, but if my guess is right, it could be worth over twenty-five thousand dollars."

Carolyn let out a long whistle. "Wow, what's a four-year-old doing with a book like that?"

"It's a family thing. I'll explain it over dinner next weekend."

Ryley came around the corner and pinned Addie with a flash of her dark eyes.

"Well, does she have it?"

"Nope, said she left it on the nightstand right where it was when the two of you were there."

"Oh dear." The blood in Addie's face dropped to meet the pit of her stomach. "Then we seem to have another problem here."

Chapter Ten

Addie ran her hands over the smooth, worn wooden surface of the arms of the chair. It was like coming home. There had been so many hours spent sitting here across the desk from Marc that at one time she had fondly thought of this chair as hers. Now as she gazed across the desk at the raven-haired detective who occupied his seat, she grasped just how much had changed over the past year.

All of Addie's earlier bravado evaporated when Ryley set her dark, piercing eyes on Addie and tapped a ball-point pen on the yellow lined notepad in front of her. Ryley had made it clear from the moment she escorted Addie into the *chief's* office that the free-flowing casual affiliation Addie and Marc had once shared was gone. Extinct. Dead. Not wanting to dwell on that painful revelation, Addie tuned into Ryley's yammering.

"From what I can gather"—Ryley set the pen on top of the pad and leaned forward—"by everything you've told me about the book, it's missing at this point, and you have no evidence it was stolen, is that correct?"

"It has to have been stolen, can't you see?" Addie said, and shifted forward on her chair. "Gloria doesn't have it. Martha, the only other person with a key to Gloria's house, doesn't have it, and I certainly don't. There is no other logical explanation for its disappearance."

"But you say that when you went to this Gloria's home to retrieve the book at her request, you saw no sign or indication of a break-in?"

"Not that I noticed, but then again, I wasn't looking for one at the time."

"What about when you left? When you did discover the book missing? Anything jump out at you then?"

"No, I made the assumption that Martha had second thoughts and either took it when we were packing the bag or went back for it."

"Martha, the same person we're holding on suspicion of murder?"

Addie's gaze dropped. She knew full well that any kind of emotional appeal to this woman would be a waste of breath. Detective Ryley Brookes was all evidence-based in her investigations, and Addie couldn't argue with the evidence. Martha was seen having two public squabbles with the victim, who had a rocky history with Martha's youngest daughter, and the body was discovered behind Martha's bakery. However, Ryley's flippant attitude regarding the missing book was another thing. This was something Addie could press.

"Look, I know that you'd like nothing better than to think of this as just a misplaced children's book, and it will turn up at some point. But I'm convinced, because of the worth of this book, that something else is going on here. If you struggle with taking my word for it, ask

Marc. He'll tell you about my gut feelings. They're rarely wrong."

Ryley's jaw tightened. Addie had clearly struck the wrong chord with the detective. Addie stifled a laugh. It must be something taught in police academies because that was the same tell Marc had when she struck a nerve with him.

Detective Brookes pinned her dark, unwavering eyes on Addie's. "Tell you what I'm going to do. I'll send two of my officers over to have a look around at Gloria's house, and if they feel anything looks out of place or suspicious, then we'll launch an investigation."

"It's a start."

"It's the best I can do right now," Ryley said, and clicked the intercom button. "Desk Sergeant Coleman, can you come in here for a moment."

It was a demand and not a question, and Addie's heart went out to her friend as Carolyn waddled through the door.

"What can I do for you, Detective?"

"With Marc and Jerry still downstairs running interrogations, who do we have on duty that I can dispatch over to Gloria McBride's house to check on a suspected break-in?"

Carolyn leaned her hand on the back of a chair, winced, and let out a deep breath. "There're already three units at the park until the carving festival winds down, and then they'll go to the beach to join the two units stationed there until the tree burning festivities wrap up later."

"It sounds like we're spread thin tonight."

"Yeah, and the chief okayed overtime for the night

shift to come in early to assist with crowd control at the beach."

"So, bringing someone in on OT is out of the question."

"You know what a stickler for balancing the department budget the chief is, so unless you want to face his wrath . . ." Carolyn met Ryley's unwavering stare with one of her own.

"No, we don't want that." Ryley crossed her arms and sat back. Her gaze darted between Carolyn's swollen abdomen and the notes she had in front of her. "Look, I know you've been assigned desk duty until you go on maternity leave next week, but we seem to be in a bind here. If I don't follow up on Addie's claims, and it turns out to be warranted, then—"

"Then you'll face the chief's wrath anyway."

"Exactly," Ryley said, standing up. "I'd go myself, except I left a witness sitting in interrogation."

Addie stiffened and glanced at Carolyn's hand ringing large circles over her stomach. Surely the detective wasn't about to suggest sending a very pregnant woman out into the field alone. Her baby was due anytime now. She opened her mouth to protest. . . .

"I can go if that's what you're saying. I am still a police officer, and if I'm incapable of performing my duties as such, then I should have gone on leave a month ago."

With her friend's coolheaded and matter-of-fact words, Addie snapped her mouth closed.

"Good to hear. This should be an easy one. Just take a look around the McBride residence and see if there's any indication that a break-in occurred." Ryley glanced at her wristwatch. "It's not quite six, and Tammy is working down in the file room. I think she's on until seven. I'll have her come up and cover the desk until you get back."

Ryley seized the pad of paper and her pen from the desktop, stalked to the door, then stopped and turned back slowly. "I hope I don't regret this . . . but take Addie with you. Heaven forbid that you go into labor while you're out in the field. Marc would kill me for sending you alone."

Yes. Addie did a mental fist pump.

"But Addie, you are not to interfere with Sergeant Coleman's investigation in any way, and you are to follow any and all of her orders. Do I make myself clear?"

Addie fought a grin that threatened to blow her non-chalant cover.

"You are a civilian, and one of the only reasons why I'm even considering this is because you are familiar with the property and perhaps can be of some assistance."

"Understood."

"Good." Ryley swung around on her heel and marched out the door.

"Understood that she's covering her behind is more like it." Carolyn slid Addie a sly grin. "If she sent me out on a break-and-enter call with no backup . . ."

"I'm not exactly backup."

"You're all I've got at the moment, so let's go, *partner.*"

"Can I drive? I've never driven a squad car before."

"Exactly why you won't be driving one tonight either."

"Can I at least operate the lights and sirens?"

"There will be no lights and sirens."

Addie put on her best little-girl pouty face, and Carolyn shook her head as she withdrew a set of keys and unlocked a cupboard. She hauled out a black case labeled CRIME SCENE. "Here, you can carry this for me."

Addie's eyes lit up. "Can I at least dust for finger-prints?"

"No, you cannot." Carolyn rolled her eyes. "Come on. Tammy, the file clerk, only works until seven, so we have just over an hour to get this finished."

They headed down the back stairwell, Addie still pleading her case—to the mocking tunes of Carolyn's laughter—to allow her to contribute more to the investigation than being on baby watch.

"Here, take my arm. The last thing we need is you slipping on the ice. Not only would we face the wrath of Marc and Ryley, but I can't even imagine how Simon or Pete would react if you ended up on your head in a snow-drift at nine months pregnant."

"I think I'll be okay." Carolyn shined her flashlight beam up the sidewalk. "It looks like a fresh sprinkle of some sort of salt mixture has been applied."

"It was probably one of Gloria's neighbors helping her out."

"Helpful neighbors in a crisis is great. There's not enough of that. But in this case, it also means that if there were tracks here not belonging to you or Martha, they're long gone now."

Carolyn's beam danced from the left and right up the path, including scanning the snow piles on either side and across the base of the house as they approached.

"I'll take that arm now," Carolyn said when they reached the steps to the covered porch. "I bet you never thought you'd be hauling a beached whale up the stairs today."

The imagery Carolyn's words evoked in both women made the task of tugging an already off-balance woman even more difficult when they both doubled over in laughter.

"This is nothing compared to the other things I've had to do lately."

"Like what?" Carolyn stopped at the top of the steps to catch her breath.

"Like fostering a dog." Addie motioned to the little head peeping over the top of her tote slung over her shoulder. "And finding a dead body in the alley behind my store."

"Yeah, that must have been tough."

Addie slipped the key into the door lock. "I'm not sure how you police get used to it."

"It's not something you get used to," Carolyn said, scanning her beam of light around the casing of the window to the right of the door. "It's just unfortunately part of the job sometimes."

"Kind of like Simon's, I guess."

"Yeah, speaking of my brother," Carolyn said as she moved around Addie to the window on the left of the door, "how's he enjoying his new set of wheels?"

"It's worked out great, him buying your truck and parking that summer ride of his for the winter. I must say there was more than once when I wasn't sure we'd make it over a few of the snowbanks we encountered. Don't get me wrong. A Tesla Roadster is a great car. They're just not made for the tons of snow we can get with our storms."

"Like your Mini is?" Carolyn laughed.

"You're right. I've been thinking of trading it in, especially after this last winter," Addie said as Carolyn aimed her beam of light over the side of the porch rail and scanned the pathway that ran to the back gate.

"Why did you sell the truck to Simon in the first place? I noticed Pete's been driving you around lately. Didn't you get anything new?"

"No, not yet. I guess Simon didn't tell you why I had to sell it?"

Addie shook her head.

"Well, Pete hasn't been getting many construction contracts lately with the weather, so money's been tight. That's also part of the reason why I opted to work until my due date and not go on leave last month. Marc was good about it. He understood and reassigned me to the desk as a precaution. Once the weather lifts, Pete's work situation should improve, and we'll look at buying something else for me to drive then. Okay, I can't see any signs of an intruder from here. Let's go in, and I'll check the other windows and backyard."

Carolyn stepped over the threshold and pulled two pairs of blue gloves from her police-issue jacket. "Here, replace your wool mittens with these just in case you're tempted to touch anything inside."

"You sound just like Marc."

"It's a standard police line." Carolyn grinned and flipped on the light switch beside her and scanned the small entranceway. "Cute house." She peeked around the pillar into the living room. "Okay, you can help by wandering around to see if you notice anything that might have changed since you were here on Friday and from when you came back today. I'm going to check the windows and backyard."

"Can I let Pippi out for a run? She gets so cooped up in the pen at my house. This is a real treat for her."

"Sure, but don't you go out with her. I want to be able to check for human footprints in the snow."

"Got it, thanks," Addie said, and made her way to the back door.

She waited until her little charge gave the signal that she was ready to come back in and scooped Pippi up in her arms. It was probably best to keep her out of Carolyn's way as she made her rounds of the rooms, checking the windows and dusting for prints. With the dog tucked firmly under her arm, Addie made her own rounds of the house, searching for anything that looked out of place. When Carolyn came in from the backyard and gave Addie the all clear, she set Pippi down on the bedroom floor.

"And you're sure that when you came back this afternoon, you didn't notice anything disturbed?"

"No, nothing."

"And now that you know the book is missing?"

Addie hesitated.

"What?"

"There is one thing . . . I just thought of . . . " Addie padded down the hallway, Pippi close on her heels, and stopped in the entrance to the living room. "Today, when I went through the photo album, it was closed on the coffee table."

"What do you mean?"

"I mean that when Martha and I were here on Friday, it was lying open. That's when I spotted the picture of her, Gloria, and Martha's ex-husband, Ken. But when I came back today, I'm positive it was closed."

"Are you sure?"

"Yes! I remember. I let Pippi outside and sat down to

look through it while I waited for her to finish her business. I flipped the cover open. I remember clearly now."

"You're positive that when you were finished up on Friday, you left it open? No one else has been in here since you came earlier today?"

"Yes, I'm certain I left it open, and according to Gloria, no one else has a key."

"Unless Martha isn't being honest with us, and she did come back later before she was picked up."

Chapter Eleven

Addie switched the defrost to high when her Mini warmed up enough to blow hot air. The spirals of ice crystals across the windshield dissolved, clearing her view, but she remained motionless in the police station parking lot. The conversation she and Carolyn had on their return drive to the station played over in her mind. It left Addie with a twisted sensation in her gut.

On one hand, she could understand why her friend thought Martha was lying about not going back to Gloria's house. As Carolyn pointed out, Addie had just informed her of the book's worth. On the other hand, as Addie tried to argue eloquently, why would Martha steal a book that belonged to her own daughter? If the value of it made her have second thoughts about it being loaned out to Gloria, wouldn't she just say so and take it back? Why lie? No, something didn't fit.

As a visual person, Addie needed to see it in black and white, and she knew exactly where she had to go to do that. She shifted into reverse and glanced at her rearview mirror. Out of the corner of her eye, she caught a glimpse of two little bright shining marbles reflecting in the parking lot lights, and stopped. The woeful look in Pippi's eyes, coupled with the fact that she had Baxter's ear clamped between her tiny jaws, told Addie she'd had enough adventure for the day. It was time to head home.

Addie chuckled. "Okay, you win. The blackboard at the bookstore can wait until tomorrow. I've had to make do at home in a pinch before, and I'm sure I can do it again."

She missed having Simon and Serena around to bounce her ideas off. Serena and Zach were at the tree burning festival—an event Addie didn't think she could cope with after the day she'd had—and Simon . . . well . . . she assumed since she hadn't heard from him, he was still working in the lab at the hospital. For a fleeting moment, she considered heading there now, but just as quickly pushed the thought away. Convincing the clerk at the information desk that Pippi was an emotional support animal for a patient was one thing, but for Dr. Emerson, that might not bode well for Simon's professional reputation.

Addie pulled up in front of her house, snatched the basket off the front seat, and bounded up the wide porch stairs. There was no sign of lights on anywhere in her three-story Victorian, which meant Kalea was out and the conversation Addie needed to have with her was put on hold, again. Addie wasn't looking forward to it, but her cousin had gotten out of control lately, and it was wearing not only on her at home, but also with Paige at the store. After today, Paige definitely didn't need the added stress of Kalea's I-me-mine attitude. At the first opportunity, Addie would have to make that clear to her cousin. Kalea needed to hear the shape-up-or-ship-out speech before Addie lost Paige over the whole thing. In Addie's mind, Paige was worth a dozen Kaleas, relative or not.

After eating her kibble and taking a trip out to the dog run, Pippi hunkered down on a warm rug in front of the crackling fire Addie had lit, her eyes following Addie's every movement. Addie proceeded to haul out a large roll of brown paper and masking tape from the bottom of her 1880s antique French Baroque carved hutch buffet. This very paper had come in handy in the past, and it didn't take her long to fix a sheet by all four corners to the wall on the left side of her fireplace. After a quick search through the top drawer of her aunt's antique desk, she found a black felt-tipped marker and was ready to roll.

Addie stared blankly at the sheet of paper. She crossed her arms and glanced down at the relocated Pippi asleep in her dog bed beside the sofa. Her head snuggled on top of Baxter's. "Some help you're going to be," Addie said, and refocused on the blank sheet. "Think, Addie, you have two mysteries here, and they're unrelated. So, where do you start? You take it one at a time." Addie drew a vertical line down the center of the paper. At the top of the left column, she wrote *Murder*, and on the right column, *Book*.

Under the *Murder* heading, she started with what she knew, which wasn't much. Not having a direct pipeline to Marc anymore made it more difficult to get information, but she knew there might be something here that could help her eventually see the big picture.

Victim—Brett Palmer—Paige's ex—Emma's (Martha and Ken's granddaughter) father

Murder weapon???
Murder scene???
Crime scene—alley behind Martha's Bakery
Victim involved in two very public family
 disagreements—Brett, Martha, Ken Stringer
 (Paige's father/Martha's ex)

And . . . Addie stood back and studied what she'd written. Those were the only people she had noticed caught up in the shouting match at the park on Friday night, but what about on the beach Saturday? She wracked her brain to visualize the scene. *Right!*

Keith—husband to Mellissa (Paige's eldest sister
 and son-in-law to Martha and Ken) broke up
 fist fight between Brett and Ken

Her hand wavered over the paper, but there was someone else there. Addie replayed the scene over and over: Paige left in tears, followed by Elli, both girls disappeared into the crowd on the boardwalk, Addie turned around to see what was going on with the fight and . . . That was it.

Unknown woman???

Whoever she was, Martha had made it clear she wasn't a welcome participant when she had wagged her finger in the woman's face and shouted at her. Addie added beside *Unknown woman???—Martha had altercation with . . .*

She made a mental note to find out who she was and how she fit into this family drama scene.

She stood back and reread her notes. There wasn't much to go on, but it was a start, and hopefully, Simon would be able to add some answers to the question marks once he completed the autopsy. She moved over to the right side of paper under *Book*.

> *The Secret Garden—belonged to Paige and*
>   *Emma, gift from Ken, Martha's ex—Paige's*
>   *father—on loan to Gloria*
> *Gloria fall—in hospital*
> *Book last seen—Gloria's nightstand—by Addie*
>   *and Martha*
> *Martha informed of 25K value of book*
> *Spare key to Gloria's house—Martha*
> *Book gone—Martha denies any knowledge—no*
>   *indication of a break-in*

Addie stopped writing and considered how many times over the course of filling in clues in both columns she had written Martha's name. "Wowsers!" She dropped the pen. Her eyes darted between columns and she did a quick mental calculation. "Maybe Carolyn was right after all."

She jumped when the doorbell buzzed, and Pippi shot out of her bed, barking madly as she raced to the front door. Addie followed behind, laughing. In all the time she had lived here, only one person ever used the antiquated door ringer. She opened the door and flung her arms around Simon, who gave a startled laugh and hugged her back.

"And to what do I owe such a warm greeting from both of my favorite girls?" He reached down and playfully rubbed Pippi's ear.

Addie tugged at his coat and pulled him into the foyer, closing the door behind him. "Because I've missed you"—she stood on tippy-toes and kissed his lips—"and I need your brain."

"That sounds a bit ominous." He gave her a sidelong glance and hung his jacket on the coatrack behind the door.

Addie willed herself not to laugh at the expression of mock horror on Simon's face, but it was hard not to. "Don't worry. I haven't turned into a zombie or anything," she said, managing not to look at him while she regained some semblance of control. "Can I get you a coffee, tea—"

"I think . . . after the day I've had, I need something a bit stronger." A smirk replaced his feigned frown of suspicion as he headed across the living room to the antique walnut liquor cart, grabbed a bottle of scotch from the bottom shelf, poured a drink, knocked it back, and poured another. "Ah, much better." Simon settled onto the overstuffed sofa and laid his head back.

Addie slid onto the thread-worn, wide arm of the sofa beside him and gently stroked his taut brow. "Bad day?"

He rolled his head to the side and set his blue eyes on hers. A weak smile tugged at the corners of his lips. "More like frustrating."

"How so?"

He raised his head and took a sip of his drink. "Because I still have more questions than answers."

"Like what?"

"See that question mark on your note beside 'murder weapon'?"

"Yes."

"Well, I still don't have a clue what was used to kill the victim."

"Nothing?"

"No. I couldn't match it to any known tools. I checked databases for common gardening tools, woodworking, construction equipment, and contemporary weapons. Nothing. I came up completely blank on all of it."

"What about the murder scene? Did the autopsy reveal what you suspected, and Brett was killed somewhere else and then moved?"

"That was the only positive of my day." He swirled his drink and set it on the coffee table. "With the volume of blood loss, Martha's Bakery, at least outside, wasn't the murder scene. I haven't heard back from Marc yet, so I don't know if the crime team found anything inside the bakery. If there's no evidence there, the police have to cast a wider net to find something that might shed light on all this." He picked up his drink and took a large swallow. "See what I mean about a frustrating day? I hate it when an autopsy doesn't yield any conclusions."

"You'll figure it out. You always do." She placed her hand reassuringly on his shoulder. "At some point, it will all click into place, and then you'll see the missing piece to the puzzle." Her gaze settled back on the sheet of paper. The question marks jumped out at her, but so did the eleven mentions of Martha's name. Something else popped off the page. It wasn't what she had written on the board, but what she hadn't written. She jumped up, seized the pen from the floor where it had fallen, and scribbled:

Cliff—found missing house key in area <u>already searched</u>!

She underscored the last two words for emphasis.

Chapter Twelve

Addie glanced over her shoulder from the makeshift crime board, and a grin crept across her face. Simon had fallen asleep, and snuggled in his arms was Pippi, her head nestled under his chin. Addie tiptoed behind the sofa and draped a blanket over the sleeping duo. She inched her way over to the sheet of paper and slowly peeled back the corners of the tape to remove it from the wall. She wasn't sure if her cousin was coming home tonight, but why leave her evidence sheet out to distract from the more pertinent conversation they had to have?

She glanced at the sheet of paper clutched in her hands as she made her way to the kitchen, where she could fold it and not worry about the noise waking her sleeping guests. She wasn't certain why she had the compulsion to hide it from her cousin's sight. There was no mention of Kalea on it and if her self-absorbed cousin were to see the paper and realize her name wasn't written on it, she'd probably forget it even existed anyway.

However, just in case, Addie slipped the folded paper into the straw tote along with baggies full of kibble in preparation for the following day at the bookstore. She flipped off the light, crept up the stairs, and collapsed onto her bed, kicking her slippers free. The thought of washing and changing into pajamas was more than she could bear. It was no wonder Simon had drifted off. It had been a long, strange day for everyone.

Addie snuggled deeper into her pillow. Out of recent habit, her hand reached out beside her and patted . . . nothing. *Pippi?* Her eyes flew open, and she bolted upright. Daybreak peeked through the curtains, and Addie's still fully clothed body reminded her of the exhausted state she had been in. As she tossed the duvet back, she vaguely recalled hearing the pop, boom, and whiz of fireworks at some point during her sleep. That must have been when she pulled the blankets up and retreated into a deeper dreamless sleep, because she remembered nothing after that.

She wedged her feet into her house slippers, stumbled to the bathroom, threw some cold water over her face, brushed her long hair up into a ponytail, and padded out into the hallway. She paused. Kalea's door was ajar. Her ears pricked for signs of life coming from behind it. Hearing nothing, she peeked in. The bed was unmade but empty. Addie had no idea if her cousin had been home last night because, judging by the clothes in crumpled heaps around the room, making her bed and tidying, like most domestic chores around the house, wasn't on her cousin's list of accomplishments.

Addie swung around the bottom of the banister railing and glanced into the living room at Simon still on the sofa. The gentle fall and rise of his chest accompanied by intermittent soft snores reassured her. At some point in the night, Pippi had drifted onto her own bed beside the sofa and to the comfort of her buddy, Baxter. She must have sensed Addie's presence though because her ears perked, and she scrambled toward Addie, down the hall, through the kitchen. By the time Addie caught up to her, she was wagging her tail in a frantic dance by the back door.

Morning mission accomplished, Addie dropped a pod into her coffee maker and waited for it to brew. As Pippi munched happily on her breakfast of Kibbles 'n Bits, Addie settled onto a counter stool and pulled a sheet of paper toward her.

*I had to go to Boston Saturday afternoon, got
back late last night, but had to go out early today.
I won't be into the store.
Don't hold dinner for me.*

Love, K

The paper may have been white and Kalea may have drawn a blue heart after her first initial, but Addie saw red. She crumpled the note into a ball and flung it across the kitchen with such force that it bounced out the door and into the hallway.

Simon peered around the doorframe. His dark hair looked adorable all tufted askew. "Do I enter at my own risk?"

"Yes!" she snapped. "This is a highly explosive area." Addie seized her coffee cup and took a large swig, but she couldn't help laughing at his sheepish expression and tussled hair. Coffee snorted out her nostrils. "Ouch!" She grabbed her burning nose. "See what you've gone and made me do?"

"Really?" A grin that engaged his dimples spread across his face. "You're going to blame that on me?"

"I have to. Kalea's not here, and I have to be mad at someone."

"On one hand, I'm relieved it's not me you're upset with considering I fell asleep on you last night." He slid onto a stool beside Addie's. "On the other, do I dare ask what she's done this time?"

"She just up and took off again without even checking if it worked for Paige or me at the store."

"In her defense, she might not have heard about what happened yesterday and had no idea that Paige wouldn't be around today. Maybe Kalea simply thought it would be business as usual, and it wouldn't matter."

"That's not the point. She's an employee, and she just can't come and go as she pleases. Something, for whatever reason, she's recently decided it's okay to do." Addie swirled her coffee around in her mug. "The real kicker is since she has such a sense of entitlement and always has, she'll expect a full paycheck in the middle of the month, and the argument will be on about that, too."

"One day at a time. That's not for over a week. Things might turn around for better by then."

"I don't see that happening." Addie shook her head. "I knew when I gave her a job and took her into my home, there would be challenges, but I did it because she's family, and I thought—no, hoped—that she had grown up since college, and we could make it work." Addie stared down into her cup. "But this week, she's really pushed it too far, and the note she left this morning is the final straw. She's done. The bind she has left me in at the bookstore again today is one too many family ties tested."

He reached over and laced his fingers with hers, his thumb stroking small circles over the back of her hand. "The last few days have been tough, and until this is all sorted out, I don't expect things to get better for you, or for anyone involved. Don't make a rash decision today that you might regret in the future. As you said, she is family and one of the last remaining blood ties you have."

"Blood tie, maybe, but family? No." Her gaze captured his. "You, Serena, Zach, Paige, Catherine, Carolyn and her brood. You're my real family."

He leaned in. His lips brushed hers, and he pressed his forehead against hers and whispered, "I love you."

His words made her stomach flutter. She opened her mouth to utter the words back to him—words that had, until now, been so hard for her to repeat. The screech of a siren split the air between them, and the moment was lost . . . once again.

"Darn it!" He dug his phone out of his trouser pocket and glanced at the screen. "Of course it's Marc." He shoved it back into his pocket. "His timing is always impeccable. He seems to have an uncanny sense of when it's the perfect moment to interrupt us." He rose to his feet. "I gotta go. They found something in Martha's Bakery." He bent down and kissed her cheek. "I'll call you later." With that, he swept out the door and was gone.

Addie touched her cheek. The touch of Simon's lips lingered there. Yes. She had been about to utter the words back to him that he desperately waited for her to say. She was certain this was the moment that it would have happened, but the gravity of what else he said hit her. She dashed upstairs, showered, grabbed Pippi and the tote bag, and raced to her store.

She made a left turn off Birch into the alley and slammed

on the brakes. The area behind the bookstore and bakery were still cordoned off, and Marc's car was parked in the extra space behind Serena's tea shop. Addie swung around, managed a tight U-turn, and headed back out, taking a left on Birch. She would cut across on Ash Street and go up the road to her bookshop toward Main Street from the back end. Marc's car, in addition to two other police cruisers and the back door to Martha's Bakery being propped open, indicated that parking on the main road in front of her store might be at a premium also. Fingers crossed she'd have better luck parking farther down the street toward the back end of the park.

When she came out on the roadway that ran by her shop, it was just as she feared. The entire area around her store and the bakery was a stream of endless blue and white flashing lights. She slipped into a parking space farther down the road in front of the park and dashed across the street. Her arm pressed firmly against the basket over her shoulder so as not to jostle Pippi.

Once on the sidewalk, Addie zigzagged her way through the crowd of curious onlookers who had spilled onto the street to see what all the commotion was. As she drew closer to her bookstore, the heightened activity behind the newly erected yellow tape in front of the bakery became clearer. Blue-jacketed officers came and went as if the bakery had a revolving door. They all deposited evidence bags into the back of the police van before retreating back inside Martha's Bakery.

Addie's pace slowed when her eye caught sight of the sandwich board sitting prominently by her front door. She mentally retraced her steps on Saturday before she left. She was certain she had taken it in. As she drew closer and the OPEN sign on her door came into view, her chest heaved. *What the heck?* Now *that* she was positive she had changed to CLOSED before leaving to meet Simon. When the door opened freely in her hand, her breath caught in her chest, and then the aroma of cinnamon chai tea wafted past her nostrils. *Of course.* A smile touched her lips. This time of the year it was Serena's most popular blend, and her friend did have a spare key in case of emergencies. She must have figured out the bind Addie would be in today and came to help out. Addie stood on tiptoe and scanned the store for any sign of her redheaded friend. "Serena? Are you in here?"

A blond head poked out from the last aisle of books along the wall.

"Paige? What are you doing here?"

"I'm working," she said, pushing the book cart around the corner. "I do still have a job, don't I?" Her face reddened. "That is . . . unless you've fired me?"

"What? Why would I fire you?" Addie placed the basket on the floor, setting Pippi free, and met Paige's tear-filled eyes. "Oh, honey, come here." She opened her arms wide and hugged the girl tightly to her. "Of course you're not fired. I was just shocked to find you here today. I thought—"

"What? You thought that I was still in jail like both my parents are?"

Chapter Thirteen

Addie swung around, flipped the sign back to CLOSED, and locked the deadbolt. "Come on," she said, removing her jacket and tossing it on the end of the front counter. "Sit down, talk to me, and explain why it's so important for you to be here today when it's clear that you're grieving."

Paige glanced at the door and then at Addie. "But what about the customers?"

"You're more important to me than they are. Now sit, please." Addie patted the stool beside her.

Paige reluctantly abandoned the book trolley. Addie noticed Paige stumble before she dropped with a thud onto the counter stool.

Addie clasped Paige's frigid hands in hers. "Your job here is safe," Addie said, sweeping the girl's hair from her face. "You don't have to worry about coming in when there's so much more going on in your life. You need to take the time to grieve. Brett and you were close once, and he was Emma's father. . . ." Addie hesitated and swallowed. "Your daughter's father was just killed. That must be devastating for you and her. You need to be together now, not here."

"You're wrong." Paige held Addie's gaze. "Brett and I never were a real couple. I was a naive freshman, and he was an attractive college professor who took advantage of that. I don't mean to sound heartless because it is sad that a death occurred, but him dying isn't what's shaken me."

Addie tried to grasp what Paige was saying. Her assistant had always been a very private person, at least when it came to sharing her personal life with Addie. Now whether that was because of the employer-employee relationship, Addie didn't know, but to hear her words and the matter-of-fact tone Paige spoke them in rattled her a little. She knew from the tidbits Paige dropped over time that she and Brett weren't close, except for the link they shared with Emma, but this was not the reaction she expected. "What is it then?"

"It's what's going on next door, and the fact that the police could even think my mother had anything to do with what happened."

This is what Addie had originally thought, too, but then came the message Simon had received a few hours ago from Marc. She glanced out the window at the police van. Now a shiver raced across her shoulders, and any encouraging words she might have offered Paige in that moment vanished. "What about Emma? Surely she needs to be with her mommy today, or haven't you told her anything yet about . . . well . . . her father being gone?"

"Her father?" Paige let out a short, harsh laugh. "She doesn't know him as her father. He's had nothing to do with her since she was a baby. My brother-in-law Keith is the only father figure she's ever had. She never even had *my* father much in her life until this past week. Both of them are strangers to her. No, Emma's fine. My sister's babysitting today, and I'm sure she'll see Uncle Keith later. She's happy, don't worry," Paige said, her words firm.

"That's a relief."

"Oh!" Paige covered her face with her hands and sobbed. "I just wish I had gone home Saturday night, and then Mom wouldn't be a suspect. She'd have an alibi."

"What do you mean you didn't go home Saturday?"

"I stayed at Elli's. Her grandmother Vera was baby-sitting Emma, so we could work down at the beach. When the fight broke out, and I left, we went back to her house. Emma was sound asleep, and we decided it was best if we just left her and I stayed over, too."

"Is that why you were released after they took you in for questioning?"

Paige nodded. "But Mom drove herself home on Saturday night and was alone in the house. There was no one there to confirm what time she had come home, or that she didn't go out again during the night. Don't you see if I had only gone home with her and not slept over at Elli's, Mom wouldn't be—" Sobs overtook Paige.

Addie knew from past experience that the police would not consider Paige acting as her mother's alibi and Martha hers airtight. Especially since both of them were also involved in two earlier heated incidents with the victim and were now considered persons of interest.

"Paige, I think the only reason you were released as quickly as you were was because you had more than one non-involved witness to verify your whereabouts Saturday night. Both Vera and Elli weren't part of what went on in the park on Friday or what occurred on the beach Saturday."

"You know about those?"

"Unfortunately, I saw both altercations."

"As did half the town, which doesn't help Mom or even my dad."

"No, it doesn't." Addie studied Paige's face, pain clearly etching lines that hadn't been there before. "If you don't mind me asking, though, who was the other woman involved in the argument on the beach?"

"That was Amber Carr, Brett's latest girlfriend." Paige all but spat out the words. "She's older than most of his past string of women, so I doubt she'll be around long."

Addie shifted on her stool when movement in front of her window caught the corner of her eye. Two officers, heads together, were reviewing something the taller one had in his hand. "I know it's none of my business, but the arguments appeared pretty intense. What were they about?"

Paige lifted her head, her eyes swollen and red. "Brett decided he and that woman were going to be a regular part of Emma's life. He actually *demanded* I give him joint custody!"

"Wow."

"Yeah, wow is right. Can you believe it? He hadn't given Emma a second thought since she was born, and now because his new girlfriend thought it would be fun for them to play mommy and daddy, he wanted custody." A tear trickled down Paige's cheek.

It was clear to Addie why Martha would be driven to stop that from happening, but if Ken hadn't been part of Paige's life for so long either . . . "Where's your dad staying? Why are they still holding him?"

"He's staying at my great-aunt Ettie's house."

"Can't she confirm with the police when he got back there Saturday?"

Paige shook her head. "She's deaf now and goes to bed by eight. There's no way she would have known what time he came in, or if he left again later."

"So, neither of them can prove their whereabouts late Saturday night?"

"No"—Paige stared out the window—"but still. It's no reason to tear the bakery apart, is it?" She waved her hand wildly in the air, motioning to the officers on the street. "I just don't understand what brought all that on."

Addie thought back to her own arrest and knew a certain amount of what was taking place next door was part of a routine investigation. Combined with Simon's cryptic message from Marc, though, it appeared the discovery of something in the bakery had escalated the search to more than routine evidence gathering.

"Well"—Paige swiped the tears from her face and rose to her feet—"those shelves aren't going to straighten themselves, and since Kalea didn't come in with you, I'm assuming it's only the two of us again today."

"You know if you want to leave you still can. Maybe go visit your mom. I'm sure she's in a state over all this and could use the company."

"Thanks, but no. They only let me talk to her for about two minutes last night when they released me. Even then, that Detective Brookes hovered over my shoulder every second of it. To be honest, I'd rather be here. It helps keep my mind off it, and maybe I can hear something from someone about what's going on in there."

Addie watched as Paige disappeared around the corner of a bookshelf. The creaking of the book trolley's wheels was soon the only sound in the store. Addie's gaze drifted back to the activity outside. She rose to her feet, strolled over to the bay window, and peered out. The police barricade extended to the left side of her doorway. This most likely would deter all but her most die-hard customers from entering the bookstore today. Perhaps it was best Kalea hadn't made herself available. All Paige or she needed right now was to listen to the constant whining of a bored prima donna.

Addie caught sight of a dark figure beside the old maple by the park entrance. It was Bill, which meant he'd been released from police custody and hopefully taken off their suspect list. He appeared fixated by the goings-on at the bakery, but his body huddled against the tree told her he also wanted to remain out of sight. *If he'd been cleared of charges, why the hesitancy?* She bolted out the door. "Bill," she called as she dashed across the road toward him.

He spun around and started off in the opposite direction.

"Wait, I just want to talk for a minute." He stopped when she skidded up to his side. "I see you've been released. That's great. I knew Marc would see that you just happened to be in the wrong place at the wrong time, kind of like me."

"They're wrong you know, *just* Addie."

"About what?"

"About Miss Martha. She had nothing to do with that guy ending up dead." Something in his voice told Addie he knew more than he had said he did before.

"I know you and Martha are friends, but what makes you so sure that she had nothing to do with this?"

"Cause there was a man there." Bill's face paled. "Never mind, I gotta go."

"Wait, Bill." Addie rubbed her hands up and down her

arms for warmth. "Who else was there on the beach when you were collecting bottles?"

He turned back toward her. "No one. Forget I said anything."

"Did you tell the police?"

He shook his head. "I can't ever go back there."

"Where, the police station?"

"I can't go back to jail, ever."

"But Bill, if there was someone else there besides you and Brett, the police have to know. They won't lock you up just because you have information."

"No, I've said too much already. It was just some guy. I don't know who he is and can't give a description anyway. So, it doesn't matter, but just so you know, it wasn't Miss Martha he was fighting with that night."

"Whatever it is you saw, you still have to tell the police. It could help Martha."

"I saw nothing. I just heard something. That's all. Could have been a dog for all I know. No more police." He turned and fled through the park.

Addie thought for a moment of going after him. If he had information about another potential suspect, he needed to tell Marc, but as he disappeared through the library parking lot, she knew it was useless to try to force Bill to talk. He had made it clear he wasn't going to say anything else about it, at least not today. He had appeared frightened, and she couldn't help wondering exactly what he did see, or if he did recognize the other man on the beach late Saturday night with Brett. Maybe she could track him down later and ease more out of him, but right now, she was freezing and needed to get back inside.

As she started back to the road, she hugged her icy arms around her middle and studied the flow of pedestrian traffic. It was clear the police tape was not only a hindrance to her shop but also Serena's. People were crossing the road when they came to the flower shop on the other side of Martha's, and then they'd walk along the park sidewalk to the dressmaker and alteration store on the far side of Serena's before crossing back to the shops.

This is going to be a long day. Addie pulled the door open and stepped inside to be greeted by the familiar scent of old books, leather, and fresh-brewed coffee.

Paige, who had been hovering by the window, handed Addie a steaming mug. "When I saw you outside without your coat on, I figured you'd need one of these."

Addie took a sip. "As usual, you read my mind. Thank you."

"I saw you speaking with Bill. Is everything okay?"

"Yeah, no, I'm not sure. He seems to be really spooked about something to do with all this"—she motioned to the window—"but he won't tell me."

"That sounds like Old Bill. Say, have you come up with a new plan for the window displays now that the festival is over?"

"No." Addie rubbed her temple in an attempt to keep up with Paige's abrupt shift in focus. "I haven't even thought about it."

"I just so happen to have an idea."

"Please share, I need help right about now." Addie eyed her young assistant warily and wondered if Paige's erratic thought pattern was a sign that she wasn't coping with all this as well as she pretended.

"You know how the book club is discussing *The Secret Garden* later this month."

Addie's chest tightened. With everything else going

on today, she had completely forgotten about Gloria's book. "Yes."

"Why not do an entire display around that theme. We could re-create the garden scene and showcase the book. I could even get my old copy back from Gloria, and we could use it as a centerpiece, not to sell of course, but we still have a dozen copies in the back we could unload with that display. What do you think?"

Addie reached a hand behind her and made a grab for the counter to support the unexpected wobble in her knees. "Paige, I guess you never heard," she said, and went on to relay the information about the missing book.

Paige shrugged. "It doesn't matter. It was just some old book my dad gave me. The embossing on the cover is pretty cool, and I did want to give it to Emma when she was a little older, but it's no big deal if it's lost. I'll buy one of the other copies for her."

"Paige, I saw that book. Mind you, I didn't have time to fully appraise it, but from the brief look I did have, it's a first edition."

"And?"

"And, it's worth about twenty-five thousand dollars."

Addie scrambled to grab Paige before she hit the floor. "Here, sit down. I'll get you some water."

"No, I'm fine. Are you sure it's worth that?"

"Pretty sure."

"I can't believe it. My dad left it for me when he took off. I always assumed it was just some old book he had lying around and wanted to get rid of so he didn't have to pack it. But—"

"But it appears he left it for you as an inheritance, something for your future."

"And you say it's missing now?"

"Yeah."

"Then he didn't leave it as an inheritance. Knowing what I do about him, it was more like an insurance policy that he'd want to collect on some day, and I guess that time is now."\

Chapter Fourteen

"Paige," Addie said as she shifted on her stool, struggling to keep her voice even in an attempt to conceal her shock, "do you really believe your father has something to do with the missing book?"

"That's exactly what I think."

"But both your mom and I saw it on Gloria's bedside table, and there's no evidence of a break-in. How would he have gotten it?"

"Who knows? He was over at our house a few times last week. Maybe he stole the spare key Mom had, used it to get the book, and then put it back before she missed it, or . . ."

"Or what?"

Paige shrugged. "It's possible he's had a key since high school. They were all friends back then and still later when they went to college."

"Has Gloria lived in that house that long?"

"Yes, it was her parents' house. She's always lived there. From the little bits of conversation I've heard between Mom and Gloria over the years, that's where they all partied for a while. He could have had a key from back then. I doubt in all these years she's ever had the locks changed. Heck, it's only been the last ten years or so that some people in town even started locking their doors when they went out."

Addie glanced at the book cart filled with copies of *The Secret Garden.* "I'm going to take one of these to Gloria, so she has something to read in recovery, and I'll ask her if he or anyone else could have a key from back then."

"Yeah, but if it turns out that it was Dad who took the book, there's not much I can do about it. After all, he gave it to me. I guess that means he can take it back, too."

"It doesn't work like that with gifts."

"You don't know him. He's never been a man of his word, so this doesn't surprise me."

"If that were the case, why wouldn't he just ask for the book back?"

"Maybe he was afraid I knew its value and wouldn't give it to him. This way, he's sure to get his hands on it and make off with a tidy sum, isn't he? Look, I'm going to go in the back and go through the boxes of props we use for displays to see if I can find something to create a secret garden with. That is unless you want me to stay up front?" She stacked books from the counter onto the cart.

"No, you go ahead. I think by the activity on our doorstep, it might be a slow morning anyway." Addie slipped a ten-dollar bill into the cash drawer to cover the cost of the book she was giving to Gloria and glanced out the window, noting all the shoppers on the other side of the road. "What do you think about us running a January sale? We have lots of calendars, candles, essential oils, and some other Christmas-themed knickknacks we can clear out."

"It is that time of year, and the Emporium on Main is running a huge sale. So yeah, it's a great idea."

"Okay, I'll pull some merchandise when I get back." Addie slid into her coat and gave Pippi a scratch. She looked up at Paige. "Do you mind if I leave the princess here? I'll only be gone a few minutes."

"No, she's great company. She can stand guard at the back-room door and let me know if anyone comes in." Paige grinned and scooped the little dog into her arms and headed for the back.

"Guard dog? Hardly." Addie chuckled softly and put the book into her purse. She turned to leave just as the door opened, and a ginger head appeared around the edge of the door.

"Keith, hi."

"Hey. Paige isn't at Elli's or at home. I was wondering if she came here today."

"Yeah, she's in the back."

"Of course she is." He stepped inside and closed the door. "That girl, I told her to take a few days off. With all she's been through this past week with Brett and that woman and now with Martha . . ." He glanced at the street. "Anyway, I wanted to make sure she and Emma were doing okay."

"Other than being a bit of a scatterbrain right now and all over the place in her thinking, she seems to be coping okay. Although, my guess is that what she's experiencing is still shock, and it hasn't all hit her yet."

"Yeah, that's my worry, and when it does, she won't be any good to herself or little Emma. I want to make sure she knows that in spite of . . . well, other things. I'm still here for both of them whenever they need me."

Addie guessed that the other things he referred to were

the fact that he and Mellissa, Paige's sister, were now living apart. "You're welcome to go back and talk to her. I tried to get her to go home, but—"

"She can be stubborn." A low laugh rumbled in his chest.

"Yes, she can." Addie's laugh mixed into a chorus with his. "Well, I have to pop out for a few minutes, but you can go back. She's just sorting through some boxes."

"Thanks."

"Fingers crossed you can talk some sense into her and get her to take some time off to process all this."

Addie could hear his low chuckles all the way to the back room as she stepped out onto the street. She clasped her jacket tight around her neck to fend off an icy ocean windblast, and with head down, strode over through the park to the hospital.

Paige's words gnawed in Addie's gut. *Could Paige's father really be behind the disappearance of the book?* The thought was unfathomable to Addie, but from what little she knew about that family, she did know there were deep-seated problems. Perhaps Paige was right. She tried to wrap her head around it and recalled the first time she saw Ken and Brett. They were familiar to each other, which stood to reason. Brett was Ken's granddaughter's father, but there was something more to the animosity between them. *Or am I only imagining that given one is dead and the other's in jail?*

Addie snaked around a group of decorating committee members who were hard at work taking down the ice festival decorations. She made some small talk as she passed through—all the while keeping one eye open for Bill. If he had information to prove that someone else was on the beach at the time, he may well have been the last person to see Brett alive other than the killer. She would have to convince him to talk to Marc. How she would manage that, she wasn't sure, but she knew in her gut that he knew more than he was saying. Perhaps if she could make him understand that withholding information about a crime was far more serious than the trouble he thought he would be in for disclosing it, that would help sway him to come forward.

With no sign of Bill, she made her way into the hospital, up to Gloria's room, and peeked around the door to make sure she wasn't sleeping.

"Addie, come in. You just missed Cliff. Look at the gorgeous flowers he brought me."

Addie glanced at the bouquet lying on the bedside table. She still couldn't shake the feeling she'd had when Cliff miraculously found the keys in spite of the thorough search she'd conducted. For Gloria's sake, she forced a smile. "They're beautiful. I'll go to the desk and see if they have a vase we can put them in."

"That's okay. The nurse was by and said she'd bring me one when she comes back in a few minutes with my pills." She glanced at Addie's handbag. "Where's my baby?"

"I'm sorry. I left her at the bookstore to play guard dog for Paige."

"My Pippi a guard dog?" Gloria snickered. "That would be the day."

"I just thought it would be quicker if I left her there while I popped in to drop this off for you." Addie slipped the copy of *The Secret Garden* out of her bag and placed it on the table beside the dozen long-stemmed roses. "It's pretty special to receive a dozen roses from a gentleman. Are you sure that you and Cliff—"

"Oh you." She swiped her hand in the air. "Don't start that again. Cliff and I are just old friends, and he knows roses are my favorite flower."

Addie raised a teasing brow as she took a seat on the bedside chair. "If you say so."

"Yes, I do say so." Gloria's face glowed with a healthy flush, and she crossed her arms, a mock look of indignation in her eyes as she peered sideways at Addie. "Thank you for the book."

"No problem. I know it's not the copy you had, but until we find that one, I thought at least you could still read it before the next book club meeting."

"And it will be such a relief to have something else to think about other than dwelling on everything that happened and beating myself up for being so stupid on Friday."

Addie reached over and slipped Gloria's cool hand into hers. "You can't think that way. It was an unfortunate accident. That's all. You didn't do anything wrong."

"I shouldn't have been on that ladder in the first place. As soon as it started to shake, I knew I must not have made sure it was stable before I climbed up. I was just in such a hurry to get everything done . . ." She buried her face in her hands and moaned, "Stupid, stupid, stupid!"

"Now, now, it's in the past, and what you have to do is move forward and think of it this way. You have a brand-new shiny hip, and you'll be back to climbing ladders again in no time." Addie hoped her smile looked authentic. In truth, she wasn't certain if her words rang true or not. She really wasn't familiar with the procedure of hip replacements or the recovery after. The last thing she wanted was to give her friend false hope.

"I keep replaying it over and over in my mind, and I

guess the only good thing to come out of that moment was seeing how helpful people in this town really are in an emergency. Like the fellow who was at my side as soon as I hit the ground. Now I know who he is." She picked up a folded newspaper lying on the bed and pointed to a photo. "As soon as I saw this picture it came back to me, and I remembered. He was the dark blur crouched over me, making sure I was comfortable. He even readjusted my parka, so it wasn't bunched up underneath me." Gloria flung the newspaper back onto the bed. "But it says here that he died on Saturday, so I can't even thank him for being so kind to me."

Addie reached over and seized the paper. She stared at the photo of Brett Palmer on the front page and then glanced at Gloria. Her chest constricted. "Are you sure this is the man who was the first on the scene after your fall?"

"Yes, as soon as I saw his face, it came back to me. He had such kind soft-brown eyes."

Addie sat back on the chair with a thud.

"What happened to him? Was he hit by a car or something? All it says here is that Brett Palmer has been identified as the person who was found in the alley off Birch." Gloria's eyes widened and filled with horror. "That's yours and Martha's alley, isn't it?" She shifted to support herself up on one arm and locked her gaze on Addie's. "Is that why Martha hasn't been by? Is she the one who hit him?"

Given the fact that Gloria had no recognition of the name Brett Palmer told Addie that if Martha ever discussed Emma's paternity with her friends, she must have used far more colorful language than his name to describe him with—something Martha was famous for.

It was also clear that Gloria, being in relative isolation from the outside world these past few days, wasn't aware of what had happened or that her friend was sitting in a jail cell under suspicion of murder. That was a testament to the fact that Cliff or any hospital staff which came and went weren't spreading rumors or gossip either. Addie gripped the chair arms. She had hoped that by now Martha herself would have been released so she could explain everything to her friend. But she could see by the look on Gloria's face it was up to her.

Addie drew in a deep, slow breath and relayed everything she knew about Brett's death, where the body was discovered, and the hardest part—the reason this woman's lifelong friend couldn't come to visit. When Addie finished, she sat back in the chair, her gaze fixed on Gloria's expressionless eyes.

"Hmm"—Gloria fluffed the pillow under her head—"I'd say we have a bit of work to do to get her out, don't you think?"

"I'm not following you."

"I've read my fair share of murder mystery novels, and you seem to be a magnet for bodies, and if I remember correctly, have had a hand in solving one or two murders lately, right?"

"Well"—Addie wrung her hands in her lap—"I guess I have led the police to solve them in one way or another."

"You did more than that by my recollection, but that's neither here nor there. We have a mystery to solve, and it affects my best friend and her future. I know she didn't have anything to do with that scoundrel of a man winding up dead behind her store, so how are we going to prove it?"

"To be honest with you, I don't know. Between trying to find your lost book and everything else, I haven't been able to focus on Brett's death. I told you what the witness said about the state Brett was in on the beach Saturday night, and that he was on the phone, arguing with someone. But I spoke to that same witness not long ago, and he said there was someone else there that he hadn't told the police about. I think until I can persuade him to talk to me and come forward with his information, there's not much we can do but let the police do their job."

"Who's this witness you're referring to?"

"I shouldn't say anything until I can get more information."

Gloria's eyes narrowed on Addie's.

Addie shifted uneasily in her seat. "Okay, if you must know, it's Old Bill."

Gloria tossed back her head and laughed. "Old Bill, as everyone refers to him, is no older than Martha or me. As a matter of fact, he was part of our group back in the day."

"Really?" Addie blinked in disbelief.

"Really. He used to have such a crush on Martha, followed her around like a puppy dog. He'd have done anything for her."

Her words turned Addie's blood to ice water. "Would *anything* include killing someone he thought was causing Martha stress or pain?"

"If that were the case, Ken would have been dead years ago. No, Bill's a good soul. Lovestruck still maybe, but he wouldn't harm a fly."

"Was Bill afraid of Ken?" Addie recalled the look on Bill's face when he realized he had said too much to her.

"Afraid? No. Well, perhaps a bit. You see, Bill Unger was a fringer. He hung around with us, always sort of in the shadows but never really part of the group. He was a Vietnam vet. Did you know that?"

"No, I wasn't aware."

"Yeah, he always wanted to be a chef and to go to culinary school, but the day Martha and Ken announced their engagement, he went straight to the closest recruitment center and signed up. He served a couple of years and spent part of that as a prisoner of war before the troops pulled out. When he was released and got to come home . . ." She laid her head back, her eyes reddening. "Let's just say, he was never the same. He avoided all of us and didn't even show up to his own welcome-home party that I threw for him at my house."

Addie couldn't believe what she was hearing. It all made more sense now. If Bill had been a POW, that explained so much about his fear of the police and of going to jail. "Has he been on the streets since then?"

"Not really. It was gradual. He worked wherever he could find it, doing odd jobs and such. I think he even tried his hand at being a line cook for a while when he first came back, but he couldn't hold a job. Finally, it seems whatever died inside during the war also killed his spirit, and that's when . . . well. You've seen the results."

Addie nodded and took a deep breath as she shifted uncomfortably on her chair and squeezed Gloria's hand. "I understand more now. I also understand that most of the partying back then went on at your place, the house you still live in. Is that true?"

"Yeah." Gloria turned her head toward Addie. "My parents were killed in a horrific car accident up there on the switchback by Pen Hollow when I was a senior in high school. Since I had just turned eighteen, and they had left me the house in their will, the courts allowed me to stay. I was in rough shape for a long time and took it out by partying pretty hard. We all did. Since everyone lived at home, and I had no parental supervision, my house was the place to be in those days."

"Did anyone else in the group have a key to your house?"

"A key? Heavens no! The house was always open. Nobody locked their doors back then. The world was a different place than it is today."

"But could it have been possible for someone to have had one and have used it recently?"

"I suppose so, but I don't even remember needing to use a key myself then. The locks have never been changed in all these years." Gloria raised her head and stared at Addie. "Why, what are you thinking?"

"I'm trying to figure out how the book from your bedside table has gone missing when there are no signs of a break-in."

"You know that? Have you been speaking to that Detective Ryley, too?"

"Actually, I was with Carolyn when she went to look for evidence when I couldn't find the book."

"My, my, you have been busy with all of this, haven't you?" Gloria said, dropping her head back on the pillow. "The detective told me that the book was missing and asked me a ton of questions, but what she didn't tell me is why such a fuss over it?" She pinned Addie with a glare. "What is it you're not telling me, and does this have anything to do with my friend rotting in a jail cell?"

"That's what I'm trying to figure out. I don't think the book has anything to do with Brett being killed, but . . ."

"But what?"

"The book Paige loaned you is actually a first edition and worth over twenty-five thousand dollars."

Gloria let out a low whistle. "You don't say. This book was on my nightstand, and now it's gone?"

"Yes."

"Ken!"

"What?"

"It had to have been Ken. He gave that book to Paige. He knew she had it. I bet ten-to-one when he found out the value that he's the one who went in and took it."

"That's what Paige is thinking, too, which is why—"

"Which is why you wanted to know about the house key?"

Chapter Fifteen

Addie pressed her back against the wall in the hallway outside Gloria's room. Paige wasn't the only one who needed to process all the information being thrown at her lately. Granted, Addie's wasn't as monumental as a person once close to her winding up dead; her parents being held as prime suspects; or having been faced with the possibility of losing the most important person in her life, her daughter; or her valuable book going missing. Nevertheless, it all seemed to involve, in one way or the other, many of the people Addie cared deeply about. She needed Simon. He always offered a clear perspective to these situations.

She tapped out a quick text to Paige and told her she'd be a little longer than planned and waited. The reply was a thumbs-up. Taking that as meaning all was still quiet at the bookstore, Addie headed down the elevator to Simon's office. Her phone buzzed with another text from Paige.

Serena was just here. She said she needed to talk to you. Wouldn't say about what, but she seemed upset. I told her you'd be back soon if she wanted to wait, but she left.

Addie's thumbs flew across the keypad. Thanks, I'll phone her.

Addie sat on the bench beside the elevator on the lower level where Simon's office was located and waited for Serena to pick up.

"Hi, Paige said you were looking for me . . . I dropped a book off for Gloria at the hospital and was about to go find Simon, why . . . slow down, what happened? . . . Really? . . . That's what he said?" Addie's stomach twisted into a knot. "Okay." She took a deep breath to ease the tightening in her throat that threatened to dislodge itself into her chest. "I'll try to find out . . . yeah, thanks . . . will . . . bye."

Addie crammed her phone into her coat pocket, hurriedly made her way down the corridor to Simon's office, and banged on the door.

The door slowly opened a crack. "Is someone out here dying?" Simon's brow rose tentatively as he peered out.

"No"—she pushed past him and stepped inside—"but it's urgent."

He placed his hands on both her shoulders. "There is nothing more urgent than someone dying. Take a deep breath, and tell me what's wrong. Oh, and hello by the way." He kissed her cheek.

"Hello." Her lips turned up at the corners in a sheepish half smile, and she dropped her gaze. "Sorry to barge in, but I just hung up the phone with Serena and . . ."

"And what? Something she said has clearly upset you?"

Addie met his gaze. "It did. She told me that two of the officers tearing the bakery apart were in the tea shop, and she overheard them talking about the blood residue that was found by the sink." Addie swallowed. "Does that mean Martha did kill Brett and—" Her breath caught in her throat and a half sob escaped.

"No, no, it's okay." Simon wrapped Addie in his arms and pulled her close. "You came at the perfect time. The results came back a few minutes ago, and they aren't a match for Brett's." He nuzzled the top of her head.

She pulled away and stared at him. "Does Marc know?"

"Yeah, I talked to him a minute ago."

"So, they can stop with the inquisition and release her?"

"That's not exactly how it works, but they're no longer considering the bakery as the *only* possible crime scene."

"Then they've expanded the search?"

He nodded.

"Where else are they looking?"

Simon looked away.

"Tell me. Her house? The beach? Surely you heard Bill tell Marc about seeing Brett on the beach late Saturday night, and that he was on the phone arguing with someone."

"You know I can't discuss the details of an investigation with you."

"You sound exactly like Marc."

"What I said was in your best interest."

"Pfftt."

"Look, if I tell you where the searches are being conducted, you know as well as I that as soon as you're out the door, you'll be performing your own investigation. You have to stay away, at least for now."

"I wouldn't do that."

"Really?"

"Okay, maybe you're right. I do want to go down to the beach and have a look around on my own."

"But you can't. If Marc saw you down there, he'd . . . he'd . . ."

"What? Sic his watchdog, Detective Brookes, on me?"

He gave a surprised laugh, and pressed his face to her forehead, still snickering. "I do love you, you know," he whispered. "Why, I have no idea, because you drive me crazy most of the time."

"Trust you to start teasing me during a touching moment."

"Would you want it any other way?" He gazed deep into her eyes.

Her heart hammered against her chest wall, and all she could do was shake her head to break the spell his sea-blue eyes cast over her. "I'd better go. I have to tell Paige that the invasion of the bakery was a wild goose chase, and things should be cleared up soon."

"Not exactly." He released her from his arms.

"What do you mean?"

"Just because the blood didn't match Brett's, doesn't mean that the bakery still didn't play an important part in the events leading up to the murder."

"That doesn't make sense."

"The problem is we still haven't been able to identify the murder weapon. The wound pattern shows it was caused by something with almost a serrated edge, but not completely. It did leave a jagged impression on the surrounding tissue though. The width and depth of the penetration point indicate a cylinder or cone shape, and by the chemical composite I found embedded in the wound, whatever it was contained a mixture of organic substances. The weapon or tool was well weathered. Needless to say, it has me stumped. There were a number of appliances found in the bakery kitchen that have, well, rather unusual edges or forms to them. As I'm sure you saw, the police are removing anything suspect from the bakery, so I can test it in the lab to see if they have any trace evidence or match the wound formation."

"But they wouldn't be weathered, would they? It's a bakery, and Martha keeps her kitchen spotless."

"That's one of the mysteries, isn't it?"

"What have you found so far?"

"I haven't had a chance to run any tests yet on her kitchen appliances. Perhaps it's one of the antique bread cutters in Martha's collection or something similar. Anyway, that's what I'll be doing the rest of the day and most likely into the evening unless, of course, I find a match."

"And if your tests don't match anything at the bakery, what then?"

"Then the bakery is released as a possible crime scene and we continue to investigate other possible sites and look for a matching weapon."

"Hmm . . ."

"Don't get any ideas. You heard what I said about Marc catching you snooping around."

"I know, but—"

He placed his finger over her lips. "No buts. Marc is a trained officer, let him and his people do their job."

"Okay"—she nodded—"but if you won't tell me where else they're conducting investigations at least tell me if you've determined the exact time of death yet. I heard you tell Marc at the scene that the autopsy would give you a better idea."

"As close as I can calculate, it appears, he was killed sometime between one and three a.m. Why?"

"Given the police investigation and Marc seeming to believe the bakery is important to the murder, I'm just trying to figure out how Martha would have lured Brett into the bakery at that time of the night. It doesn't make sense to me. Does it to you?"

"Nothing about this case so far makes sense."

"You're right." Addie tried to digest what he had said, but his words left a bad taste in her mouth. In Marc's eyes, Martha was still the prime suspect, but something was wrong with the theory that the murder weapon came from the bakery, especially given that it was weathered. It didn't make sense logically, but then again, murder was never completely logical.

"I guess I won't be seeing you later."

"I guess not. It seems you really have your work cut out for you." She held his gaze and hoped her disappointment didn't show. Not only was she missing him desperately these past few days, she really needed his keen fresh eyes on her board of clues. There were so many, and she was struggling to keep them all straight in her head. It was though she had the puzzle pieces from two different boxes dumped on a table and mixed together. She couldn't quite figure out if the scattered pieces went with the book mystery puzzle or the murder puzzle.

On the way back to her bookstore, Addie replayed the conversation she'd had earlier with Gloria and tried to figure out if someone else in the old group of friends could have been behind the theft of the book. She came up with a couple of possibilities and made a mental note to add their names to the list on her board later.

Her mind wandered then to what Simon had revealed about the murder weapon. It was curious to her that nothing had come up as a match so far. If she could figure out the weapon used, it might lead them to the killer and/or book thief. Right now, she still wasn't certain both crimes were related, but if she didn't do some sleuthing on her own, that connection, if there was one, might be missed and Paige would lose her and Emma's inheritance for sure. But Simon had also made it clear to her that he was worried she would go off and investigate potential weapons on her own, and invoke the wrath of Marc by interfering in the investigation in some way. *It wouldn't be the first time.* She did an inner eye roll with that thought.

However, she smiled to herself as she hopped over a snowbank by the library parking lot. He never said she shouldn't use her wicked research skills on the computer, did he? She had the Earth mapping app, and she had an online catalogue of ancient weaponry from when she worked at the Boston Library and the British Museum. She put her head down and forged through the park. It was time to go twenty-first-century sleuthing.

When she flung open the door to her shop, she stopped short at the sound of a child's giggles and peeked around the doorframe. There was mother and daughter sitting cross-legged on the floor, a stack of Lego blocks between them. Pippi's ears perked at the jingling of the bells, and with one look at Addie, she scampered toward her, yipping all the way. Addie picked up the wriggling fur ball and was rewarded with doggy kisses. Addie turned her head away and caught sight of Keith sitting at the counter.

He raised his cup in a hello gesture and grinned. "I bet you never thought you'd walk into this when you came back."

She laughed and pushed Pippi's head away from her face. "Not exactly what I had in mind, but it's great."

Paige and Emma laughed as they tried to fit the blocks together without them falling apart. It was clear Emma still didn't have the hang of working with the small ones yet. Paige said she was a whiz with the larger blocks, but these were rather detailed for four-year-old fingers.

Paige glanced up at Addie and grinned. "I hope you don't mind."

"Not at all, carry on." Addie set Pippi on the floor. "I see you have a coffee, Keith. Mind if I join you?"

"Go ahead. I sure hope this isn't a problem. I thought it might be good for Paige to see Emma for a few minutes this afternoon. Don't worry, we'll be out of here soon. Mellissa had a last-minute meeting she got called to. Apparently, there's an interested buyer for her dress shop there on Main and—"

"I didn't know she was selling?"

"Yeah, she's talked about if for a while. I guess with . . . well, with all the changes, she decided that was one more she wanted to make. We set that place up nearly fifteen years ago, and it was something we both put a lot of work into. At least, I helped when I had days off from the fire department. I guess it has kind of lost its appeal for her lately." He swigged back the last of his coffee and held his hand out to Emma. "Well, cupcake, we'd better go and let these two ladies get back to work."

"Noooo, Uncle Keef. Mommy and I aren't finished building the secret garden."

"Come on." He wiggled his fingers for her to take his

hand. "I told you when we came that Mommy was working, and we could only stay a few minutes."

"But I don't want to leave. I like it here."

Addie crouched down beside Emma. "Tell you what, you're welcome to come back any time you want when Mommy isn't busy, and maybe we'll even have story time right over there in those comfy reading chairs. How does that sound?"

"It sounds good. Can I bring my new ducky book with me?"

"Of course you can." Addie laughed and ruffled her hand through Emma's golden hair.

Emma whispered last-minute instructions to her mother on how to finish the garden wall. Then she wrapped her little arms around her mother's neck and kissed her cheek. Addie glanced at Keith and swore she saw tears in his eyes as he clasped her tiny hand and walked her out the door.

Paige wrapped her arms around Addie and gave her a bear hug. "Thank you," she whispered. "We both needed that."

Chapter Sixteen

Addie slammed the top of her laptop closed.

"Is it safe to come in?"

Addie twisted around on her chair at the small desk in her back room. "Don't sneak up on a person like that. You scared the bejeezus out of me."

Serena tossed back her long waves of bright red hair and laughed.

"It's not funny, my friend." Addie mockingly pinned her with a glare. "I'm getting old, and you could have given me a heart attack."

"Yeah, you're ancient now, aren't you?" she said, hopping up onto the desk. "It must be time to look at an assisted-living facility for you."

Addie's first impulse was to stick her tongue out at her friend, but she remembered that wasn't fitting for a lady, especially one who had just declared herself old at almost thirty-four.

"Actually"—Serena eyed her with a shifty glint—"placing you in a senior's facility might just be the answer to my prayers."

"What?"

"Then your house would be vacant, and Zach and I

could move in, and perhaps my future mother-in-law would approve of me."

"I thought you got along great with Zach's parents."

"His father, Oliver, and his mother, Melinda, Oliver's first wife, are fantastic to me. It's the current Mrs. Ludlow I have problems with."

"Oh dear. I didn't realize it was that bad."

"I didn't either until lately when she kiboshed every single wedding plan Zach and I had already arranged and *booked*. It seems *nothing* is going to be good enough to please that woman."

"What does your mom say about it? She's helped you plan most of what you have so far, hasn't she?"

"Mom quotes: 'It'll all work out, Serena, don't worry. If you and Zach are meant to be together, you will. Don't stress about the small stuff.'" Serena looked at her. "Remember, she comes from the peace and love generation and only wants to see the best in everyone and everything."

Addie recalled the photos she had seen, and she smiled softly. "She might be right, though. Don't let this woman get to you. Go around her, and make your plans with Zach's mom. She's the one you really have to get along with in the end. He is her baby after all."

"Easier said than done, I'm afraid. *Veronica* Ludlow runs *everything* now. Zach told me she has even weaseled her way into the family business and is attempting a coup to have Melinda ousted as the chief financial officer. For Pete's sake, she helped Oliver start that company over thirty-five years ago, and she's still a major shareholder."

"I really don't know what to say except to parrot your mother's words."

"I know. I know. It'll all work out, and the wedding is still five and a half months away." Serena thumped her heels against the side of the desk. "What are you working on back here while your manager is up front playing with Legos, killing time like me? It's been a painfully slow day, hasn't it?"

"I was attempting to use my top-notch research skills in a little sleuthing venture, but as you heard when you walked in, it is not going as well as I'd hoped."

"What are you researching?"

"Ancient tools and artifacts that might have a somewhat serrated or jagged edge but is more like a cylinder or cone shape. Simon has researched modern tools and come away empty. I thought this might be a lead, but I've got nothing."

"You lost me there. I haven't a clue what you're talking about."

"At this point, I don't either. There're just too many clues to all this that don't add up."

Serena glanced up at the tarp-covered blackboard on the wall. "What have you got on there?"

Addie followed her gaze. "Nothing on there yet, but I did start a list at home last night. As a matter of fact . . ." She removed the folded brown paper from the straw basket at her feet. "Here it is."

"Open it up, and let's take a look."

"What about your shop? Don't you have to get back?"

"No, Elli's in, and there definitely isn't enough work for two today."

"Why not send her home, then?"

"She's worried about what's going on in the bakery and wants to keep an eye on Paige in case it all goes south. Besides, she's been great at getting information out of that young recruit officer"—she narrowed her eyes in thought—"Curtis, I think his name is. Anyway, he seems to be taken with her and has been in at least a dozen times to pick up tea for the *guys*, or so he says. Given how many times he's used my washroom facilities, I'm thinking it's an excuse to see Elli."

"Elli is sort of on a recon mission?"

"Oh yeah, and she's good at it. I gotta give her credit. She's sharper than I ever thought she was."

"I got that impression on Saturday night when she and I were partnered up after Simon had to leave."

"She's young, that's for sure, but she's got smarts up here." She pointed to her head. "So, I got all the time in the world this afternoon. Show me what you got on there."

Addie unfolded the brown paper and laid it open on the desktop.

Serena's gaze scanned over the two columns Addie had written and nodded approvingly. "Did you learn anything else today to add to this?"

"Actually, I have. Hold that up for me so I can copy it." Addie picked up a piece of chalk from the ledge and began copying:

Murder
Victim—Brett Palmer—Paige's ex—Emma's
(Martha's and Ken's granddaughter) father
Murder weapon???
Murder scene???
Crime scene—alley behind Martha's Bakery
Victim involved in two family public
disagreements—Brett, Martha, Ken Stringer
(Paige's father/Martha's ex)
Keith—husband to Mellissa (Paige's eldest sister

and son-in-law to Martha and Ken) broke up
fistfight between Brett and Ken.
Unknown woman???—Martha had an altercation
with

She moved over to the right side of the board and wrote under *Book*:

The Secret Garden—belonged to Paige and
Emma, gift from Ken, Martha's ex—Paige's
father—on loan to Gloria
Gloria fall—in hospital
Book last seen—Gloria's nightstand—by Addie
and Martha
Martha informed of 25K value of book
Spare key to Gloria's house—Martha
Book gone—Martha denies any knowledge—no
indication of a break-in
Cliff—found missing house key in area already
searched!

As she wrote the final words, Serena darted past her and pointed to Cliff's name. "You can't be serious about this one?"

"I am because I found it funny that after I conducted a pretty thorough search of the area, he just happened to find them right at the base of where the ladder had stood and where Gloria had landed. Don't you find that weird?"

"It is uncanny, but I can't believe Cliff would take her keys, sneak into her house, and steal a book. Does he even know how to appraise a book? Why would he do it if he didn't know the value? Paige had it for years, and she didn't know what it was worth. No"—she shook her head—"I'm not buying that one."

Addie folded her arms across her chest and studied what she had written. "You know, I'm not sure if I am either. I discovered that he and Gloria were high school sweethearts, and the way he behaves around her and talks about her, it wouldn't surprise me if he still doesn't see her as the one who got away. But the fact is Cliff found the keys and could have gone in and taken the book. He also might have been the one who closed the photo album. Maybe a picture he saw upset him. Gloria also eluded to their breakup carrying a lot of baggage with it. Perhaps taking the book was out of revenge or something?" Addie shook her head. "No, even that sounds too farfetched once I say it out loud. You might be right. He's not a viable suspect, but until I have more evidence against someone else, his name stays as a remote possibility."

"That's fair, I guess. Did you learn anything else today from Simon or Gloria that you can add to this, or have you hit a dead-end like with the murder weapon?"

Addie braced her hand against the board, chalk primed. "Actually, there are a couple of things I've learned and remembered since last night. I'm not really certain which side of the board to put them on, so I'll write them over here on the side. See if you can figure out where they belong." She scribbled beside the notation she had about no indication of a break-in: *Searched Gloria's with police, absolutely no evidence of a break-in.* She underlined the word *no,* and on the side wrote:

Ken, Martha, Gloria all high school friends—
familiar with house

Brett, first on scene after Gloria's fall
Kalea's unknown boyfriend argued with Brett in
     park on Friday

"Speaking of your cousin, where is she lately? I haven't seen her around."

Addie gave Serena a side glance. "Your guess is as good as mine. This past week she's been coming and going at all hours of the day and night. According to Paige, this guy"—she tapped the board—"has been picking her up every day for over a week, and since Friday, she's suddenly decided she doesn't seem to think she needs to work at all."

"Maybe her new boyfriend is rich, and she thinks he's going to keep her in the manner of lifestyle she believes she's entitled to."

"By the look of the car he drives and the expensive clothes he wears, you might be right. She was exactly the same in college. I thought she'd grown out of it, but these last few days? I can see it only took a fancy car and a good-looking fellow to bring all that out in her again."

"What do you know about this guy?"

"Nothing, which is the weird part. Generally, when the black widow goes hunting, she's more than happy to expand on the details of her latest conquest, but with him"—Addie tapped the board under the unknown man's name—"she hasn't said a word, not even in passing to Paige. We don't even know his name."

Serena's eyes narrowed in on the board. "But you did see him having an argument with Brett two days before you found his body, so that means he and the victim knew each other."

"Yes, and Mr. Unknown happened to come to town the

week before, which was when Brett arrived in Greyborne Harbor too."

"When did Paige's father, Ken, show up? He hasn't been back here for years and then out of the blue—"

Addie's jaw dropped. "You're right! And whose name do I have on the board nearly as many times as Martha's?"

"Are you thinking what I'm thinking?"

"That Brett, Ken, and Mr. Unknown all knew each other, and came here for a reason other than to visit?"

Serena nodded.

"I wonder if Marc has found a link between them."

"I wonder if he's even put the three together yet. I think you have to go and talk to him," Serena said.

"Easier said than done, I'm afraid. Whenever I've dropped in, the dragon lady is standing guard, and she won't allow me passage into the inner sanctum. She's made it clear that Marc and I even remaining friends won't happen under her watch."

Serena slipped her phone out of her back jean pocket. "Then it's a good thing that you have a family connection to His Highness." Her thumbs skimmed across the keypad.

"If all it takes for an audience with His Majesty is a text, then I could have done that."

"Aw, you see this way, if she's with him, she really can't discourage him from meeting with his sister, now can she?"

"You are a devious one, my friend."

"I've learned that when dealing with her, it's the only way to be."

Chapter Seventeen

Addie eyed Serena standing with her hands on her hips as she scanned over the information they had written on the blackboard. "We still don't know who this mystery woman is who was involved in the incident on Saturday night, do we?"

"Yes," Addie said, "I have a name now," and she picked up the chalk, erased *unknown* with her finger, and wrote *Amber*. . . .

"I believe Amber Carr is her full name."

Addie and Serena spun toward Marc skulking in the doorway.

"Hey there, big brother. It's nice of you to join us."

Marc's gaze darted around the storeroom and rested on Addie. "I see nothing has changed back here"—he glanced at the board—"and the two of you are up to the same no good."

"Really"—Serena hung her head, shaking it—"that's all you have to say after I tell you we have a lead in your case."

"All right then, humor me." He sat on the edge of the

desk and crossed his arms. "What's so important for you to drag me away from the scene of an active investigation?"

Addie pinned him with a self-assured look. "Because I think we have another suspect in Brett's murder."

"Who?"

"This guy." Serena pointed to *Kalea's unknown boy-friend*.

"And why do you suspect him of the murder?"

Addie set the chalk down and moved toward him. "Because I saw him in the park having an argument with Brett on Friday, and it just so happens that he came to town around the same time as Brett. Coincidence? I think not. I think they knew each other, and whatever brought Brett to town also brought him."

"Have you got a name for this guy?"

"No, that's the problem. Kalea has never introduced him, let alone talked about him, but he drives a high-end BMW."

"Do you have a license plate number?"

Addie shook her head. He stood up, and she knew by the look in his eyes that he thought this summons for his presence was a waste of time.

"Ken arrived in town at the same time as those two," Serena said hastily. "Do you think it's all connected?"

"Connected to what?"

"Duh, Brett winding up dead!" Serena glared at Marc, a look of disbelief across her face.

Marc eased back down. "We've already established a connection between Ken and Brett, and I have someone checking into how deep it went."

"Of course they're connected." Addie glanced from him to the board. "Ken is Emma's grandfather, and Brett was her father."

"No, the connection is more recent."

"What do you mean?" Serena asked.

He dropped his gaze from Addie's. "I mean, it seems Ken Stringer is the maintenance man for the apartment building in Boston where Brett Palmer and Amber Carr just happen to live."

Addie swiveled toward the board and began scanning over the clues. "That's it!"

"What's it?" Marc came to her side. "What are you seeing in all this that I'm not?"

Addie picked up the chalk and drew a line from the *Book* column to the *Murder* side of the board. Bits of chalk dust flew off when she stabbed the end of the joining line. "It has to be about the book that was stolen from Gloria's."

"But you were there when Carolyn conducted a search of the property. There was no indication of a break-in."

"I know but . . ." Her gaze flashed across the board. "This morning, Gloria identified Brett as the man who was the first on the scene after she fell."

"So?" Marc shrugged.

"So?" Addie paced back and forth in front of the board. "So, she said he was kind enough to adjust her coat from under her to help make her comfortable."

"That was nice of him." He looked at her with reservation.

"That means he may have gone through her pockets and removed her keys."

"I thought you got those back." Serena searched her face. "You have Cliff down as a suspect."

"I know, but it makes sense when you put it all together. Brett took the keys, and then after he took the book, he went back to the scene of the fall and buried them in the snow so it looked like they had always been there. That's why I couldn't find them, but Cliff did later."

Serena erased Cliff's name from the list.

"Addie, that's a lot of speculation for me to even remotely consider. The *facts* that we are working with are right here in black and white." Marc's finger stabbed at the word *altercation*. "There are witnesses to a family disagreement about Emma's custody, and you told me what Martha said about Brett and how she would put an end to it. No, unless you have more proof, that is the evidence we have to focus our investigation around, and to be honest, it's not looking good for Martha at this point."

There was an audible gasp from the doorway. Paige, her face as pale as the chalk, stood with her mouth gaping.

"I'm sorry you had to hear that, Paige." Marc raked his hand through his chestnut-brown hair and rubbed the back of his neck. "But if it's any consolation, your dad is being released."

"My dad? In my mind, he's more of a suspect than my mother is." The force of her words matched the flash of venom in her eyes.

"Maybe, and through our investigation that will be determined, but when two of my officers canvassed the neighborhood, they found a witness that saw him arrive at your aunt's house about ten. This witness said the lights in the house went out shortly after that and swears his car never left again all night."

"That sounds like a pretty convenient witness, don't you think?" Addie scoffed, her face clearly illustrating her skepticism.

"She's a *credible* witness. That's all I can say at this point. Like I said before, if you have proof for this other theory"—his hand waved toward the board—"then by all means bring it to me. Until then, I have to follow the evidence because the evidence doesn't lie."

"Maybe not"—Addie flipped her head—"but sometimes it doesn't tell the whole story."

His brown eyes softened, and he looked back at Paige. "You mom's bail hearing is set for tomorrow at nine a.m. That's when the circuit judge is here. Now, if you'll excuse me, I have an investigation to get back to."

After Marc left, Paige dropped into the desk chair. Pippi jumped out of the basket by her feet and stood in a gopher stance on her hind legs, imploring the distressed girl to pick her up. Paige obliged, hugged the little dog close, and sobbed into the back of Pippi's furry neck.

"Oh, honey." Addie rushed to Paige's side and gently stroked the girl's back. "It'll be okay. You'll see. I have a theory—"

"And we just have to find the proof of a connection, and your mom will be released, free and clear," Serena said, finishing Addie's sentence.

"That's right." Addie tilted Paige's chin up and gazed reassuringly at her. "Don't worry. It just might take a day or so, but we'll get her off."

Paige held Addie's gaze, her eyes swollen and tear stained. "Promise?"

"Promise."

Paige puffed out a deep breath. "Okay." She set Pippi back into the basket. "I trust you. You've never been wrong before, and I have a garden to finish." She stumbled zombie-like out to the front of the shop.

Addie's gaze caught Serena's. Her friend's eyes said it before her words did. "You've never been wrong before?" Serena rolled her eyes.

"Never completely wrong. Sometimes maybe I've

headed down the wrong path to start with, but it eventually came back around, and we figured out who the killer was."

"Do you think this murder connection to the book is the right path this time?"

"For Paige and Emma's sake, and Martha's . . . I hope so." Addie focused her gaze on the blackboard. She didn't know what else to say to Paige and hoped she wouldn't have to break her promise to prove Martha didn't do it. However, the one thing she did know was the answers were somewhere on her board. If it was proof Marc wanted, then it was proof he'd get.

She stepped forward and wrote beside Ken and Brett's names:

Knew each other in Boston
Came to town the same time
Did Ken tell Brett about the book prior?

"Are you thinking they planned to steal it together, and then one got greedy and wanted it all for himself?" Serena asked.

"It's a possibility because Ken knew about the book and had access to Martha's house this week on the pretense of visiting his daughters. But when he found out it was on loan to Gloria . . ."

Serena's eyes lit up with an aha moment. "Then Brett took matters into his own hands and tried to double-cross Ken, and so he killed him." She scanned the board. "What about this Amber? Do you think she fits into it somehow?"

"I think if there was a plan to steal the book, then she certainly knew about it, but it's highly unlikely she killed Brett."

"Unless she was only in the relationship with him for the money and decided twenty-five thousand dollars wasn't enough to share three ways." Serena snapped her fingers. "That could also be why Brett's body was found behind the bakery. If she could implicate Ken in the murder, he'd go to jail and with Brett dead . . ."

A soft chuckle bubbled up from Addie's throat. "You have more of a wild imagination than I do."

"Think about it, and what about this mystery man? How does he fit into this new theory?"

"Who knows what his relationship to Brett was? We don't even have a name for him."

"But you saw them arguing in the park, which means they knew each other."

"True, but for all I know, Brett may have knocked into the guy in the crowd, and Mystery Man was mad about it. I did see them arguing but don't have a clue as to why. I think until we can find out who he is, he remains a question mark."

"He did show up in town at the same time. Seems suspicious to me." Serena glanced sideways at Addie.

"So did a thousand other people. The Fire and Ice Festival was on, remember?" Addie tapped the chalk stick in her hand. "I guess at this point, we're only speculating, so anything is possible. I need to pin Kalea down and find out who this guy is and speak to Paige more about her father's visits to Martha's house this past week. I need to find out if he showed interest in the book before it went missing."

"I don't think right now is a good time, do you?"

"No, it can wait until tomorrow." Addie placed the chalk on the blackboard ledge.

Serena's phone buzzed. "Gotta go. Elli has some news. I'll let you know if it's anything helpful." She made her way out of the shop, the bells announcing her departure.

Addie took a final gander at the board, grabbed the tarp, threw it over to cover it from prying eyes, and walked to the front, straightening shelves as she went. She wasn't certain why she was as there had only been about three customers in all day. *Habit*.

Addie slid up beside Paige, who was bent over the backdrop she'd created for the window display "Paige. You're a rock star! This is magical. It looks exactly like the secret garden when it was in full bloom as depicted at the end of the book."

Paige's eyes blurred with tears. "Emma's last words to me today before she left were, 'Make it a happy place for us, Mommy.'"

Chapter Eighteen

Addie eased onto the ice-cold driver's seat. A shiver quivered through her. She set the beach basket beside her and tugged a corner of a towel from the bottom around Pippi to help keep the chill off. Addie bounced her legs, and she jostled in her seat to keep warm as she waited for the frosty glaze to clear from her windshield. Her mind raced with information overload.

She wasn't certain if the constant gnawing in her gut was from hunger or the fact that she still didn't have a big-picture image of the situation with Martha, Brett, Ken, or the book, and how or *if* it all fit together—whatever the cause, it sat unsettled in her. She knew it had been a long day only made longer by the fact that they'd only sold four books in total.

The investigation next door had taken its toll. And as far as she knew and confirmed by Simon, the blood evidence discovered in Martha's Bakery wasn't the victim's. Given the amount of apparatus removed from the shop for testing, combined with her not having heard from Simon, it was clear he was still working in the lab and had come up empty on discovering the weapon. As far as she could tell, the entire day hadn't yielded any results in the case other than putting a damper on the surrounding businesses, which was good news for Paige and the rest of Martha's family.

On the journey home, it became clear that all her erratic thoughts were wearing on her ability to concentrate. On her way up the hill to her home, she had glanced at Pippi and nearly rear-ended her neighbor's car parked on the street. Enough was enough today, and she struck five items off her mental to-do list for the evening, leaving only food, a hot bath, and much-needed sleep.

When she turned into her driveway, she slowed to a crawl. It appeared Kalea was home, but she wasn't alone. Parked in front of the house was the black BMW. "Maybe we can get at least one answer to all those question marks, hey girl?" She grinned at Pippi, shouldered the basket, and headed up the wide porch steps. Before she could get to the door, it flung open and Kalea flounced out. Addie darted to the side to avoid the impending collision with her cousin and her companion.

"Oh, hey there, Cuz. You startled me." Kalea patted her chest. "I didn't expect you home so soon." She gave an awkward side glance to the striking dark-haired man accompanying her as he stepped out onto the porch. "Well, have a wonderful evening." She waved a bottle in her hand and linked her arm through the man's. "We're on our way to a business dinner and have to run."

"Hold on a minute." Addie locked in on the bottle of champagne that she'd been saving for a special occasion and then pointed that gaze to her cousin, who looked everywhere but at her. "I think we need to talk, and soon, don't you?" Addie pinned her with her best *don't-be-afraid-of-me-but-I'm-going-to-scratch-your-eyes-out* look and flicked her gaze from Kalea's flushed complexion to the man's bewildered expression. "I need a few minutes of your time, *now*." Addie would have stomped her foot for emphasis but refrained in fear that in the frigid evening weather it would shatter like glass. She settled for grabbing Kalea's jacket sleeve as she attempted to descend the top step.

Kalea shrugged off Addie's arm. "You know I'm busy, and I can't always drop everything to help you solve whatever little problem you're having at this moment. I'm sure it's something you can work out on your own *this time*, but like I said, we have a meeting to get to. People are waiting for us."

The man produced a silver business card holder from the inside pocket of his black lamb's wool trench coat, slipped a card out, and dropped it into Addie's straw tote bag. "Call me when you get back on your feet. I'm sure I will be able to help you get set up again."

He followed Kalea down the stairs and placed his hand on the small of her back as she strutted across the driveway to the BMW, her long amber waves swinging in time with her hips.

Addie overheard the man saying, "I must say, you do have an exquisite taste in champagne, my dear. I'm certain it will be the hit of the evening."

"Of course I do, darling. This is a celebration after all, isn't it?" Kalea cooed and leaned into him. Addie could almost hear Kalea purring.

"True, true." His lips nuzzled her cheek as he leaned past her and opened the car door. "And, I will say after meeting your cousin, I clearly see how unselfish and noble it was of you to invite her to come live in your fabulous home. I certainly hope she comes to appreciate all you've done for her in time. That little bit of tough love you showed back there was probably exactly what she needed given how needy you've told me she is."

Addie looked aghast at the man, and her mind struggled to process what he was saying. Her mystified glare caught Kalea's. Her cousin's eyes flashed with a burst of horror. It was clear that Kalea could tell by the look on Addie's face that she'd heard everything Mystery Man said. Kalea reached for the door handle, glanced away, and slammed it closed. Addie stood frozen on the spot. *Did that just happen?*

How dare her cousin treat her like that and lead this man to believe that this house was Kalea's and Addie was the houseguest. Addie flung the door open, set the basket on the floor, and kicked off her boots. To heck with food. She needed a stiff drink after that little show. She stomped into the living room and stopped short.

There on the coffee table were the four first-edition books Addie had recently discovered in one of the many remaining boxes in the attic and had been appraising. Except now, instead of being neatly stacked with a sheet of vellum paper placed between each book to protect the fragile leather covers, they were strewn across the coffee table, as though they were mere corner-store magazines.

"I'm done. If I have to, I'll change the locks on the doors." She spun around and had started toward the kitchen when a knock on the door halted her steps.

"What?" she spat as she flung it open.

A wide-eyed Serena stared back at her. "I come in peace, really." She held out a foil-covered pan clutched in her hands.

"Oh, Serena, I'm sorry." Addie stepped to the side.

"Please come in. I'm just seething over my cousin's latest antics and really didn't mean to snap at you."

Serena set the pan down on the side table in the large foyer and removed her jacket and boots. "I saw her leaving with that fellow and wondered if you'd finally gotten the opportunity to put a name to the face."

"I got more than I bargained for." Addie glanced at the tray. "Is that lasagna from Mario's Ristorante by chance?"

A full-mouthed grin spread across Serena's face. "It is. I stopped and picked us up some on my way home. That is unless you've already eaten?"

"No, I was going to forgo food and just drink before"— Addie sniffed in a deep breath—"I smelled that."

"Come on, then. Let's dish up, and you can tell me what Kalea's done this time."

"Do you have all night?" Addie marched to the kitchen and skidded to a stop at the door. "I can't believe this."

Serena strode over to the kitchen island and picked up an empty wooden box of hot-smoked imported salmon, pushed aside a half-eaten tin of Siberian caviar, and flicked at a White Stilton Gold cheese wrapping, whooshing it across the countertop. "Wasn't all this in that exotic gift basket Jonathan sent you from who knows where, for Christmas?"

Addie fought back the tears burning behind her eyes. "Yeah, and in it was also the bottle of French champagne that she left with." Addie waved her hand over the island. "All this I was keeping to serve at your wedding shower this spring. Except the champagne. I was keeping that for another special occasion, but it doesn't matter. She knew that, and she had no right."

"No, she didn't, but it's too late now." Serena pulled a trash bag out of one of the drawers and dropped the refuse from the counter into it. "You'll have to wait until she comes home to speak to her about crossing boundaries and all that. Remember the talk you had when she first moved in? I think it's time for a refresher course." The can of caviar kerplunked on the wooden salmon box in the bottom of the bag.

"Talk to her?" Addie rinsed a kitchen cloth under hot water and scoured the top of the counter. "I don't even know who she is anymore. You should have heard what was said tonight." Addie proceeded to relay the odd conversation that took place, as Serena set out two place settings on the counter and pulled out the stools.

"I have no idea what she's up to." Addie cut into the pan of lasagna, and using a spatula, plopped two servings on the plates. "But knowing her, it's to no good, especially if she's lying to the guy."

"Does this guy have a name yet?" Serena glanced over the top of her water glass at Addie.

"Neither of them said, but—" She jumped up and dashed down the hall to the front door and returned, waving a business card in her hand and her laptop in the other. "He did leave me this when he told me to call after I got myself together."

"He actually said that?"

"Maybe not those exact words but something similar." Addie sat back down and turned the card over in her hand. "Jared Munroe—Private Financial Broker." She looked up at Serena. "Why would Kalea need one of those?"

"Does she have any money you don't know about?"

Addie thought for a minute. "If she does, she's never mentioned it to me."

"You did say they appeared to be romantically involved,

so it's most likely not a business relationship," Serena said, before scarfing the last bits of her lasagna down.

"But she said they were on their way to a business dinner, so it doesn't make sense."

"What does it say on the computer about him?"

"Give me a minute." Addie swallowed and wiped her fingers on a paper napkin, scrunched it into a ball beside her hand, and typed across the keyboard. "This must be him." She clicked on a link. "Yes, this is the guy." She swung the laptop around toward Serena.

"Wow, he's *GQ* cover material, isn't he?"

"Would you expect less from my cousin?"

"No, I guess not." Serena pointed to a line on the screen. "But look, it says he has an MBA from Harvard and currently works as a private fiduciary financial advisor and investment broker. His firm has a five-star rating with a number of large corporations. See here, they're all listed on the sidebar." She glanced at Addie. "What does fiduciary advisor mean?"

"It means he's actually licensed with the United States Securities and Exchange Commission and state regulators. He's the real deal, and not just some run-of-the-mill financial advisor. Look, his corporate office address is in Boston, but it says there's a satellite office in Salem." Addie sat back and stared at the screen. "I bet he lives in Salem, at least part-time."

"That would account for him being in Greyborne Harbor on business, wouldn't it?"

"It could, but why would Kalea be going to a meeting with him?"

"Maybe she's gone to work for him?" Serena said, as

she cleared the plates from the counter and rinsed them in the sink.

"It could be. She was a paralegal, so that might make sense."

"It also could be the reason she doesn't care about her job at the bookstore anymore. She's got something better now."

Addie closed the laptop. "If that's the case, then she should have talked to me and explained instead of pulling what she did, and it doesn't account for her behavior tonight, or the fact that she's misleading this guy into thinking this is her house. My gut tells me she's up to something else."

"There's nothing I see here that is relevant to the missing book or the murder, so we can probably take his name off that board of yours. I'd say after reading this, his being in town is a coincidence and most likely related to a business investment. You were probably right. The argument you saw between Brett and Mr. GQ was over something else. However . . ." Serena's eyes flashed with a mysterious gleam.

"What? Don't leave me hanging."

"Elli did come through today. That girl sure can turn on the charm when she needs to."

"Something I believe she learned from her mother, Maggie. In her real-estate dealings, she's known to flip on and off that same charm in an instant."

"I don't care how Elli got it, but all she had to do was bat those false black lashes of hers and that young police recruit, Curtis, was singing his heart out to her."

"Stop with the dramatics. What did he say?"

"He said . . ." Serena sat down beside Addie and toyed with the scrunched-up napkin on the counter.

"Serena, for you to torment me like this, it better be good."

"Blood residue was found by the sink in the bakery, and it appeared that someone had tried to clean it up, but it still glowed under that special light the police use."

"I heard that, but Simon told me this afternoon it wasn't a match to Brett's."

"Did Simon also tell you Brett's fingerprints were all over the bakery?"

"I know he was there. I saw him and Ken coming out of the bakery Friday morning, so it stands to reason his prints would be found."

"Did you tell Marc?"

Addie thought back to the statement she'd made on Sunday and shook her head. "I can't remember."

"Maybe you should because now they're working on the premise that there was a third person involved in committing the murder, and if they can identify who the blood belongs to, they can figure out who Martha's accomplice was because it's not a match for Martha's either."

"It seems that nothing that turns up helps her case, does it?"

Chapter Nineteen

Addie scanned over the brown paper she'd lain out on the breakfast nook table.

"Are you sure we're not missing anything that we added to the shop board earlier?" asked Serena, leaning over her shoulder.

"Not as far as I can see."

"You can probably take that black marker and strike out 'Mystery Man' since we now know who he is, and that he's here for legitimate reasons."

Addie's hand hovered over the notation on the paper and drew it back. "Yeah, but I can't shake the feeling I had when I saw them arguing in the park. There was something about Jared's and Brett's body language that told me they weren't strangers."

"That's most likely because Brett ended up dead two days later, so you're looking at everyone as a suspect."

"You're right because I can't believe Martha did it, and I'm desperate to find someone else to sic the police on." She made a firm, bold stroke through *Mystery Man*. Addie's gaze read through the notations. "It also means we have even less than we did before, and nothing here is going to help Martha or Paige."

A text alert pinged on Serena's phone, and she fished it out of her jean pocket. "It's Zach. He got off early and is on his way home."

"Tell him we have some leftover Mario's lasagna if he's hungry."

Serena's thumbs tapped out her reply, and she grinned. "He'll be here in five. I'll heat it up for him." She retrieved the pan from the refrigerator, scooped out a serving onto a plate, and slid it into the microwave. "He's not a fan of nuked food, but"—she shrugged—"what can he expect at nine p.m.?"

"I'll put the kettle on and make a pot of tea. What kind are you in the mood for?" Addie searched through a small cupboard filled with assorted packages of SerenaTEA blends.

"My old standby in the evening is still Heavenly Delight unless you prefer another one, like the Beddy Time blend?"

"No, I need to relax but not conk out. I think that one has valerian root in it, doesn't it?"

Serena grinned. "Look at you, learning your tea blends. I'm impressed."

"Only the ones that taste like dirt." She smirked and gave Serena a little hip check.

"That'll be him. I'll get it." Serena scampered down the hallway at the sound of knocking.

"Hey, Zach." Addie waved from a counter stool. "It's nice you could get off early tonight. Was the Grey Gull Inn slow?"

"Yeah, the large police presence around today didn't

help." He settled his lanky body onto the stool beside Addie.

"Why? What happened?" Serena's voice warbled as she set his plate in front of him. "Are you okay?"

"I'm fine. It's just that apparently the fellow who was killed was staying there, and his girlfriend still is. So, the police have had a couple of units searching their room and questioning everyone in the inn who might have had contact with them." He dug into the pile of juicy tomato, noodles, and cheese. "This is so good." He bent down to scoop in another mouthful, and his elbow bumped Addie's laptop. It flickered back onto the last opened page. "Sorry, I'm just so hungry. None of us got a dinner break because we had to take our turn talking to the police and had to cover each other for that." He glanced at the screen. "Hey, I know that guy."

Addie's eyes flashed to the screen. The photo of Jared Munroe stared back at her. "This guy?"

"Yeah, I've seen him around a few times lately and saw him again tonight, too."

Serena looked at Addie and then back at Zach. "Is he staying at the inn?"

"Not as far as I know, but he's been there a few times. Like tonight, when I took a bag of trash out before I left. He was having an argument with the dead guy's girlfriend in the parking lot."

"What!" Addie and Serena cried in unison.

Addie's eyes flashed. "Did you hear what it was about?"

"Not much, I was too far away. Except that guy"—he motioned with his fork—"yelled, 'I want my money,' and then got real close in her face and said something else that made her flinch back. I hung by a car to make sure he didn't get physical with her."

"Did he?" Serena clasped his arm.

"No, he left, and after a few minutes of sitting in her car, she did, too."

"Was Kalea with him?" Serena asked, her fingers gripping his arm tighter.

He twisted his arm to release her hold on him. "No, I didn't see her."

Confusion seeped through Addie. "So, she wasn't in his car with him when he left?"

"He never left in a car. He went inside the main door." Zach's gaze went from Serena's to Addie's. "What's this all about?"

"That's the guy she's dating now and the one she left here with earlier tonight." Serena sank onto the other stool.

"Oh . . . well, I never saw her with him and when I went back inside that guy"—he motioned with his head to the screen—"was talking to Bruce, the manager, outside of one of the meeting rooms they rent out, and then he went in and closed the door behind him. Maybe she was in there?"

"Yeah, maybe." Addie's gaze flitted from the screen to Zach. "And you have no idea what else he said to Amber in the parking lot?"

"I wish now I'd paid more attention and had gotten closer when a truck started backing into the loading dock. At the time, I only wanted to make sure that this guy wasn't going to hurt the poor woman whose boyfriend got killed. I never thought that he might have had something to do with it."

"We still don't know if he did, but that does prove.what I saw in the park on Friday wasn't happenstance. Jared knew Brett and Amber." Addie scrolled down the page. "Who is this guy? He looks so upstanding on his company web page and is a major player in the investment field. At least according to the large corporations that have given him endorsements." She continued to read. "Hmm, this is interesting. It says here, near the bottom under the services his firm offers, that it also can arrange for business loans and financing."

"So, he's like a banker, too?" Serena asked.

"It doesn't look like he's connected to any actual banking institutions, but it does say his firm can provide financing if required." Addie glanced at Serena. "The wording on his site is fairly vague about the details so my guess is, given what Zach overheard him say tonight to Amber, licensed with the Securities and Exchange Commission or not, his private investment company might operate its financing division a bit on the shady side."

"You mean, he's like a loan shark, the kind of guy who goes around breaking kneecaps?"

"Who knows, and if the stakes are high enough, they have been known to commit murder, too."

Zach leaned on his elbow and met Addie's gaze. "But if he killed the people who owed him money, then how could he expect them to pay it back?"

"Unless it wasn't Brett who owed him the money, but Amber, and killing Brett was a warning to her. A sign that he was serious."

Zach motioned to the screen. "But would a guy like that do the dirty work himself? Wouldn't he hire a hit man?"

"You're probably right. Maybe he was only delivering the personal message to Amber to let her know he was around and watching her." Addie scrolled farther down the page, stopped, and glanced back at Zach. "You know, you might not be far off in suggesting a hit man. That could be why Simon hasn't been able to discover what the murder weapon is. Professional killers use a lot of methods that the typical murderer wouldn't be aware of."

"Wow. A shakedown in a parking lot certainly isn't the kind of business meeting I imagined your cousin was running off to," Serena said, and yanked her phone out of her pocket.

Addie pushed her phone down. "Wait. Who are you texting?"

"Marc. We have to tell him all this."

"But none of this proves anything. We're only guessing. Jared might be completely innocent of everything we *think* we know."

Serena's thumb hovered over SEND. "Are you willing to take the chance that your airhead cousin isn't in danger until we, a couple of amateurs, can get absolute proof of what we figured out and then take it to him? It might be too late for Kalea by then."

Addie dropped her hand. "You're right. Tell him, and let him decide if it's fact or fiction and worth looking into."

Serena pressed SEND. "There, let's see what he has to say after he takes a look at all this."

Within a minute, her phone rang, and she glanced at Addie. "Wow, that was fast, and he's obviously interested in what we have to say because my message garnered a phone call from His Highness and not a reply text." She grinned and answered, "Hello . . . yeah, we came across some information about that mystery man Brett was arguing with in the park on Friday. His name is Jared Munroe, and I think you should come to Addie's and take a look at it." She gave Addie a wink. "What? . . . Oh, okay, sure . . .

just a minute." Serena looked apologetically at Addie, and she stepped out into the hallway.

Addie glanced after her and then at Zach. "I wonder what all that's about?"

Zach shrugged. "They're pretty busy at the inn tonight questioning everyone. Maybe he can't get away."

"But why all the secrecy to their conversation?"

"Secrecy . . . or Serena being overly dramatic?" His brow quirked.

Addie chuckled. "You're right. Can I get you anything else? Want some tea?"

"No, I'm not much of a tea drinker." Zach rinsed his plate and put it in the dishwasher.

"Does your bride-to-be, you know, the local tea merchant, know that?" Addie laughed and poured herself a cup.

"Oh yeah, she swears she's going to convert me, but tea has never been my first choice in after-dinner beverage, but I could go for a cup of that coffee blend you use."

"Okay." Addie opened up a cupboard and plucked a pod of dark-roast coffee from a box and dropped it into the coffee maker. "It'll just take a minute."

"Great, thanks." He leaned his elbows on the counter. "Say, I wanted to ask you something."

"Shoot." Addie took his brewed cup and placed it in front of him and pointed to the creamer and sugar. "Ask away."

"Has Serena said much to you about my stepmother?"

Addie took in a slow, silent breath. *What to say, what to say*? She gulped. "Not really, why?"

"It's just that Veronica and Serena don't seem to like each other, and I'm afraid Serena is going to change her mind about marrying me because of all the stress Veronica is causing her." His forlorn gaze caught Addie's.

"Serena loves you. There's no way she would change her mind about marrying you."

"I know, but they can't agree on anything about the wedding, and Veronica is a very domineering woman. I'm afraid she's going to make Serena run."

"The Serena I know isn't a jackrabbit. She's not going to run, but maybe you need to step in and speak to your father about the . . . well, the tension his wife is causing and remind him whose wedding this is."

"I did, but he's blinded by that woman. It's like she's cast a spell over him."

"What does your mother say?"

"She said that she'd like nothing better than for Veronica to disappear, never to be seen again."

"I guess that's understandable after what happened in their marriage, but seriously." Addie took his hand in hers. "Just be there for Serena, and show her your support and stand united against Veronica."

"It's hard sometimes. She's so—"

"That was interesting." Serena swept back into the kitchen. "He won't be coming. When I told him what we had discovered, he said he already knew. As far as he could tell and Ryley could dig up, Jared Munroe is exactly who he says he is, a very *rich*, private financial investor and, therefore, not a suspect in anything related to the murder case."

"What about him threatening Amber tonight? I saw it," Zach said.

"I told him, and he said it didn't prove anything, but he would keep it in mind should something else pop up."

"Why all the secrecy to your conversation?" Addie asked.

"Oh, that." Serena waved her off. "He wanted to put

me on speakerphone with Ryley, and I . . ." Her gaze dropped. "Thought it best."

"Is that all?"

"Yes, well, plus he went into his usual rant about keeping our noses out of police business."

"Okay, I'll take your word for it, but if I find out you've been conspiring with Ryley behind my back . . ."

Serena responded with a dramatic eye roll.

Zach drained his coffee cup. "Well, if that's the end of the action tonight, then I'm heading home. It's been a long day, and I have to be at the clinic by eight tomorrow." He set his cup in the sink and glanced at Serena. "Are you coming now, too, or are the two of you going to rehash what we learned tonight?"

"I think since Marc isn't coming, all we're going to do is exactly what Zach said." Serena glanced over at Addie. "Or have you any new theories?"

"No, I'm all out of theories, and if the police are aware of everything we know, then all there's left for me to do is try to get some information out of Kalea. Maybe she knows something about him that she isn't aware means something else. My gut tells me his being here isn't a co-incidence, and Brett ending up dead and his threats on Amber are all related to the book and/or murder."

"Just be careful. You know your cousin, and if you go asking too many questions, she'll get suspicious and might say something to Jared. Then . . . well, you could be in danger if what we suspect about him is true."

"I'll be careful. I promise." Addie started to close the door as Zach glanced back at her and then hastily at Serena. His eyes pleaded for Addie to say something before he turned, and his long legs took him down the porch stairs.

"Wow, he's in a hurry to get home," Serena said. Her voice strained as she watched him march across the driveway to their apartment above the garage. "He didn't even wait for me."

"He probably just wants to get warm. It's freezing tonight, so don't worry." Addie grabbed Serena's coat sleeve. "But he is afraid that his stepmother is going to make you change your mind about marrying him."

Serena's eyes widened.

"Just reassure him and present a united front to her. Let him know you're not going anywhere."

"Thanks. I had no idea he was feeling that insecure, but that's how she manipulates. Divide and conquer. Yeah, we need to talk." Serena bolted down the stairs after him.

Chapter Twenty

Addie ambled to the kitchen, grabbed her teacup and the brown paper from the table, switched off the lights, and returned to the front living room. She spread the paper across the coffee table and settled onto the antique horsehair-stuffed sofa. Pippi hopped up beside her and curled into a ball. "Well, my friend, as usual there are too many question marks here. Like this one." She pointed to the paper and glanced at her softly snoring roommate and smiled.

She refocused on the paper. "Hmm." She went to the desk, rummaged around in a drawer until she found a notepad and pen, and returned to the sofa, pen primed in her hand.

"If Brett stole the book, and someone knew it and wanted it from him badly enough to kill for it, why are all my top suspects still in town?" She tapped the pen on the coil-ringed pad. "Amber would have taken the book and fled if he had it or at least given it to Jared to pay off the money she owed him and then left if that's what he was arguing with her about tonight. She would have been long gone before the body was discovered late Sunday morning, wouldn't she?" She glanced at her sleeping friend. "You're no help, are you?"

Pippi's ear twitched.

"Okay, and what about Ken? If he and Brett were partners in all this, and he killed him, so they wouldn't have to split the money, why didn't he bolt right after either?" Her gaze narrowed on what she had written. "If Jared had killed Brett for the book or the money, if Brett was the one who owed him, and he had it, he wouldn't be threatening Amber or sticking around, regardless of Kalea's charms. No, none of this makes sense, does it?" She glanced at Pippi, who was so deep in sleep she jerked and softly yelped in a dream.

Addie looked back to where she had written *Brett book thief?* and drew a circle around it. "My guess is Brett stole the book. Gloria ID'd him as the first one on the scene, and I think his attempt to assist her was, in fact, a cover-up for him rifling through her pockets for the keys."

Her chest squeezed with another thought. "He might have even pushed the ladder over to cause the whole thing. After all, didn't Gloria say it shook just before she fell?" Addie shuddered and glanced at her notes. "So, if I'm right, they all have an interest in the book, for whatever reason, but none of them could have it now. Given that all three of my main suspects are still in town, they don't know where it is because whichever one of them killed Brett, did it before he could tell them where he hid it. They're all hanging around, trying to find it." She frowned and bit her bottom lip. "Which also means Brett might have been killed for another reason than the money. Because dead men can't talk, so if one of them had killed him for the book, then they'd never learn where it is." Her gaze flitted between the brown paper and the notepad.

"Think, Addie, think. You've been assuming the motive was money for the book and that someone wanted the twenty-five thousand dollars so desperately they were willing to kill for it. What are other motives that can lead a person to kill?" She sat back, lost in her thoughts, to the tune of the pen clinking on the metal notebook coil, and then began frantically scribbling.

Monetary
Passion
Revenge
Personal Vendetta
Self-defense and in-defense
Anger
Hatred
Jealousy

She stopped scribbling and read over what she had written and moaned. "That leaves even a bigger window of *what-ifs*." She tossed the notebook on the table and picked up her teacup, sipping the now-cold brew, and stared at the brown paper. "I don't even know where to start."

Pippi jerked, looked up at her through sleep-blurred eyes, and nestled her head on Addie's lap. She stroked the small dog's head and tried to picture in her mind what all her notes were trying to tell her, but it was no use. She needed more information, and at this point she couldn't even be positive that it was Brett who stole the book. Because it didn't make sense to her that someone would kill him for it and not know where it was to retrieve it.

Addie refocused and glanced back over her notes about the other motives for murder, trying to sort each one of them into an image in her mind with each of her three suspects: first Ken, then Jared and Amber, based on Jared's threat toward her. Which *other* murder motives fit each suspect? But it was still no use. She didn't have enough information about any of them to see a motive other than the book and money. She looked at the *other* motives she'd just written and muttered, "Well then"— she gulped—"Martha fits a couple of those to a T."

Her eyes scanned the notebook. *Personal Vendetta,* check. *Anger,* check, *Hatred,* check. After all, Martha told Addie herself that she was furious with Brett for threatening Paige with a custody dispute, especially as he'd shown no interest in Emma or paid Paige any child support for nearly four years. That alone would be enough to set a mother bear like Martha into full protection mode of her baby bear Paige.

Addie scratched her head as she thought her theories through. She had told Martha the ballpark worth of the book. What if Martha figured out Brett was the one who stole the book, depriving Paige and Emma of their inheritance? Would Martha, could she, have killed him? She had to speak with Paige in the morning to find out if Brett even knew about the book and had learned somehow that Gloria had it.

She shuddered, folded the paper, and dropped it into the doggy bed along with the notepad and Baxter to take it all upstairs. She then went to the table in front of the window, turned off the light, and peered into the darkness. Her gaze focused on the fluffy falling snowflakes, and her heart fell, too. That meant any evidence left behind at the bakery or at the original murder scene—wherever that might be—would be lost. She'd begun to turn away when headlights started up her driveway, and as a car pulled up, she recognized it as Jared's BMW. Addie dropped the blind, scooped Pippi into her arms, and held her snug, clasping her fingers over the small dog's snout to keep her from barking. She needed answers and maybe eavesdropping in the dark would be one way to get them.

The front door flew open, and the entry was filled with the sounds of soft laughter and deep, breathy moans. Addie flinched. She was most definitely going to have to make her presence known before things between Jared and Kalea went too far and she found them in a compromising position.

As she moved closer to the double-wide living room door, she cringed when Jared pushed Kalea against the wall beside the marble foyer table. His hands and mouth searched out her body. "Should we take this celebration upstairs?" his smoky voice murmured as he kissed Kalea's neck.

A soft laugh escaped Kalea's throat, and she pushed him away. "I can't. My cousin's here and heaven knows what gossip she'll spread around town about me."

"Do you care?" He nibbled behind her ear.

"No, I don't. However, my late aunt had a sterling reputation in this town, and I don't want to be the one to tarnish it." She ducked under his arm and sauntered toward the door out of Addie's eyesight.

He moved toward her. "But my love, this is an occasion worth celebrating."

"And we will when I visit you in Salem. It just can't be celebrated in that way here, now." Kalea's sulky voice held a rich, seductive edge, a technique she had honed over the years. Addie could picture in her mind that her cousin was holding his jacket collar and cooing, her long lashes fluttering as she looked into Jared's eyes to tease him about what would come and to appease him now.

"If you think it's best. I can wait. I know a good thing when I find it, and my dear, you are not a disappointment so far."

With that, the door creaked and a cold wind gust swept around Addie. She shivered as a car started outside, and she heard the front door click closed. She drew herself up stiffly, let out a deep breath, and stepped into the foyer. "What was all that about?"

"Addie!" Kalea's hand flew to her heaving chest. "You scared the bejesus out of me!"

"What was that all about, Kalea?"

"What?" Her cousin feigned innocence as she hung up her jacket.

"That little scene, and what do you have to celebrate?"

Kalea's gaze averted Addie's and dropped to Pippi locked in Addie's arms. "I was going to tell you. I just didn't want to until it was official, but . . . but I'm going to be the new owner of the dress shop on Main Street."

"What! Where did you get the money to buy it?"

Kalea, still avoiding Addie's dagger-filled eyes, toyed with the candelabra on the side table. "Jared has arranged financing for me."

"He has, has he? And you don't need any money of your own to put in?"

"Well, I will. He's . . . it's more of a loan just until . . ."

"Until what, you kill me and steal mine?"

"No!" Her eyes filled with horror. "How could you think such a thing?"

"Because for some funny reason, he seems to be under the impression that all this and what I have is yours, isn't that right?"

"Perhaps he got that impression."

"Perhaps? I've heard the two of you talking. How do

you plan on paying him back? This kind of money doesn't come without strings or a personal guarantee. No one just hands over the amount of money it would take to buy a business!"

"I'm hoping we can work something out when the time comes."

"What time is that? When he's going to kill you because he finds out everything you told him is a lie?"

"Don't be silly. Jared couldn't kill anyone." Addie's thoughts went to Zach's words about a hit man, and she shuddered. "By then he'll be so in love with me, he won't care about the money, and besides, the deposit was only a hundred thousand."

"Oh, chicken feed in your eyes, the woman who works part-time and lives in my house, eating all my food. What if he doesn't fall in love with you, what then?"

"I'll worry about all that then."

"It's a hundred thousand dollars, and you don't have it. I checked him out online, and he appears to be a very successful financial broker. Do you really think he's just going to hand over all that money without doing a background check on *you* first? Think about that one."

"Well, he did give me the money, so obviously he hasn't checked me out, or he would have said something. Look, I'm tired. I need to go to bed." She started for the wooden carved staircase.

Addie grabbed her dress sleeve. "Where did you meet him?"

"He came into the bookstore one day, why?"

"Was he looking for anything in particular, or just browsing?"

"Actually, he was interested in some first editions we had. I told him I kept my rare book collection at home.

He asked if he could see it sometime, and that was it. So, you see, that little fib led to the rest of it." Her gaze dropped. "We've been seeing each other since, and then one day I was mad because Paige was being so bossy and wanted me to sort through some dirty old boxes. I told him I was thinking of giving you the bookstore to run and starting a new business. I couldn't help it if he thought I was serious, and before I knew it, he found the opportunity of the dress shop, and we went ahead with it."

"So just like that he gave you the money."

"Not exactly." She played her foot over the carpet runner on the bottom step. "I told him my money was tied up for a while, and he said he'd take care of it until I could cash in on my investments. We signed some loan papers, and he made the deal with the sellers. We signed the purchase agreement tonight."

"Kalea, what you've done is fraud, and if Jared discovers you're not good for the money he's arranged interim financing for, then you could be arrested or worse." Addie's mind rushed to the look on Brett's face when she discovered his body.

"Trust me. I know what I'm doing. Jared adores me. He'd never press charges."

"Maybe not, but there are other ways he can make certain he gets what's owed to him."

"Stop being so dramatic. You sound like Serena right now."

"Maybe so, but think about it. Men like Jared don't just give their money away to every pretty face they come across."

"Relax, you heard what went on tonight. I'm pretty sure I have him exactly where I want him."

"For how long though? You can't really think you can continue this charade and—"

"I'm going to bed. We can finish this discussion in the morning." She started up the stairs. "Good night."

"Were you at the Grey Gull Inn tonight?"

Kalea stopped mid-step and glanced back down at Addie. "Yes, that's where the meeting was, why?"

"Was Jared with you?"

"Yes."

"All evening?"

"Yes, well, except when he went out for a few minutes to get some fresh air. Why does any of that matter?"

"It's just that"—Serena's words of warning about sharing too much with Kalea right now rushed back at her—"you don't know anything about running a business."

"I can hire people, which are one of the perks of being the owner."

"It's not that easy."

"Come on, I've seen how you do it. It can't be that hard."

"Kalea, stop!" Addie's voice came off as shrill, but she didn't care. "You're going to have to find someplace else to live."

Kalea's knuckles whitened around the banister. "What are you talking about?"

"I can't be a part of this ruse you're pulling, and it's time for you to leave."

"But we're family." Kalea's tear-blurred gaze caught Addie's fiery one.

Addie shook her head adamantly. "No, this is the last straw. You've pushed me too far this time. You have until the end of the week to find something else, and tomorrow you can stop by and pick up your final paycheck."

"You're firing me, too?"

Addie crossed her arms and stared in disbelief at her cousin. "You have your own business to run now. With what you've done lately, I don't want you to have any part of mine *or* my life."

"But Addie—"

"It's gone too far this time. I won't be digging you out of this mess you've created. One week, and that's it." Addie spun on her heel and stomped into the living room.

Chapter Twenty-One

Addie backed her Mini out of the garage. Serena's Jeep was already gone from its sheltered spot inside, and so was Zach's older Honda CR-V from the driveway. She glanced at the furry head poking out the top of the straw tote bag. "See what happens when you take your time playing in the snow? Now we're going to be late opening the shop today." With a chuckle, she ruffled Pippi's head and cranked the wheel to turn down the driveway. A sharp rap on her passenger-side window made her jump. Kalea stood, peering in, a travel mug in one hand and a grin spread across her face. Addie rolled the window down. "What is it?"

"You forgot me."

"I didn't forget you. I fired you last night, remember?"

Kalea's grin withered. "I thought you were joking."

"No, I was completely serious, and as a reminder, you have one week to find someplace else to live."

"Come on, we're family."

"Then you should have thought about that before you stole my identity and created a con with your new boyfriend as the mark." Addie shifted into drive. "Now, if you'll excuse, I have a business to run."

Kalea's hand gripped the doorframe around the window. "But I don't take possession of the dress shop for another month. If you let me go now, how will I live with no income?"

"You'll have to figure that one out on your own. You seem to think you have everything else figured out. Or . . . you can ask your new boyfriend for it since you think you have him exactly where you want him. But it's not my problem, and I won't be part of whatever it is you're doing, because aside from being legally wrong, it's outright deceitful."

"But where will I go?"

"Frankly, I can think of some place, and you won't need your winter coat there." Addie stepped on the gas, bumped over the tire ruts in the fresh-fallen snow, and turned left to head to town. One look in the rearview mirror at her openmouthed cousin standing rigid in the driveway told her that maybe Kalea's new reality was starting to sink in. "Good riddance," she muttered.

Addie pulled up the alley and was relieved to see the crime scene barricade had been taken down. She grabbed Pippi's carry bag and headed inside her shop. She hoped that also meant it was business as usual out front, too. However, with one look through the bay window at the yellow tape blowing in the wind, her heart fell.

Paige was sitting on a stool at the front counter reading the paper and closed it as Addie approached. "Good morning." A smile that missed her eyes pulled at the corners of her mouth. "I see our sometime employee isn't with you. Is she a no-show again today?"

"She won't be an issue for either of us anymore. I fired her."

Paige's eyes lit up.

"I see the bakery is still sealed off. Does that mean the judge denied your mother bail, and she remains in police custody?"

"Actually, she's out and next door if you can believe it."

"What, after spending all this time in a cell, she didn't go home?"

"Oh, she went home and had a shower, then came right in to see what was left of the bakery."

"The police have cleared her to be in there?"

"Carolyn's with her to make sure she doesn't touch anything."

"Carolyn? My goodness, she's ready to pop any minute. I hope it doesn't happen while she's there alone with your mom."

"If she does, remember my mom has given birth to five babies herself, so she's probably in good hands."

"True, she'd know what to do." Addie set Pippi on the floor, who immediately raced over to get her morning cuddle from Paige. "How's your mom doing? You know, mentally through all this."

Paige peered at her over the top of Pippi's head. "Not good. I tried to convince her to stay home and sleep today and not to worry about the bakery until all that"—she waved her free hand toward the window—"was gone, but . . ."

"But what? She wouldn't hear of it, and for you, it was like looking into a mirror, and you saw where you get your stubborn streak from?" Addie said with a chuckle.

"No." Paige's eyes flew wide open, and then she bit

back a laugh as her cheeks reddened. "Yeah, you're right. I guess I'm more like her than I want to admit."

Addie's gaze scanned the bookshop, and from where she stood, it appeared the intrusion of the barricade was going to mean another all too quiet day for them. "Would you mind if I left you alone for a while to check in on Carolyn and see how your mom is holding up?"

"Nope, go ahead. I have my guard dog," she said with a giggle as she set Pippi on the floor.

Addie looked at Pippi's wiggling back end and tail. "Ankle biter is more like it. Aren't you, girl?" Addie crouched and gave her furry roommate a scratch. "Okay, I won't be long." She grabbed her bag, headed outside, and ducked under the police tape.

Addie pulled the bakery door open and poked her head inside. One never knew what kind of greeting they'd receive from Martha. Given the circumstances, she expected the worst this morning. She glanced across the empty storefront to the high glass-shelved countertop. Paige had tried to convince her mother to set up four to five tables so customers could relax and have a coffee or tea with their pastries, using Serena and her tea shop as an example. Martha—in her usual Martha style—had harrumphed the idea, saying she didn't like people hanging around all day and wouldn't hear of it. However, when an elderly customer collapsed one hot day due to standing too long in the lineup on cinnamon roll day, Martha relented and placed a wooden bench in front of the window. A very tired-appearing Carolyn now greeted Addie from that utilitarian seating.

"Addie? Hi, you are aware this area isn't open to the public." She made a strained effort to rise to her feet.

"Sit, please. I'm only here to check on Martha." She dropped her voice. "Paige is concerned."

"I bet she is. I don't think the woman slept more than two hours since she was taken in Sunday afternoon."

"Where is she?"

"In the back."

"Shouldn't you be—?"

"Don't tell Marc, but I think I'm . . ." She winced.

"Are you okay?" Addie dropped down beside her on the bench. "Should I call someone?"

Carolyn shook her head. "No, pretty sure it's Braxton Hicks"—Addie's brow rose in question—"training labor pains. They're normal," Carolyn said with a chuckle. "I'm fine, really. I just need to sit for a minute. Could you go back and make sure my charge is behaving herself, though?"

"Sure, call out if you need me."

"Oh, I will. Don't worry."

Addie peered around the doorway into the kitchen area, and her heart lurched in her chest. Martha sat on a shipping box marked FLOUR, her head in her hands, her shoulders heaving with sobs. Addie stood motionless. She knew the woman needed consoling, and if Catherine Lewis were here, that's exactly what her dear friend would do. Oh, how Addie missed her at times like this.

Addie silently cursed Jonathan Hemingway, her late fiancé's father—a man, who had David not been killed, would have been her father-in-law—for taking her old friend on a whirlwind tour of Europe, or wherever they were. Catherine wasn't even allowed, by the confidentiality of Jonathan's work, to reveal where she was meeting him on Christmas Day. She hadn't even been able to tell Addie what day she'd return or from where. It was all so hush-hush, and Addie hated it, especially at times like this. Catherine was like a mother to her, and right now she needed her guidance. Catherine knew how to deal with the cactus lady, something Addie was still learning.

Addie drew in a deep breath, held her head high, and took a step forward. Martha's head snapped up, and her tear-blurred eyes focused on Addie's. Addie skidded to an abrupt halt.

"Have you come to gloat?" Martha barked, her voice sounding stronger than she appeared.

"Not in the least, I was . . . Paige was worried, and I only came to see how you were holding up."

"Just peachy." She swiped at her eyes. "Darn right peachy."

Addie flopped down on a box, wrapped her arm around Martha's round shoulders, and squeezed. "I can't imagine how you're feeling, but I do feel your pain and confusion right now." She stroked her back.

Martha glanced sideways at her. "I seem to remember you spending time in that very jail cell, so I'm pretty sure you do know how I'm feeling."

"True, but my situation was a little different."

"Was it? All the evidence pointed to you, too, if I remember."

"It did, and I worked hard to find new evidence to prove my innocence, which is exactly what we're going to do for you."

"Well, good luck with that, because as far as Chief Chandler and his ex-FBI watchdog figure, it's an open-and-shut case against me."

"I don't believe that. Marc's known you his whole life. He doesn't really believe, deep down, that you could have killed Brett. We just have to be able to find enough evidence to prove who did to change the DA's mind."

"How are we going to do that, Miss Smarty-Pants?" Martha folded her arms across her massive chest.

"First off, it appears that Brett's murder may have had something to do with Paige's book, *The Secret Garden*. I suspect he took Gloria's keys when he was pretending to help her after she fell. What I can't figure out is how he knew she had the book."

"What?" She wrung her hands in her lap. "Oh no, then it *is* all my fault."

"How? What did you do?"

"It was me who told Brett about the book, well sort of. He asked about it, and I told him Paige had lent it to Gloria. Then she ends up in the hospital and him dead. Oh, what have I done?"

"Wait a minute. When did you tell Brett about the book?"

"The evening he arrived in town, he came to the house to see Emma. Paige was out with the young fireman she's been seeing, and there was only Emma and me there. I wasn't going to let him in at first but figured it wouldn't hurt. After all, scumbag or not, he was still the child's father."

"This was *before* I told you how much the book was worth?"

Martha nodded. "He asked about it right off. I figured Paige had told him about the book her father had given her when Brett and she lived together for a short time when Emma was a baby. He said he only asked about it because Emma wanted him to read it to her before she went to bed. So, I blurted out that he'd have to find another storybook because Paige lent it to Gloria."

"Did you tell him who Gloria was or where she worked or about her being in the park with the decorating committee at any time?"

"I'm afraid so. As he was reading another book to Emma, he said Gloria was a very lucky woman to have friends who loaned out their books. He said he treasured all his so much they were like his babies, and he never trusted anyone with them. I thought he was being a jerk and trying to get a dig in at Paige, so I stuck up for her and in no uncertain terms told him what an upstanding member of the community Gloria was and how she was even the volunteer coordinator for the park decorating committee, and she'd make certain no harm came to Paige's old book."

"And from there, it wouldn't have been difficult for someone else in the park to point Gloria out to him and maybe offer a little more information like where she lived and all that."

"Probably. Everyone loves Gloria and is proud to serve her. No one would have thought harm might come to her by bragging about what they knew of her. Like me." Martha's sobs began anew.

Out of the corner of her eye, Addie saw a dark shape and looked up at a pale-faced Carolyn, a puddle pooling around her boots. "It appears my water broke."

Martha jumped to her feet, and in one motion took Carolyn's arm and seated her on the box of flour.

"I can't sit here. What if the flour is ruined?"

"Pish, it can be replaced. You sit tight. Addie, call an ambulance and then Pete. I'll get a cool cloth for her head," Martha ordered, and went to the sink. "Darn it, there's no paper towels left. That idiot Betty must have used them all when she cut her hand, reaching for them when she put out the fire."

Addie hung up with the 911 dispatcher and stared at Martha. "The blood they found in here was Betty's?"

"Yes, fool that she is." Martha found an apron in the cupboard, drenched it with water, and placed it on Carolyn's brow. "Apparently, when the oven fire started, she grabbed for the roll of towels but sliced her hand over a knife sitting on the counter beside them. After she got the fire out, she stopped the bleeding and cleaned up. The police and *I* only just found all of this out when they went to her house to ask a few questions about me. Of course, she, having just been fired, was less than flattering toward me when she spoke to them, which doesn't help my case."

Martha crouched down in front of Carolyn and fixed her gaze on hers. "Now, you relax and take some deep slow breaths. You know the drill. You've had nearly as many babies as I have." She held out her hands. "Now, take these and squeeze them when a contraction starts and keep squeezing until it stops. Can you do that?"— Carolyn nodded—"Good, okay, here we go. I'll count the time between them."

Martha's hands turned white as Carolyn did what she was told, and then the color slowly reemerged in them. "One," Martha said breathlessly, "two, three, four, five, six, seven, eight, nine, ten . . . another one already? Okay, squeeze." Martha looked up at Addie. "Maybe you should go out front and show the paramedics back when they get here."

"Are you going to be fine on your own with her?"

"Oh yes, we're doing great, and Addie," she whispered, "tell them to hurry."

When the ambulance arrived, Addie hung back in the front area of the store. Between the carts of cooling racks and the boxes of supplies that hadn't been put away since Saturday's delivery, there was barely enough room for the two burly paramedics, a stretcher, and her. She paced the floor and frantically checked the time on her phone clock. Visions of Pete rushing to the hospital to meet the ambulance raced through her mind. Why weren't they taking her? Couldn't they tell she was going to deliver soon? They were running out of time.

Cries of a baby filled the air. Tears streamed down Addie's cheeks as the paramedics wheeled mother and baby past her. Addie's gaze sought out Carolyn's, a wide grin across her damp face.

"It's a girl! Tell Simon he has a new niece," Carolyn said, and hugged the tightly swathed bundle in her arms closer to her chest.

Addie glanced over at Martha, who followed the procession out of the kitchen. Her cheeks were covered in droplets of freshly shed tears.

"Are you okay?" Addie raised a questioning brow.

Martha nodded. "For the first time in a long time, these are tears of happiness," she said, and openly sobbed.

Chapter Twenty-Two

Paige burst through the bakery door, fear etched across her face. "Mom, are you okay? I saw the ambulance and—"

"Oh, honey, I'm fine." Martha wrapped her arms around her little girl. "I just delivered a baby." She stood back at arm's length, and her face lit up like the fairy lights in Addie's window displays.

"You did?"

"Yes, it was the best thing that's ever happened to me, aside"—she stroked Paige's cheek—"from birthing my own. And I'll tell you, I sure couldn't have done it if Addie hadn't come in to check on me." She glanced at Addie with gratitude.

"I didn't do anything. I've never even been around puppies being born."

"Yes, but without you here, I would have had one heck of a time calling the ambulance and delivering that wee one at the same time. It all happened so fast."

"Well, well, Miss Greyborne," Marc said from the doorway, a teasing glint in his eyes, "can you imagine my relief at walking into a scene, seeing you, and knowing there's no dead body for me to investigate."

"I imagine it is a relief." Addie couldn't stop the grin spreading across her face. "You know I don't always have the bad luck of being in the wrong place at the wrong time." She glanced at Martha. "Actually, sometimes I can be in the right place at the right time."

"Let's keep it that way in the future." He skirted past her to the back room, poked his head in, and turned to Martha. "I'll get someone in to clean up back here. Why don't you head home now? The tape should be down in the next day or so. Come back then."

"I don't have my car. I came with Paige."

"One of my officers can give you a ride. Jefferies," he called, "please see that Martha Stringer gets home safely."

"Yes, Chief."

Martha shuffled to the coatrack behind the counter, retrieved her handbag from a cupboard, and kissed Paige on the cheek. "I'll see you at home later," she said, and nodded at Officer Jefferies. "I'm ready, but I do have one favor to ask."

"Sure, what's that?" he asked, pulling the bakery door open for her.

"Is it possible for me to sit in the front seat? I don't want all the townies to think I've gone and gotten arrested again."

"Umm . . ." He glanced at Marc and chuckled at his nod. "Sure. No problem."

"Well, Paige and I should get back to the bookshop." Addie glanced at Marc. "See you around." She dashed out the door. "Martha, wait a minute," she called as Jefferies started to close the front cruiser door.

"What is it, dear?"

Addie leaned down and kept her voice low. "Remember what we were talking about before all the excitement?"

"Yes, why?"

"I'm working on a theory, and maybe you can help me put a few missing pieces to the puzzle together."

"Sure, if I can. What do you need to know?"

"What time did you leave the beach on Saturday night?"

"Well"—her gaze followed Jefferies as he slipped his way through the snow piles around the hood of the car toward the driver's side—"I'm not exactly certain. I had it out with Brett's latest hussy, and she took off in tears. Then I went back to the refreshment table and cleaned up. Ken helped me pack my car, and we left."

"Together?"

"No, heaven forbid! Except when he wants something from me that man is as useless now as he was twenty years ago." She pinned Addie with an unyielding gaze. "Not sure what he's after this visit, but I got my eye on him so gonna keep him close until I know. So no, he was in his car, and I in mine. I only happened to follow behind him until he turned off on Hemlock Street to go to his aunt's, and then I went on up the hill to my house."

"And you have no idea what time that was?"

"Probably close to ten because by the time I unloaded the car and put the coffee urn and everything in the garage and got inside, the kitchen clock said ten-twenty."

"I guess you wouldn't have any idea what time Amber went back to the Grey Gull, would you?"

"No, and I didn't care where she went at the time. I was just happy she had left the area. She was the one pushing for custody of Emma, it seems." Martha bit her lip, no doubt to stop the flow of tears behind her eyes.

"I know that according to what Amber Carr told me," Jefferies piped in as he leaned over in his seat and looked up at Addie, "and confirmed by witnesses when I questioned her, she went up to her room about nine-thirty and ordered room service. At about midnight, another guest at the inn was walking down the hallway and heard shouting, but he said it sounded like the woman was by herself, so she must have been on the phone."

"Thank you, Officer." Addie smiled and squeezed Martha's shoulder. "We'll talk later."

Addie couldn't contain the butterflies in her tummy. That midnight phone call confirmed that Amber must have been the person on the phone Old Bill overheard Brett arguing with. Now she only had to track down Bill and somehow make him reveal the other man on the beach. She loved it when pieces started to fall into place.

Martha pulled the door closed, and the cruiser pulled out into traffic. Addie spun around to head into her shop and jumped. "Marc, I didn't know you were behind me."

"It sounds like Jefferies didn't either."

"Don't be mad at him. He didn't share anything about the investigation. He only answered a question that may not have anything to do with the case."

"You really expect me to believe that?"

"What?"

"How many times do I have to tell you not to—"

"Save your breath. I know the rest of the standard line."

"Do you?" A harsh laugh erupted from his chest.

She flipped her ponytailed head, spun around, and marched into her shop to the tune of his laughter and the overhead bells ringing.

"It sounds like you and Mom had a pretty exciting morning?"

"Yes, yes, we did." Addie smiled. "It was amazing

actually." She took off her jacket and laid it across the wooden countertop.

"You missed some excitement in here, too."

"Really, what happened?"

"Kalea came in looking for her final paycheck."

"I forgot all about that in the commotion. Was she upset that it wasn't ready?"

"A little. Then, of course, she went on to whine about her tragic life."

"I bet she did. She didn't happen to mention where she and Jared were on Saturday night, did she?" Addie dropped a pod into the coffee brewer.

"As a matter of fact, she did."

"You're kidding?"

"No. She said she wondered if one of the reasons you were angry with her was because she didn't let you know she was leaving town on Saturday and didn't come home. She went on to tell me"—Paige's eyes held a glimmer of mischief—"that it hurt her if that was the only reason because she and Jared had such a lovely evening in Boston, and to know that her happiness upset you was more than she could take." Addie's neck hairs bristled. "She huffed at that point and said she thought you'd be proud of her, not angry, because she was finally making something of her life and trying to prove to you that she wasn't the same girl you knew in college."

"Oh, I'm angry with her, but not for just that night, and it tells me she really hasn't changed." Addie shook her head. A sardonic chuckle formed in her chest. "Because last night I told her exactly why I was mad at her, but obviously none of that part has sunk in yet." Addie eyed Paige. "Look, it's not busy, and most likely won't be until that police barricade comes down and stops detouring foot traffic past our door. Believe it or not, Kalea's little talk with you has helped fill in a few of the puzzle pieces. Do you want to be my set of fresh eyes on the crime board?"

"Me? Shouldn't you call Serena or Simon for that? I've never helped before. I wouldn't know where to begin."

"Nonsense, you read as many mystery novels as I do. Come on. It'll be fun." Addie scooped Pippi into her arms, and they headed toward the back room. Addie regaled Paige with Kalea's latest antics and the deception she was attempting to pull off with Jared.

Paige stood in the doorway of the back room. Her fingers whitened around the wooden-frame molding. "She bought my sister's dress shop? I didn't realize Mellissa was actually serious about selling it. She told me she was only thinking about it."

"It seems she did more than think about it. Keith told me since he and Mellissa . . . um . . . separated that her heart didn't seem to be in it anymore."

"Keith is such a sweetheart. He's been like a father to both me and Emma, and a right-hand man to Mom since he first started dating my sister. They used to be so close until word got out that he left the Ship 'n Anchor with a local barfly and were spotted later by the lighthouse in a compromising position, to say the least. Still, Mellissa must have rocks in her head to even think about divorcing him. She's never going to find a better man than he is, and once Mom gets over being mad at him. I'm pretty sure she'll tell her the same." Paige flopped down on a wooden crate. "I just wish she wouldn't be so rash and hold off selling their shop until all this settles down, and she clears her head."

"First off, having her husband cheat on her must have been a big blow and—"

"Yes, it's tough, but not impossible to work out. It's not like it was an ongoing affair. She was just some drunken-spur-of-the-moment fling."

Addie's brow rose. "Still, his indiscretion hurt your sister deeply, and—"

"But to sell the dress shop after they both worked so hard to make it successful."

"I'm not sure this sale will go through once Jared discovers Kalea isn't good for the money he fronted her. Because"—Addie's eyes narrowed as she thought hard about what she'd said to Kalea last night—"I can't imagine a businessman with his standing didn't check out Kalea thoroughly before he fronted her money."

"Good, maybe by then Mellissa and Keith will get counseling and be able to work it out. They have two kids." Paige's eyes filled with tears. "This isn't fair to them."

"No, it's not, but there's nothing we can do. It's between Mellissa and Keith to work out."

"You're right." Paige's shoulders shuddered with a deep breath. "Okay, let's focus on getting Mom off the list of suspects. Maybe we can salvage at least one of my family members here."

"That's my girl," Addie said, flipping the cover from the board and then standing back to review what she'd previously written.

Paige gasped when she read the title of the first column on the board.

Murder

And then she continued to scan down the list.

*Victim—Brett Palmer—Paige's ex—Emma's
    (Martha's and Ken's granddaughter) father*
Murder weapon???
Murder scene???
Crime scene—alley behind Martha's Bakery
*Victim involved in two family public
    disagreements—Brett, Martha, Ken Stringer
    (Paige's father/Martha's ex)*
*Keith—husband to Mellissa (Paige's eldest sister
    and son-in-law to Martha and Ken) broke up
    fistfight between Brett and Ken*
Amber Carr—Martha had altercation with

Paige's eyes widened as her gaze pored over the information written in the *Book* column on the right side.

*The Secret Garden—belonged to Paige and
    Emma, gift from Ken, Martha's ex—Paige's
    father—on loan to Gloria*
Gloria fall—in hospital
*Book last seen—Gloria's nightstand—by Addie
    and Martha*
Martha informed of 25K value of book
Spare key to Gloria's house—Martha
*Book gone—Martha denies any knowledge—no
    indication of a break-in*
*Searched Gloria's with police, absolutely no
    evidence of a break-in*
*Ken, Martha, Gloria all high school friends
    familiar with house*
Brett, first on scene after Gloria's fall
*Jared Munroe, financial investor—Kalea's
    boyfriend argued with Brett in park on Friday*

Ken and Brett knew each other in Boston
Came to town the same time
Did Ken tell Brett about the book prior?

"Addie, I have no idea where we even start with all this."

"We look at each clue and figure out if it tells us a connection to the murder and how strong of a connection it is, given means, motive, and opportunity. But before I forget a thought I just had . . ." She plucked the chalk stick from the ledge and added beside Jared's name: *money to Kalea, and excuse to stay in town???*

"This list over here"—Addie said as she scrawled the heading *Reasons to Commit Murder* beside the second column. She continued to talk to Paige while she scribbled—"is generally the main reason why a person commits murder. That is aside from serial killers or psychopaths who do it for fun or sport or other sick reasons, but I'm pretty sure that's not what we're dealing with here."

Monetary
Passion
Revenge
Personal Vendetta
Self-defense and in-defense
Anger
Hatred
Jealousy

"The most important thing you have to remember is with any murder case, the key is to look at the"—she wrote across the top of the two columns—"*means*, *motive*, and *opportunity*, and then figure out which one of the suspects best matches all three."

Chapter Twenty-Three

"We have to be missing something," Addie said, scanning the board, "because according to this, everyone on here had a motive to kill Brett but what I don't see is who had the opportunity."

"You mean, besides my mom?" Paige said. "We've been at this for over an hour, and we're no further ahead in proving her innocence. It still looks like she's guilty because all the other suspects on here were somewhere else at the time of the murder, and have alibis."

"I'm afraid you're right. It does appear that given the coroner's estimated time of death each of the other suspects have witnesses for where they were."

"Yeah," Paige said in a huff, crossing her arms. "Because Kalea and Jared were in Boston, someone saw my dad at my aunt's house and swears he never left, and according to staff and another guest, Amber was at the hotel. Unfortunately, it looks like, at least according to the information we have so far, no one but Mom had a motive to kill Brett, *and* also had the opportunity to do it at that time of the morning."

Addie's eyes narrowed as she studied the board further.

She tried to hide her uneasiness as they reviewed the clues, but Paige was right. According to everything on here, Martha, without an alibi, was the only one that could have killed Brett, and the whole town knew by now that she had more than one motive.

"I told you I was no good at this. I haven't been able to come up with one single new theory to add. Should I call Serena and ask her to come? She's good as your second set of eyes."

"It's not that. I think we're stuck on your mother as the guilty party because we still don't know this important piece of information." She circled *means*. "Yes, we know the result. Brett is dead, but we don't know what killed him, and that would give us our lead to the rest of it. The murder weapon can tell so much about a case. If only Simon could come up with something, anything that might give us a hint."

The bells at the door jingled. "I don't believe my ears. Has someone really braved the detour to come in?" Paige poked her head around the corner. "Oh, it's Mrs. Jamison. She ordered a couple of books last week. They're at the front. I'll go."

Addie stood back and read over what she had written, and then clapped her hands with excitement. "Duh. That's it! Martha aside, I've only been focusing on these three other suspects"—she tapped her finger on *Ken*, *Jared*, and *Amber*—"and the likelihood that one of them killed him for the book."

Addie discovered after her father—an ex-NYPD detective turned antiquities reclamation specialist for an insurance company—was killed, that if she worked through a problem verbally, it was like he was working through it with her. Generally, between the two of them, they came up with the next steps or the solution. She glanced up and then back at the board. "Okay, Dad, if you're listening, I really need help with this one."

She focused on the names she had scrawled and tried to remember the theory she and Serena had discussed previously. "If any of them were guilty, they would have left town after the murder, right?" She studied the board. "Okay, I started out thinking the book and murder weren't related, but then had second thoughts about that and started working on the premise that they were. What if my first instincts were right, and they're not related? Is that what you're trying to tell me, Dad, and why I can't figure it out? That his murder has nothing to do with the book at all?"

She reread the notes she had scribbled on the side of the board. "If I look at taking the most common reasons why a murder is committed into consideration, then . . . then . . . ?"

Monetary
Passion
Revenge
Personal Vendetta
Self-defense and in-defense
Anger
Hatred
Jealousy

She dropped the chalk on the ledge of the board and sat down at her desk. "It means the same as it did before. It either comes back to Martha and the custody issue or I have a larger pool of suspects that I haven't even considered and no clue as to where to start." Because, as far as she could figure out by reading over all her notes, it well could have been someone in town for the festival. Perhaps Brett's car broke down that night, and a stranger gave him a lift, robbed and killed him, and just happened to dump the body behind the bakery, and none of it was connected to anyone or anything in Greyborne Harbor, but completely random.

"Arg!" she cried, and scrubbed her hands over her face. "But then where is the book?" Her head popped up. "Unless of course that's what Mister X, the random guy, stole from him." She shook her head. "Then we'd never find him or it unless it showed up on the black market." She closed her eyes and took a deep cleansing breath trying to clear her erratic thoughts.

Arms wrapped around Addie from behind. A familiar musky-amber fragrance wafted over her, and soft lips nuzzled into the crook of her neck. "Mmm." She tilted her head back, her eyes still closed. "I sure hope this is my knight in shining armor riding in on his white steed to save the damsel in distress."

"Sorry, he was busy saving a damsel who *needed* saving. You never have, so he sent a very tired doctor in a black pickup truck in his place. I hope that's all right for milady," he whispered, and nibbled her earlobe.

"It's more than all right." Her lips sought out his. "I've missed you."

"And I you." He stood upright, swept his hand across his midsection, and bowed low from the waist. "This humble servant is at her ladyship's service. Your wish is my command."

"How very bold and brave of you, dear Knight of the

Black Truck Order, and since you're offering, I want your head."

Simon's jaw tensed. "Very well, milady. Would you like it on or off my body?"

Addie let out a snort when she tried to stifle a giggle, but his words and deadpan expression produced laughter from both of them as he swept her into his arms and kissed her. It felt good to laugh with him after the events of the past few days, and in that moment, Addie knew why she felt the way she did about Simon. He wasn't perfect, but he was perfect for her.

He rested his forehead on hers and sighed heavily.

"What's wrong?" She pulled back and glanced up at him.

"I hear that you've added to your résumé."

"What on earth are you blabbering on about?"

"Aside from rare book researcher, appraiser, and book-seller, you've now taken up midwifery?"

"Be serious."

"Like I was being serious before?" His eyes searched hers. "Unless, of course . . . you were and really do desire my head?" He gave her a wry smile.

"Don't be ridiculous. Your head is perfect exactly where it is. It's your brilliant brain I'm after."

"What's with you and my brain lately? You know, I am starting to worry about that whole zombie—"

"Stop it," she said with a chuckle. "In all seriousness, how could I be a midwife? If you're referring to the birth of your new niece, then please know the facts, Doctor. I did nothing except call the ambulance and Pete to meet Carolyn at the hospital. It was Martha who did all the work. I wasn't even in the room when the baby arrived."

"Whatever your contributions were to the events of this

morning, my sister and Pete have seen fit to give you second billing. I've just come from visiting mother and baby Marta Addison Coleman."

"Really?"

"Yes, really. Pete wouldn't agree to Martha as a first name." Addie's brow rose questioningly. "It seems he has an aunt named Martha, who is as tetchy as our Martha can be. So, they compromised on Marta, but Carolyn put her foot down on the middle name because she said without you, things might not have gone as well as they did. There's also something about you being the little one's godmother."

"Wow," Addie said, "I'm a namesake and a godmother just because I know how to use a phone?" She grinned until her face hurt. "This is an amazing day, isn't it?"

"If it's so amazing, why were you looking so glum when I snuck up behind you?"

"Oh, it's all this." She waved at the blackboard. "I've hit a major roadblock and have no idea where to look."

"Okay, we've been at a standstill before." Simon perched one hip on the desk. "Tell me where you're at, and we'll see if I can offer a new perspective."

Addie ran through the information she had gathered about everyone's whereabouts Saturday night and pointed out the fact that no one except Martha had the opportunity to kill Brett within the window of time of death. She stressed her disbelief that Martha could have lured him into the bakery at that time of the night to kill him. "So, you see how none of these other puzzle pieces fit now?"

"Yeah," he said, rereading her notes. "This whole thing is like two puzzle boxes that have been mixed together, and the job is to figure out which pieces match which picture."

"Exactly! I've only been focusing on the fact that the murder had something to do with the book. But now I'm thinking that they are two separate crimes, with Brett, for some unknown reason, being the link between both the theft and his murder." She gazed at the board.

"If, in fact, Brett was the one who stole the book, which is something that hasn't been proven yet. It's only a suspicion you have."

"You're right. No proof, no evidence. Only suspicion based on conjecture."

Simon moved to the board and pointed to *Amber*, *Ken*, and *Jared*. "Even though all these people have a motive, their alibis, like you pointed out, show they didn't have the opportunity. The fact that all of them are still in town and not on the run tells us to exclude them."

"Which means the killer isn't on the list. The reason I was looking . . . what did you call it? Glum? Yeah, glum, is when you came in I realized there are just too many other people who could have done it for another reason—" She purposely left off telling him her runaway theory of Mister X, chalking that one up to the rambling mind of a crazy woman, or at least that's what she feared Simon would think at this point.

"This brings us right back to Martha," he said, "and the only other name on the list."

"Exactly! Now you see where I'm at."

"And if we believe there was no way Martha did this, then we have to figure out who else would want Brett dead," Simon said, scanning her notes. "There has to be someone we haven't suspected yet, or someone whose alibi is less than airtight."

"And that someone obviously wanted to make it look like Martha was the killer because they went to a lot of trouble to stage the body behind the bakery. But who haven't we thought about? Who would hold a grudge like that against Martha?"

"Given her personality, it could be half the town, but let's look at it like all the major players are pieces on a chessboard. We just have to figure out where to place each one."

"Okay, so these three"—she underlined *Amber*, *Ken*, and *Jared*—"have alibis, which place each of them nowhere around Brett at the time of death, leaving 'Martha' the only other name on the board as the probable killer." She glanced sideways at Simon. "So, we're no further ahead."

"You're right. Martha's piece is the only player on the board still standing."

"Come on, there's one person who might be able to shed some light on this mess." She grabbed her handbag and jacket and stood waiting for him in the doorway. "Well, don't look so leery. Have I ever taken you on a wild goose chase before?"

Simon rolled his eyes. "Normally, I would follow you anywhere, but I'm exhausted. I've been in the lab day and night, trying to figure out what the murder weapon is, and this morning I had to do my weekly check at the homeless shelter—"

"You were at the shelter this morning?"

"Yes, it's part of their town licensing requirements.

A doctor has to check on the residents once a week for communicable diseases and make sure there's no—"

"Did you see Bill?"

"He wasn't there. Reggie Gardner, the shelter manager, told me he hasn't been back since Saturday night. When he didn't show up on Sunday, they held his bed another night, but then when he didn't come back again, they had to give it to someone else. Why?"

"Because I have a gut feeling he knows more than he's saying about hearing another person on the beach that night. He's the one person who can give us another name to add to this board or prove that one of the three main suspects' alibis isn't airtight."

"What makes you so sure he knows something?"

"Because the last time I spoke to him, he told me there was someone on the beach that night besides him and Brett."

"Did he say who it was? Did he or you tell Marc?"

"I tried to convince him to go to Marc, but Bill was really scared. I'm thinking he knows who the other person was and appeared scared of that person. Even though he denies it, I think he knows who it was. Now you're saying he hasn't been back at the shelter since Saturday night." Her gut churned. "Simon, we need to find him now. He could be in danger if he's still . . ." She gripped the doorframe. "I don't even want to think about that."

"If Bill withheld information important to the case, and he hasn't come forward with it, then you have to be the one to tell Marc about this. He's the one who can find Bill and get to the bottom of it. That's his job, not yours."

"You're right. It's quiet now. Maybe I should."

He placed his hands on her shoulders. "Not maybe but definitely." His gaze locked on hers. "Promise?"

"Yes, can you come with me? You know how he gets whenever I tell him anything about a case."

"I'd love to, but I have to get back to the hospital and do rounds. I missed them this morning because of the shelter visit and then Carolyn's baby. Plus, Gloria's last test results are back, and I'm thinking she can be discharged soon, perhaps even later today."

Addie's chest tightened, and she glanced down at the straw basket under the desk. "That's wonderful," she said, forcing the words past the cotton balls forming in her mouth. "I'm sure Gloria is excited about the prospect of life getting back to normal."

"Not normal for a little while yet. She'll still have physiotherapy appointments, but at least she can convalesce in the comfort of her home. Also, I'm fairly certain that having Pippi to look after will help with the rehabilitation process, too."

Addie's handbag slipped from her hand. Simon studied her. "Oh no, you've become attached to Pippi, haven't you."

Addie nodded and swiped at a tear threatening to leak from her eye.

"I'm sorry to blurt that out," Simon said. "I never thought in such a short time that you—"

"I'll be okay." She straightened her shoulders. "I've gotten used to her, and it will be a change, but it's the way it is, right?"

"Maybe we can go to the animal shelter and look for the perfect dog for you."

Addie focused on the basket. "No, it's fine. Pippi will be with her mommy again, where she belongs, and life will get back to normal for me." Her words caught in her throat. "But since you're going to see Gloria, could you ask her if she has any idea where Bill might make camp since he's not at the shelter?"

"Why would Gloria know that?"

"Because they all grew up together. Maybe she knows of a favorite place he used to go when they were teenagers. Or"—she shrugged—"something else that might help me find him."

"Addie, please take this to Marc and let him and his officers do the footwork."

"I will, but Bill doesn't deal well with the police, so if I could get to him first, perhaps I could convince him to go in and tell Marc everything he knows."

"Addie, you need to take everything Bill told you, including where he might be hiding, to Marc. I hate to say this, but aside from Martha, he's the only other person on the board who doesn't have an alibi for the time in question. Not to mention that he was on the scene when you arrived and discovered the body."

"Simon!" Her eyes widened. "This is Old Bill. He would never hurt a fly."

"What is it you told me your father used to say? *Everyone* is capable of committing a crime, even murder, given the right circumstances." His eyes fixed on Addie's. "Remember that, and go speak to Marc, now."

"All right, I'll see if I can get past his watchdog and see what he says."

"That's my girl. Chin up. I'm fairly certain you can slay this dragon yourself, milady." His lips brushed hers. "I'll text you after I speak to Gloria."

Simon strode to the front of the shop and said goodbye to Paige. The bells rang out his departure.

Addie glanced down at Pippi, who was sitting by the door, tail excitedly sweeping the floor. "Need to go for a walk, girl?" The little dog yipped. "Good, let's get you into your doggy coat to keep you nice and snug, and we'll take a quick walk through the park before we go see Marc. It'll give me one last chance to look for Bill before I go and tattle on him."

Chapter Twenty-Four

Addie peered over the edge of the last garbage can in the event area of the park. Like all the others before, among the normal candy bar wrappers and other unrecognizable refuse, there was a mixture of soda bottles and cans. Bill had apparently not been making his usual rounds to collect them.

Her mind raced with a number of what-if scenarios, and none of them ended well. The first one was that the other person Bill saw on the beach had found him and silenced him. Second and least disturbing was that Bill was so afraid of this person he had gone into hiding. Then there was the scenario Simon presented, one she didn't want to consider: Bill could be the murderer. Gloria had said he would do anything for Martha because he still loved her. Had he killed Brett because of the custody disagreement and how upset Martha was over it? Did he know Brett had stolen Paige's book, and in trying to get it back, things escalated and ended badly? Was he on the run or in hiding?

Any way she looked at it, Simon was right. This may have been Bill's secret she had hoped to pull out of him without involving the police, but she couldn't keep it any longer. It was time to share what Bill had told her and leave it up to Marc to figure out. She only hoped that it wasn't too late.

Addie cut through the library parking lot to Main Street and headed for the police station in the middle of the long block of municipal buildings. With Pippi tucked under her arm, she dashed up the stairs. When she reached the glass door, it flew open, and Amber raced out, nearly knocking Addie off her feet as she pushed past her.

"Amber, wait! Can I talk to you a minute?"

Amber clutched her coat tight around her neck and hustled down the steps. "I have nothing to say to anyone, especially a reporter."

"I'm not a reporter. I'm a friend of Emma's family."

Amber halted at the bottom and glared up at Addie. "Oh, you mean the family of that horrible woman accused of killing Brett?"

"That's what I'm trying to find out. I just have a couple of questions, and you can answer them, so we can all get to the bottom of this."

"Okay, if talking to you can help get Brett's body released. What do you want to know?"

"I have no connection to the police department, so I can't help you with that," Addie said as she walked down the stairs and met Amber's cynical gaze. "But I know Brett owed money to Jared Munroe."

A look of fear replaced the cynicism in Amber's eyes, and she turned and started to walk away.

Addie grabbed her coat sleeve. "Please, don't you want to find out who really killed the man you love?"

Amber stopped, but she didn't turn around. "Yes," she

said, her voice no more than a whisper, "he owed him money."

"And a source tells me that Jared threatened you about that money."

Amber spun on her heel and pinned Addie with a glare. "Are you sure you're not a cop or a reporter?"

"I swear." Addie crossed her heart.

"Yes, Brett owed him money, and we figured out a way to get it, so he could pay back that bloodsucker once and for all. Every time Brett made a payment, Jared upped the interest, and it seemed we'd never be free of the debt."

Addie locked her gaze with Amber's. "Did that plan include stealing Paige's book? Is that how you figured out a way to pay off the loan?"

"You sure you're not a cop?" Addie nodded. "Well . . . yes," Amber choked, and broke her gaze from Addie's. "Ken told Brett about the book he'd given Paige one night when they were drinking. I overheard them talking, and according to what Ken said, it sounded like it might be worth some serious cash. I did a little research and found out what it might be worth."

"So, Brett came to Greyborne Harbor with the sole intent of stealing the book?"

"Partially." She twisted her gloved fingers around the strap of her purse. "I found out the week before that I couldn't have children of my own. We'd been trying for a year, and we thought maybe we could share custody of Emma. I was pretty shaken up by the news from my doctor, and Brett thought that might help me feel better. He knew Emma's birthday was coming up and decided that would be the perfect time to visit and inform Paige we wanted at least partial custody and . . . well, to steal the book."

"Did he steal it? Or had someone beat him to it?"

"No, everything was going as planned except he discovered Paige had loaned it out, but he got hold of that woman's house keys, went in and got the book, and hid it until we could sell it to get the money to pay Jared."

"But he didn't pay Jared, did he? That's why after Brett was found dead, Jared threatened you, right?"

She nodded.

"Do you know what happened to the book after Brett took it?"

Amber shook her head. "He just told me it was safe, but then he told me the plan had changed. We weren't going to sell and pay Jared. We were going to keep the money." She put her face in her hands and sobbed. "He never told me where the book was, and Jared kept coming at me for the money. I'm going to end up dead, too, because Jared must have found out Brett was going to double-cross him."

Addie wanted to reach out and comfort the distraught woman, but Amber's confession to the theft made Addie recoil instead. "Did Jared know where the money was coming from? Did he know about the book?"

"I don't know if he knew, but that's why I'm so desperate to get Brett's body released so I can get out of here, get him buried, and go into hiding. But why am I telling you this? Although, it feels good to tell someone, finally." Amber glanced over her shoulder. "Look, I gotta go. I don't want Jared to see me around and come after me again. I've been holed up in my room at the inn ever since Sunday."

"Do you really think he would kill you?" Addie stared at the woman. "If he did, then how would he get his money? No, my guess is that he likes to scare and threaten, but murder isn't his style."

"That's what Brett said Saturday night when he called me to tell me there was a change of plans."

"Is that what the two of you were arguing about on the phone around midnight?"

"How did you know that?"

"There were a couple of witnesses."

"You know, for someone who says she's not a cop or a reporter, you sure sound like one."

"I'm just invested in my community, you might say." It was all Addie could do to keep a civil tone with this woman.

"Yeah, that's what we argued about. My last words to him when he told me the new plan was that he was going to get himself killed . . . and the next day . . . so, you tell me Jared had nothing to do with it, and then I'll relax, until then—"

"Did you tell the police any of this? About Jared's threats or Brett taking the book?"

"Are you kidding me? And if *you* do"—she poked her finger into Addie's chest—"I'll deny this conversation ever took place and come after you. Do I make myself clear?" She sneered and darted to her car in the parking lot.

Addie stood on the sidewalk, staring at the sandstone wall of the police station as she mentally checked off one big question mark on her blackboard. "That means Marc doesn't know Brett was the book thief." She dashed up the stairs and through the waiting room to the front counter. "Hi, Jerry, I need to talk to Marc. It's important."

Jerry looked at her from under his bushy brows. "Will Detective Brookes do? I guess she's in charge of the investigation now."

Addie thought she had managed to keep her mental cringe just that, but it must have shown on her face because Jerry quickly added, "I'm sorry, I'm only following orders."

"I guess if they're Marc's orders, you have to oblige."

He glanced over his shoulder, leaned forward, and lowered his voice. "Not his, hers. At least, that's what she has decreed regarding any information *you* might turn up." He gave a helpless shrug.

Addie flinched with his words. So that was how Ryley was going to play it from now on. Was she trying to keep Addie away from Marc or was she hoping Addie might bring her something that would help crack the case and then claim the fact gathering for herself? There was a lot about this detective Addie didn't like, but she, just like Jerry, was helpless to do anything about it.

The murmur of Marc's voice behind his closed office door made Addie miss the days when she could have skirted past the desk and plopped down in one of his chairs and vented her latest theories about a case. She glanced back at Jerry, who was eyeing her anxiously. "No, that's okay. It's not that urgent, so I wouldn't want to bother the detective with it."

"I shouldn't tell you this, but I know you, and I know you're doing some sleuthing on your own anyway." Jerry stood up, leaned over the counter, and whispered, "If your news has anything to do with Bill's statement about hearing that dead guy arguing with someone on the phone, it's just been confirmed who he was speaking to at the time."

"I know what you're going to say." Addie put her hand up in a *stop* motion. "I don't want you to get into trouble over me. I spoke with Amber outside before I came in."

"You did? I didn't know you knew her."

"I don't, but Paige told me she was Brett's new girl-friend." Addie met Jerry's searching gaze. "When she was in here, did Amber tell you why she and Brett were argu-ing or say anything about who she suspects killed Brett?"

"No, she seemed scared, maybe thought we would start looking at her again, but the staff and a guest at the inn verified she was in her room all night. Why? Do you have information about who the killer is?"

"No, I'm at as much of a loss as you guys seem to be. I have a couple of suspects, but they all seem to have air-tight alibis, so"—she shrugged—"I don't know where to look now. That's why I spoke to Amber when I saw her. I hoped she could shed some light on a few of my ques-tions."

"She told the detective"—he jerked his thumb, motion-ing behind him—"that they were only having a lovers' spat. Is that what she said to you?"

"Basically." Addie bit her tongue. "Anyway, I saw her coming out and wanted to confirm what Bill said to me was true about overhearing his arguing on the phone."

"Speaking of Bill"—Jerry's voice dropped to a mere murmur—"his statement isn't adding up anymore." He glanced over his shoulder.

"Why, what happened?"

"It seems that when he said he heard Brett on the phone arguing with . . . well, as it turns out . . . Amber . . . there were a lot of other people on the beach. We had a unit down there chasing off a few late partiers, and a couple of fire department members were still running their electrical check on the bandstand. Bill told us there was no one else there when he saw Brett, but that isn't true."

Bile churned in Addie's gut and rose to the back of her

throat. She swallowed hard. "Really. Well, you know Bill doesn't own a watch. Perhaps he was confused about the time."

"Except," said Jerry, "Amber and another witness confirmed that the argument with Amber occurred at midnight."

"Maybe he argued with someone else later, and that's what Bill overheard."

"Maybe, but anyway, the chief wants us to find Bill and bring him back in for more questioning."

"He does, does he?" Addie gripped the edge of the counter pretending to adjust Pippi in her arms.

"Yeah, have you seen him around anywhere lately?"

"Nope, I haven't seen him recently."

It wasn't exactly a lie, she told herself. He had asked if she'd seen Bill lately, and she hadn't, at least not since Monday when Bill told her there was another man there. Jerry didn't need to know that now. She needed to find Bill herself. He either killed Brett, or he saw the person later on the beach who did, and it was someone he was terrified of. *The beach!*

Why hadn't she thought of that before? It made perfect sense as to where the original crime scene must be. If so, then it couldn't have been Bill. He didn't have a car. How on earth would he have taken the body to Martha's bakery, and why would he? He loved her. No, Bill held the key to this, and she had to find him before Marc's officers did and go off and arrest him again. With his obvious fears about captivity and confinement after what Gloria had said about him being a POW, a second arrest would certainly send him into a full mental collapse, and he'd shut down for good.

"Are you okay, Addie? You went a little pale."

"I'm fine, just so much swirling around in my head. It would really help if I could . . ." She looked longingly at Marc's door. "Are you sure there's no way I can get in to see him?"

"I'd like to, but she'd have my head, and I'm up for promotion to lieutenant next month."

"Is there a problem here, Sergeant?" Ryley's icy voice sliced through the air behind Jerry.

"No, Detective. Everything's fine."

"Addie, is there something *I* can help you with?" She stepped around an unyielding Jerry and pinned her dark eyes on Addie.

"Nope, I was only stopping by to see how Marc was after all the excitement of the morning, that's all."

"That's right, the baby." Ryley's guarded facial features relaxed as she folded her arms across her chest. "How is Carolyn doing, by the way?"

"Mother and daughter are fine." Addie forced her lips into some semblance of a smile. "I only wanted to tell Marc that Carolyn and Pete gave her the name Addison as her middle name. I thought he might get a kick out of that."

Ryley's jaw muscle twitched. "I'll be sure to pass it on to him."

"You do that." Addie's cool gaze left the detective's equally cold one, and she glanced at Jerry, nodding her appreciation. She shifted Pippi into the crook of her arm and dashed out the door and down the steps.

When they reached the sidewalk, her phone pinged a text message. She clipped the leash on Pippi before setting her down and tugged her phone out of her pocket.

I hope you're at the police station??? Gloria said to tell Marc to look around the small rock cavern by the lighthouse. She's seen him hanging around in that area when she takes Pippi down there for walks on nice days.

BTW, I'm discharging her today. Martha is picking her up soon. I told her you'd bring Pippi back tonight 😞 I can go with you, if you like? I'll call you later. xxxxxx

Addic's eyes burned with tears. She jammed her phone back in her pocket. "One last walk back to the shop through the park, and then we'll go on a little adventure down by the beach before you go home to Mommy. How does that sound?"

Pippi yipped and excitedly pulled on her lead.

Chapter Twenty-Five

Addie pulled into a parking space by the old lighthouse and glanced over at the basket beside her on the seat. Her chest constricted at the sight of the two dark-brown eyes peering back at her over the top. The tears she'd been fighting slipped from her eyes and rolled down her face. She withdrew her furry friend from the snuggly cocoon and cuddled Pippi into her heaving chest.

"How on earth did I allow myself to get so attached to you in such a short time? Heck, I haven't even been able to tell Simon how I feel about him." She scratched behind the little dog's ear as Pippi's tongue lapped at Addie's tear-covered cheeks. "But somehow, a dog of all things managed to break through the shield around my battered heart in only a few short days." Addie buried her face into the soft fur of Pippi's neck and sobbed until she shed all her tears.

"Well, it is what it is, and time I pull up my big girl pants." She stepped out of the car and set her friend onto the graveled parking lot. "You have a mommy, and she loves you, too. So, let's make our last adventure a good one, what do you say?" She glanced down at the wriggling ball of fur by her feet. "How are you at tracking?" She giggled as Pippi lunged ahead on her lead and headed across the parking lot in the direction of the bandstand.

As they trudged across the open space, the icy fingers of an arctic wind gust reached under Addie's collar and sent shivers to her core. She cursed the fact she hadn't thought to wear her parka today instead of her dressy wool coat. Even though the sun was shining, the coastal winds still held on to the last remnants of the blustery winter they'd endured. For a moment as they passed alongside the stage and the rear covered shell of the bandstand, there was a reprieve from the Atlantic winter winds. However, coming out of the backside of the event area toward what, in less snowy months, would be the edge of the grass above the pebbled beach to the shore, she found the winds whipped up again. She clasped her cloth jacket tighter around her neck, glad she had remembered Pippi's little coat.

Up until this point, the walking was easy. There had been so much foot traffic on the beach over the weekend that most of the deep snow had been tamped down or worn away. Unfortunately, as they headed to the base of the lighthouse on the cliff above, it became near impossible not to slide and stumble over the increasingly large snow-and algae-covered rocks. It also didn't help that Pippi, whose footing was as equally unsure, darted every which way in her effort to find the best foothold. Addie finally relented and unclipped the leash, allowing her little friend to scamper over the rocks at her leisure.

Having to keep her mouth buried in her jacket collar to stop the winds from stealing at her breath made the trudge over and around the boulders more difficult. It was a good thing she knew exactly where the outcrop cavern was. This past summer, she and Simon had caught some rays, lying on the rocks following a morning of clam digging. Head down, she continued stumbling along until she heard Pippi yapping and whining over the breaking waves and the wind.

She edged closer to Pippi, who sat back on her haunches, wailing. The woeful sounds sent shivers through Addie. She tiptoed up beside her. "What is it, little one? Did a big old crab shell scare you?"

Addie glanced at a boulder in front of where Pippi sat. Her gaze narrowed as she tried to understand what she was looking at. There were dark-red crystals splattered over the rocks. She crouched down, swiped her finger over the area nearest to her, and checked the residue on her finger. The crystals melted from her body heat. It was blood. She scanned the patches of snow between the rocks. It was there, too.

Her gaze skimmed the water's edge, across the slippery, algae-covered, rocky beach, and rested on the relatively dry boulders where she stood. She was above the high-tide mark and protected from the daily surge and ebb of the waves. The exposed blood on the rocks had also only frozen and not turned black with the sun's rays. It hadn't been here that long. She checked her bearings. She was still a good fifty feet from where Bill's camp might be. Glancing back at the blood-splattered rocks, she tugged her phone out of her pocket with shaking hands. No signal! She jammed it back in, clipped Pippi onto her leash, and stumbled back toward the bandstand area and hopefully cell reception.

Addie pressed her back against the sun-warmed wall

of the back shell of the stage area, thankful to be out of the wind, and tapped out a message to Simon.

> I'm at the beach by the bandstand, found blood on the rocks. I don't know if it's Brett or Old Bill's but he's missing and I'm afraid the killer might be after him and that it's his blood. Call Marc, tell him to come, too, and bring evidence bags.

Addie drew in a series of deep breaths. Her head was whirling between the physical exertions of boulder jumping on the way back up the beach and the unnerving discovery. Her mind raced with possibilities, and she slid down the wall, plopping to the ground. As if Pippi could sense something was off, she crawled into Addie's lap and nuzzled her wet nose under Addie's hand, forcing a comforting scratch. Addie wasn't certain if it was for her benefit or the dog's, but either way, the fine, warm fur under her fingers was consoling.

She leaned her head back against the rough-planked siding of the band shell, closed her eyes, and basked in the warmth of the sun beating down on her wind-burned cheeks. A thwack of cold splattered onto her forehead and trickled across her brow. She opened her eyes and gazed upward. A smile formed on her lips.

The sun sparkling off the string of enormous icicles above her on the edge of the bandstand roof reminded her of the Christmas decorations that adorned many of the homes in town over the holidays. Her gaze followed their trail along the roofline to where it ended, and the open stage began. Her heart lurched in her chest.

"I don't believe it!" she cried, and leapt to her feet, sending her little friend tumbling onto the dry patch of grass where they'd been resting. She bolted to the side of the stage and stared up. "Could it be?"

"Could it be what?" Simon said breathlessly as he bent forward, hands on his knees, panting. "Sorry, I ran all the way from the parking lot, and the gusty wind got to me." He puffed. "So, you found blood, where? Here?" He glanced up.

"Not here, but look." She pointed. "The last one's been snapped off at the roofline."

"Okay?" He raised his brow questioningly.

"Look closely at the size and shape of the icicles. You said part of the reason you were having difficulty in identifying the weapon was because the debris particles left in the wound contained a mixture of organic substances. This suggests the weapon or tool was well weathered. Could it have been one of Mother Nature's tools?"

Simon shielded his eyes from the glistening rainbow effect the sun was producing on the hanging icicles. "Well, I'll be," he said, his jaw dropping. "Who'd have thought? It would make a perfect murder weapon. One that would melt quickly due to the blood temperature combined with the fact that the body was placed over the hot air vent making it as hard as it was to trace."

"Hey, Doc, what was so urgent?" Marc called as he jogged toward them.

"Look," Simon said, excitedly pointing.

"Yeah, so it's icicles. Where's the emergency?"

Four more officers joined them, looked to where Simon had indicated, and then glanced at each other, shrugging.

"I think . . . that Addie has discovered our missing murder weapon. That's the emergency," Simon said smugly. "One of these made the perfect murder weapon, as they dissolve and are untraceable."

"Well, I'll be darned." Marc pushed the brim of his cap back on his head and studied the hanging shards of melted, dripping snow turned to ice daggers. "Who'd have thought of using an innocent-appearing icicle as a murder weapon?"

"That's not all I found," Addie said, glancing from one man to the other. "I think I found a murder scene, too."

"What? You found it here?" Marc's brown eyes darkened with a deep shade of doubt. "My team searched the entire area and found nothing."

"Then they didn't look in the right place, did they?"

The tips of his ears reddened. "Show me."

"Happily!" Addie swung on her heel and marched toward the beach with Pippi merrily scampering alongside her.

"Jefferies, you stay here, and wait for Jerry and keep an eye on the . . . um . . . evidence. Bag one of them," Marc bellowed. "The rest of you, come with me, and let's go take a look at what Miss Greyborne *thinks* she has found. My guess is it's blood left behind after some fisherman cleaned his catch, but . . ."

The rest of his mocking words were lost to Addie as the wind whipped past her ears.

When they reached the rocks covered in crystallized blood splatter, she stood back as Simon performed the same finger test as she had and nodded confirmation to Marc. Within seconds, the other three officers fanned out over the beach, and Marc was on his police radio.

"Sergeant Fowley, you done up there yet?"

"Yes, Chief, just finishing. We took three for good measure," Jerry's voice cracked over the small speaker.

"Good, now come down to the beach and bring the black bag. I got more for you." He snapped off the radio and turned to Addie. "How is it that you came across this?"

Addie explained how Pippi actually was the one that found it. By the time she got her words out, Jerry joined them.

A large blue vein throbbed at Marc's temple as he turned toward the sergeant. "I want the names of every officer who *said* they checked this beach for evidence of a murder. Because it appears even an untrained *dog* could find it."

"Yes, Chief." Jerry nodded.

Despite the coolness of the wind, Addie couldn't help but notice tiny beads of perspiration erupt on Jerry's forehead. She stepped forward. "Maybe it wasn't here when they searched."

"What do you mean?"

"It seems Bill has disappeared, too, and that's the reason I was here in the first place. I was looking for him."

"Chief! You'd better come see this," one of the officers yelled from the cavern rock formation.

Addie's blood ran as cold as the blood crystallized on the stones at her feet.

Chapter Twenty-Six

Addie slammed her car into park, grabbed the beach bag from the seat, and bolted through the back door of her bookshop. "Paige," she yelled, "you aren't going to believe this." She dashed through the store to where Paige was standing at the front door.

Paige twirled toward her. "Where have you been? I've been worried sick. Not a word from you all afternoon!" She pinned Addie with *the look* that Addie's grandmother used when she was perturbed with something Addie had done as a child.

Addie flinched under Paige's piercing glare, feeling more like a naughty three-year-old than a thirtysomething. "I'm sorry. The afternoon kind of got away from me. I should have called or sent a text."

"Yes, you should have," Paige said with a jerk of her head. "I didn't know if you were coming back, so I decided to close. It is almost five."

"Yes, that's fine, but wait until I tell you the good news. At least, I think it is."

"Have the charges against Mom been dropped?"

Addie grinned, no longer able to contain the excitement

bubbling up in her chest since she made her discovery at the bandstand. "If they haven't, I'm pretty sure they will be soon."

"Why, what did you find? Did Bill tell you who the other person he saw on the beach was? Did they pick up the guy?"

Addie waved her hands. "I think I discovered the murder weapon. And if I'm right, there is no way your mom had the means to use it."

"What do you mean?"

"There was a huge icicle broken off from the roof that runs along the rear part of the bandstand shell up to the stage."

"An icicle? Could one of those kill someone?"

"You should have seen the size of them. And yes, given where Brett's wound was, I'd say that's exactly what killed him."

"How does this prove my mom didn't do it?"

"Because it was broken off at the base *at* the roofline, and your mom is only, what, five-foot-two or three?" Paige nodded in agreement. "And her arm reach could only be about yea high." Addie lifted her arm just above her head. "So, you see, there is no way your mom could have reached up to the shingles to snap it off at the base. Maybe she could have plucked off a piece of the bottom bit but not the top."

Paige grabbed the edge of the counter. "When will we know for sure if that's what killed Brett?"

"Simon's taken a couple of the icicles back to the lab. I'm thinking it won't be that long."

"Wow!" Paige's face lit up, and her smile reflected in her big round eyes. "That means the murderer is someone tall, right?"

"Exactly! Because if a stool or ladder was used to take down an icicle earlier, that means the killer would have known that Brett would be on the beach alone that night, and how could anyone have foreseen that? So it had to be taken as a weapon of opportunity in the spur of the moment."

"You're right and that would also clear my dad, too, because he's only about five-foot-six."

"Come on. Let's take a look at the board and go over the suspects we have. Keep in mind, right now we're only considering who would have had the means to kill him." Addie flipped the cover off the board and scanned over the names. "Here. Jared or Kalea are two that are tall enough, maybe."

"Kalea, but she said they were in Boston Saturday night?"

"Maybe they weren't."

"But your cousin . . . could she . . . would she have killed someone?"

"Oh, I don't know. Maybe she thought she was doing her new boyfriend a favor and tried threatening Brett for the money he owed Jared, and in self-defense, she ended up killing him."

Paige's brow rose. "That theory seems a bit out there, don't you think?"

"You're right, but I'm just throwing stuff out to see what sticks."

"I think that one rolled right off the board and plopped on the floor like the doo-doo it is."

"Paige! You astound me." Addie choked out a half snort, half laugh. "But, unfortunately, that only leaves Bill as the final name on the list."

"He is fairly tall."

"I know." Addie collapsed onto a box. "I just don't want to believe it."

"But you will believe your own flesh and blood is a suspect?"

"No, but it's clear, it couldn't have been your mom. I need to find Bill. He said your mother wasn't the other person he saw, and this new evidence proves he wasn't lying. I need to make him tell me who he saw."

"And there was no sign of him camping down by the beach?"

"There was a fresh campfire and some food wrappers in the rock cavern, but nothing else. Someone has been there recently. I'll tell you it was a relief when that's all they found. The pools of blood I found on the rocks close to the camp . . . well. I was afraid that it might be much worse."

"So"—Paige hopped up onto the desk—"if Brett was killed on the beach, how did his body get to Mom's bakery, and why there?"

"That's what we have to figure out. If the blood I found on the rocks turns out to be Brett's, it seems unlikely Bill could have done it, because he doesn't have access to a car. Which leaves us to figure out who hated your mother enough to want to frame her for the murder."

"And they did a pretty good job, didn't they?"

"My gut tells me stronger than it did before that Bill is the only one who can answer that. Whoever it is has him so scared he's gone into hiding."

"But where else is there to look for him?"

"I don't know."

A bang on the alley door behind them sent them both to their feet. "Who is it?" Addie called through the door.

"It's me, Simon."

"Simon?" She pushed it open. "Shouldn't you be in the lab or something?"

"I'm done for now."

"If you're done, does that mean you've made a match?"

Simon's mouth pulled back in a wide grin. "The murder weapon was indeed an icicle from that roofline, and the blood on the rocks is a positive match for Brett's."

Paige scooted over to Addie's side. "Does that mean my mom's no longer a suspect?"

He raised his brow questioningly.

"I ask that because Addie said that she's so short, she couldn't have broken the icicle off the roof."

"That's a good question. It does mean she would have difficulty with that." He glanced at Addie. "That's something I'll have to present to Marc to pass on to the DA for consideration when I file my official report."

"Fingers crossed." Paige heaved out a sigh. "But look at the time. I have to run. Emma will be having her dinner now and then going to bed soon. I have to be there to read her a bedtime story and tuck her in before I go out. She loves Aunty Mellissa coming over to babysit when I go out, but says I read the stories in the *best voices*."

"Do you have a big date tonight?" Addie asked with a teasing chuckle.

"Yes, as a matter of fact, I do."

"Is it with the young firefighter your mom told me you were seeing?"

"Yes, his name is Logan, and I guess I'm not the only sister who is attracted to a man in uniform." Paige giggled. "Elli and some guy she's started seeing are meeting us at the Ship 'n Anchor at eight."

"Is this new guy Curtis, one of Marc's officers, by chance?"

"How did you know?"

"I have my sources," Addie said with a laugh. "Go, and thanks for all your help today."

"No problem. I'll lock the door behind me."

"Have fun."

"I'm sure we will. It's karaoke night, and Logan's a great singer. It should be a lot of fun." She trotted to the front. "I'll see you tomorrow," she called. The bells merrily jangled out her departure.

"Okay, back to this." Addie turned and studied the blackboard. "If the blood on the beach is Brett's, Bill is still alive. We have to find him tonight. He holds the key to who the other person was on the beach with Brett."

"Wait a minute. Aren't you forgetting one thing?"

"What?"

"We have to return Pippi home tonight, remember?"

"Oh right."

Simon placed his hands on Addie's shoulders. "Are you ready for this?"

She dropped her gaze and nodded.

"Good, now gather up Pippi's toys that you have here. You can drive over to your house to collect the rest of it, and I'll follow along and drive you to Gloria's."

Addie's gaze traveled across the floor to where her furry little friend slept in the basket under the desk. Tears welled up in her eyes.

Chapter Twenty-Seven

"I know it was difficult, but you did see how happy Gloria and Pippi were in their reunion. You know it's the way it's supposed to be."

Addie gazed out the side window of Simon's truck. The lights of town whizzed by in a haloed blur through her tears.

"Addie? Are you okay?"

"Yeah, I'm fine."

"What would you think about us dropping into the animal shelter later this week? You know they always have puppies and dogs in need of a forever home."

"No," she said with a sniffle, "I'm fine. Maybe I'm finally learning that I can't replace a loss with the first substitution that comes along."

"Are you making an offhanded reference to me in that? You know, about David's passing and us and—"

"Not you!" Addie glanced at him. The headlights of a passing car revealed the pain etched on his face. "I was talking about . . . well . . . Marc, who was a good example of an instance when I jumped in before I was ready and . . ." Her voice trailed off.

He turned his face and glanced out his driver's-side window, an unmistakable sigh of relief escaping his chest.

"*When* and *if* the time is right, Pippi's void will be filled by the perfect successor just like it was . . . when you came into my life." She reached over and gently squeezed his knee.

There was no mistaking the grin that reflected back at her in the dim light of the truck cab. They jostled over a snow rut at the top of her driveway, sending them both into jarring laughter. Addie rubbed the top of her head where she'd bumped the cab roof and groaned as they drew closer to her house. "I really don't need this tonight."

"Is that Jared's car?"

"Yes, and a showdown with Kalea is the last thing I wanted. Oh well." She jumped out onto the driveway. "I guess it can't be avoided, but there go my plans of heating up that leftover lasagna in the freezer and snuggling with you on the sofa with a glass of wine."

"It sounds perfect, all the way around. We can only hope they're just on their way out." Simon followed her up the porch steps through the front door.

Addie stepped into the foyer and stopped. The air was filled with the sweet aroma of tomato sauce and heady cheese. "I don't believe it!"

She kicked off her boots and stomped to the kitchen. When she reached the doorway, she gripped the frame, her fingertips white with the rage coursing through her. There in the center of the island was the now-empty lasagna pan, the Mario's leftovers she'd frozen for her and Simon to share, the bottle of special-blended scotch Addie had purchased specifically for Simon, and the remnants of the last package of fondue chocolate that had been in the pantry. Another treat she'd been saving for her and Simon's next impromptu midnight fondue.

"Hi there," Kalea's weak voice came from her left. "I didn't expect you home so soon."

"I can see that." Addie pivoted and pinned her eyes on Kalea, who was cuddled into Jared's side in the corner of the U-shaped bench of the three-window-sided breakfast nook.

"I haven't had time to clean up. We just got back from Boston and were starving, but—"

"Boston again?" Addie huffed. "Didn't you get enough of it on Saturday night, at least that's where you said you were."

"Yes, we were. We drew up the preliminary papers Saturday and then had a wonderful evening of dinner and dancing and a marvelous night of . . ." She giggled and kissed Jared's cheek. Kalea wiggled off the bench and sauntered toward Addie. "But today, we met with Jared's lawyers again to sign the actual sale papers for the dress shop. It's finally done!" She squealed and clapped her hands in excitement.

Addie's hand twitched. She wanted to smack that innocent look from her cousin's face after what Kalea had put her through and finding her kitchen had once again been ransacked. From behind her, Simon's fingers gently kneaded into Addie's shoulders—his unspoken message for her to stop and take a deep breath before speaking or doing anything else.

Addie glanced at her antsy hand and folded her arms across her chest, for her cousin's safety, she told herself. "I imagine you are into your new partner"—Addie ticked her head in Jared's direction—"for quite a tidy sum, aren't you? Has he informed you yet exactly how he treats people who owe him money?"

"What are you talking about?" Jared sputtered, edged off the bench, and moved to Kalea's side.

"Yes, exactly what are you talking about?" Kalea glared at Addie and glanced at Simon. "Is she drunk?"

That was it. The gloves were off. Addie took a step toward her cousin and wagged a finger in her face. "Ask him about Brett Palmer and how he ended up dead and then this man"—she waved her finger at Jared—"was heard threatening Amber Carr about the money they owed him. Go ahead, ask him!"

"You think I killed Brett and then threatened Amber with the same if she didn't pay?" Jared tossed his head back and let out a laugh. "That's priceless. If someone owed me money, why would I kill them? It kind of makes paying it back rather impossible, don't you think?"

"That's what I thought, too," Addie snapped. "Then I realized that it might not have been Brett who owed you the money, but Amber. Killing Brett was just a warning to her that you were serious about collecting it."

"That's a very serious allegation on your part," Jared snapped.

By the look in his eyes, Addie knew she had over-stepped a line, and if she was right, she had just put them all in danger.

"Let me put it this way, Addie, is it?" Jared placed his arm around Kalea's shoulders and tugged her close to him. "I wouldn't be as high profile as I am in the financial investment world if I went around killing and threatening everyone who defaulted on their investments should a loss incur. I prefer to let my team of lawyers fight it out in the courts. They are tigers and have lost very few cases of loan default to date. So, I assure you, *Addie*, I am not the type of financial investment specialist you appear to think I am."

"But you were heard threatening her."

"Yes, and I won't deny that. I've known her a long time and wanted her to know I was tired of fooling around. Over the years, Brett had racked up quite the bill from my personal accounts, and since she was benefiting by his recent loans, she should also have to share some of the responsibility of repaying them, don't you agree?"

"She told me every time they repaid you, the price went up, and you wanted more. That's called loan sharking."

"Addie, stop it!" Kalea gasped, and glanced to a stone-faced Simon for support but got none. "Apologize to Jared, and that's enough of these accusations. Come on, Jared, we're out of here. I told you I thought she has gone over the deep end."

Jared released Kalea's grip on his arm. "No, I think your cousin needs to hear this, so she doesn't go around spreading malicious rumors about me that could hurt my business dealings. You wouldn't want the sellers to renege on the sale of the dress shop, would you?" Kalea shook her head. "Good." His steely eyes fixed on Addie's. "Now, as far as Brett Palmer is concerned, he was my late father's business partner's son. When our respective fathers passed away, Brett fell apart. He had never been any good at managing his personal life or finances, and without his father around to guide him, he was a complete and utter failure. I felt sorry for him, having known him as long as I had, and made some small loans to help him out. But those small loans never stopped. Yes, he'd pay back some of it then, but then he would borrow more.

So, you see, whatever it was Miss Carr told you, she was uninformed, or she was purposely lying. You have to ask yourself why."

Addie's mind raced. *Is he telling the truth or is he lying?* Brett being the son of his late father's business partner would be easy enough to check. Simon placed his arm on Addie's elbow, the shaking that threatened to overcome her body reduced to small tremors. None of what Jared had said was anything she had even considered.

Jared placed his hand on the small of Kalea's back and ushered her toward the kitchen door. "I think you really need to tell your cousin to be careful and learn her place."

Simon sputtered, and Addie placed her hand firmly on his arm. "Since this is my home, I think I am in my place!"

Jared set a questioning glance on Kalea. "What's she talking about?"

"Um, well . . ."

"I see by my sweet *dear* cousin's loss of words that she hasn't informed you of the truth yet?" Addie pinned Kalea with a glare.

"Kalea? Care to explain?"

When Kalea didn't reply, Jared marched down the hallway and out the front door, slamming it shut behind him.

"Now you've gone and done it. Just because that stupid murder theory you had about him was wrong, you still had to get the final dig in, didn't you?"

"How was I supposed to know you hadn't told him the truth yet? Don't blame me. It was your lie that started all this."

"You, you," Kalea gasped, and fled down the hallway and out the door after Jared.

"Thank you," Addie whispered.

"For what? Letting you drive a deeper wedge between you and your cousin or accusing an innocent man of possible murder? I hardly think I did anything worth thanking me for."

"You're wrong. You let me get it all off my chest without shushing me or stepping in to rescue me, and that's something."

"I learned a long time ago with you that you don't need rescuing, except perhaps from yourself at times. What do you plan to do about your cousin? I think a lot of damage has been done to that relationship."

"We'll get over it." Addie shrugged. "Maybe it will take another ten years, but we managed after the falling-out we had in college. We'll pull through this one, too. I guess that's what family does, isn't it?"

He placed his hands on her shoulders and pulled her to him, his lips nuzzling her still, hot, anger-flushed cheek. "Now, let's clean up this mess, and see if they left any food in the fridge for us to eat."

A text alert pinged from Addie's jacket. She groaned and read the message. "It's from Paige. She just saw Bill heading into the alley beside the Ship 'n Anchor Tavern."

"What's that face you're making?"

"I just had an idea."

"I'm not sure I like idea-face tonight."

"You will."

"Does it have something to do with eating and lighting a fire and curling up in front of it with a glass of wine?"

"You're so predictable."

"Why don't we call Marc, and he can send a patrol car down there to pick him up."

"No, Bill won't talk to the police. He started to tell me the other day, so I'm hoping I can make him feel comfortable enough to finish his statement. He won't open up to me if the police are involved. It has to be this way. You can come with me or wait here. The choice is yours." She grabbed two flashlights from the top drawer beside the sink.

"Fine. Lead on, *Idea Girl*. You know what? That's going to be my superhero name for you from now on. . . ." Simon rambled on with his nonsensical mutterings all the way down the hall and out the front door as he followed along behind her.

Chapter Twenty-Eight

"He couldn't have just vanished," Addie said.

Simon clicked off his flashlight. "Are you sure Paige said the alley *beside* the tavern?"

"I assume it also includes the one running behind it as it's on a corner. To go anywhere from here, you'd have to go down to the far end of it and up another block to the next alley."

Simon bounced on the toes of his boots rubbing his hands up and down his arms. "He has had at least a thirty-minute head start, and I don't plan on searching all the back lanes down here on the waterfront tonight. It's just too darn damp and cold being right off the water."

"I have to find him. He's the only person who can identify the other man on the beach that night, and that man is probably the killer." Addie yanked her phone out of her jacket pocket. "But let me text Paige and ask her if there's any chance he went inside, or if she was mistaken about who she saw. He can't have just disappeared. I mean, look at these dumpsters. They're overflowing, and he would never pass up a windfall like this."

"Unless . . ."

"Unless what?" She glanced up from her phone.

"Unless, whoever he's been hiding from—"

"Found him and . . . oh no." Her hand shook as she fired off a text to Paige.

Paige bolted out of the tavern door and crushed her in a hug. "Addie, I didn't think you would come. I only told you I saw him so you'd know he was still around and not dead somewhere."

"Hey, everything all right out here?" A tall, well-built, sandy-blond young man, who towered over her, slid up to Paige's side and placed an arm protectively around her shoulder.

"Yeah, it's fine. Logan Ashmore, this is Addie Greyborne and Dr. Simon Emerson. They're good friends of mine."

"And your boss, too, if I'm not mistaken." Logan grinned and held out his hand to Addie and then shook Simon's. "Nice to meet both of you. I've heard a lot about you."

"That's interesting," Addie said, "because we haven't heard a word about you."

"It's only because we haven't been . . . um, well . . ." Paige glanced up at Logan, her eyes screaming *save me*.

"Seeing each other that long," Logan added quickly, "and with all the commotion lately with Paige's family, it kind of . . ." Logan's voice trailed off as he flashed a panicked glance at Paige.

Addie's gaze flicked from one flushed face to the other, and she had to bite the inside of her cheek to keep from laughing. They looked like two little kids who'd been caught with their hands in the cookie jar. "Don't worry. I know Paige is a very private person when it comes to her personal life. I knew when the time was right she'd tell me about you and not leave it up to her *mother* to fill me in." She gave Paige a playful shoulder bump.

"Well, Paige talks about you all the time to me, more than her own sisters. I guess she hasn't mentioned me to you because she's so shy, and you're her boss and all that."

"That must be it." Addie studied the young man's face and smiled. "You seem to know her pretty well."

"I'd like to know her a lot better." His face lit up with a grin as he gazed down at Paige and drew her like a petite china doll into his burly side.

Simon's flashlight lit up the alleyway.

"Did you find something?" Addie called.

"No." He peered behind a dumpster. "I thought I heard something, but it must have been the wind." He turned off the flashlight. "If he was here, he's long gone now."

Addie turned to Paige. "Are you sure it was Bill you saw and not someone from the bar coming out for a smoke or something?"

"These garbage bins look untouched." Simon joined them. "That's not a windfall Bill would pass up voluntarily." He shot Addie a side glance.

"I'm positive it was him. We had to park down the street, and he was shuffling along here on Marine Drive in front of us and turned right into this alley."

"There's no doubt about it," Logan said. "I've seen him around a lot, and the chief's always telling us to be on the lookout for him because a lot of the camps he builds are firetraps."

"Really? Where else has he set up camp?"

"Any place he can find, I guess. There've been a few abandoned buildings, vacant lots, a quiet back alley or two. The problem is he builds his shelter out of old cardboard and scraps of wood he finds lying around. One of these days, it's all going to go poof and start a fire. Some of these buildings date back a couple of hundred years."

"Yeah, I know." Addie's gaze dropped. "That's why it's too bad the murder scene appears to have been so close to the rocky crag where he was camping. It was probably the safest place he could have set up a camp."

"I doubt he'll be returning there any time soon, though," Simon said. "Especially given the police presence and—"

"The fact that the person who he saw on the beach Saturday night might be keeping an eye on that spot since the police brought it to everyone's attention. Hey, Logan"—she looked up at him—"were you part of the fire department squad that was working on Saturday night when the volunteers were setting up for the Sunday bonfire?"

"Yeah."

"Do you remember seeing Bill?"

"Can't say for sure that I did, but he could have been there. When my crew took the engine back to the station, the police were still chasing off a few late night partiers, so the chief stuck around to make sure there were no cigarette butts tossed into the trees. He still had the safety inspection to do on the light and speaker system. You could ask him if he saw Bill or anyone else hanging around after we left."

"What time did you leave?"

"It was probably around eleven-thirty."

"That means that Keith Hubert, the chief, must have at least seen Brett because that's close to the time he was arguing with Amber on the phone. Did you see a man around the fire pit area before you left?"

"I could have. I can't really say. The police were rounding up stragglers and sending them on their way. He could have been. Look, that's all I can help you with. Paige is shivering. Do you mind if we go back inside?"

"No . . . sure . . . sorry to keep you. I'll see you tomorrow, Paige. Have fun tonight, but not too much. You still have to work in the morning." Addie flashed her assistant a teasing grin as the two headed back inside.

"We need to find Bill. I really think he's in danger." She glanced up the darkened alley. "Do you know of any vacant buildings backing onto this lane?"

"Not that I can think of. Marine Drive is pretty popular. Any commercial vacancies that happen to come along are snatched up pretty quickly. The same with this street behind it, why?"

"I just thought maybe Bill came into the alley because that's how he gets into his new campsite, but you're right. There are no abandoned buildings on this end of the drive."

"And you heard what Logan said about the fire department. If they've been harassing him over his camps, he's not going to be easy to find."

"I know, and tonight he has proven that he's a master at disappearing."

"I guess when you've lived on the streets as long as he has, it becomes a necessary survival skill. But it's too cold to be walking around out here anymore tonight. Why don't we take a drive through a few of the alleys before I drop you off at home?"

"You're right. Maybe with fresh eyes on this tomorrow, we'll think of something or a way to flush him out."

Addie pointed the beam of her flashlight out of her passenger-side window, scanned the area around a dumpster, and clicked it off. "Let's go. I think we've been down every back lane around the waterfront. We might as well call it a night. If I can sneak out of the bookstore for a while tomorrow, I might come back and take a look in the daylight."

"There's something you have to seriously consider."

"What's that?"

"That it *was* Bill who killed Brett."

"What? No, I can't believe that. I refuse to."

"Think about it. The weapon wasn't premeditated. It was something on hand in the spur of the moment. Maybe Bill broke off the icicle to defend himself?"

"What," Addie said, "then he tried to run away, and Brett chased after him?"

"It's a possibility since the blood was found on the rocks close to the campsite where it appears Bill was staying. Maybe that's where he was running to, but Brett caught up with him first."

"Then Bill, trying to protect himself, lashed out and killed Brett in self-defense. He did tell me Brett was arguing with someone on the phone, and maybe Brett saw Bill and took his anger out on him. It wouldn't be the first time a homeless person was attacked because . . . well. He makes an easy target."

"It could be that Bill isn't telling you who the other man on the beach was because there wasn't anyone else."

Addie's stomach pitched. She really liked Bill and

had always thought of him as harmless, but perhaps Simon was right. If so, then hopefully the theory about self-defense was, too. That's the only thing that made sense. Then again, Gloria had told her about Bill doing anything for Martha out of his love for her. Brett was causing trouble in Martha's family. Did Bill see it as his duty to stop it? Fingers crossed she could find Bill before the police did and figure out what exactly happened. Justified self-defense would be an easier charge to fight in court than—she swallowed hard—murder.

Addie stepped inside the foyer, securing the lock as Simon had instructed her to do when they spotted a group of older teens down the hill who appeared to be on the hunt for a party. She flipped on the hall light and pressed her back against the door, basking in the glow of Simon's tender lips on hers when they'd shared a lingering kiss at her door. However, the afterglow flush quickly slipped away. There was an eerie emptiness about her home tonight. She hadn't prepared for this. She recalled Gloria's words from earlier this evening when Pippi had leapt into her arms on their reunion: "A house without a dog isn't a home. It's just a house."

It was the emptiness that overwhelmed her now. A vacancy in the house she had never felt before, one that had unbelievably been filled by a wiggling little ball of fur of all things. She brushed away wayward tears, kicked off her boots, hung up her jacket, and slid into her slippers. It was really too bad Serena and Zach were out tonight, discussing wedding plans with Serena's parents. She wanted to call her friend and ask her to pop over. The house echoed with emptiness and the slapping sound of her slippers flopping under her feet as she headed to clean up the mess in the kitchen.

The pong of stale scotch nagged at her nose as she poured the dregs of Jared's and Kalea's drinks into the sink and loaded crusty plates into the dishwasher. Counter and table wiped down, there was only one thing left to do before she could immerse herself in a nice warm bath and drink a hot cup of tea. She glanced down at the overflowing trash bag, tied it up, grabbed a sweater from the hook beside the back door, and started down the porch steps to the garbage can. With her foot hovering over the bottom step, she paused. The light wind off the harbor shifted, and with it, the air became heavy with the scent of burning wood.

Addie strained to see in the darkness at the back of her garden. The trees bent and whipped with the shifting wind, and for a moment between the billowing branches, she caught a glimpse of a glowing light at the back of her property, near what would be, the cliff edge.

Chapter Twenty-Nine

Addie raced up the porch steps, snatched her phone off the kitchen island as she dashed past it to the front hall, grabbed her jacket from the coatrack, stepped into her boots, and raced back down the hall and out the back door. Breathless, she paused on the bottom step and tried to focus her eyes in the moonless night. The trees swayed in the gusting wind, and again she caught a glimpse of the glowing orange light. By the woodsy scent heavy in the air, there was no question that it was just as she feared. A fire. Even so, judging by the size, it hadn't grown since she first spotted it a few minutes ago. A sense of relief rushed through her—it didn't appear to be a forest fire.

Her fingers tightly gripped her phone in her jacket pocket, and her common sense screamed at her to call the fire department. She couldn't bring herself to do it, but her curiosity was piqued. She knew high-school students were still off for Christmas break, and ten to one the group she and Simon had spotted earlier had discovered her little hideaway back here. Relatively isolated from the rest of the world, it appealed to partiers. She convinced herself that if she channeled her dearly departed grandmother, she'd be able to put an end to it without involving the authorities and wasting half her night filling in a police report. She took a deep breath to set her inner grandmother firmly in place and trekked through the snow mounds across the yard toward the grove of trees bordering the cliff.

Hopefully, she could keep the element of surprise for the full effect that her appearance would have on the teens. Stealthily she crept closer to the light source. The woodsy aroma became stronger, and she could distinctly hear the crackling of a large bonfire that sent sparks floating upward and dancing on the wind gusts over the treetops. She grasped the trunk of a tree and peered from behind it but could only make out the silhouette of one person crouched in front of the campfire.

Careful not to snap a twig beneath her feet, she edged closer. Her hand held ready on her phone to call 911 if she needed to. She kept her ears pricked for any sound that would indicate how many of them there actually were, but the crashing of the waves on the rocky beach below and the crackling and hissing of the wood in the flames were the only sounds. The wind shifted and swirled the smoke into coils around the fire pit. The figure rose and moved around the blaze to the other side. The firelight clearly reflected off the intruder's face.

"Bill!" she gasped.

He jumped back, tripped over a piece of wood, and careened backward, landing hard on the frozen ground.

"Oh no." She darted over to him and helped him to his

feet. "Are you okay? What on earth are you doing here? Paige saw you down on Marine Drive not long ago."

"Miss Addie, I didn't mean no harm." He rose to his feet and brushed snow from his tattered jeans. "Are you gonna call the police on me?"

"No, but why are you here of all places, and how did you get up here so fast? You don't have a car."

"I take that path up from the beach down there."

"You'd have to be a mountain goat to get up that."

"It's not so hard once you've learned the way and done it a few times."

"A few times? How long have you been camped out here?"

"I got nowhere else to go. I can't go back to the shelter, and that fireman is always chasing me off when I do find someplace warm to sleep. I thought you wouldn't see me back here. I've been really careful not to light the fire until I saw your lights go out." He hung his head. "But tonight, I was cold and thought . . . well, never thought you'd come and check it out on your own." He raised his head and fixed his eyes on hers. "You know, Miss Addie, that was darn right foolish of you to come back here by yourself. What if it hadn't been me but someone who wanted to do you harm? You know you can't be too careful these days."

"I know it was foolish, but this is my property, and when I saw the light, I thought at first it was a forest fire, but then I remembered seeing a group of kids walking up the hill. I thought it was them partying." She shoved her hands in her jacket pockets. "But that doesn't matter. I'm so glad it is you."

"You are?"

"Yes, I've been looking for you. I was worried sick."

"You were worried about me?"

"Yes, I was and have been ever since we found that man behind Martha's. After the police discovered the blood by the rock crag where you'd been camping, I was worried that—"

"I didn't kill that guy if that's what you're thinking. I ain't hurt anybody or anything since . . . I come back from Vietnam." He dropped down on a log he had placed as a seat beside the fire pit. Clasping both sides of his head with his hands, he began rocking back and forth. "You can ask Miss Martha. She knows me. I don't like killing."

"It's okay." She patted his shoulder. "It's only that you had told me there was someone else on the beach that night, but you wouldn't tell me who it was. I was afraid that someone saw you, too, and that's why you were hiding."

Bill shook his head vigorously. "No, no, I can't say." He sat with his arms locked around his shins, rocking, but wouldn't look at her.

"Please, the police think it was Martha, and she could go to jail for a long time. You don't want that, do you?"

He shook his head.

"Tell me . . . who was there? Who killed the man?"

"Is Miss Paige and her little one safe now?"

"Yes, why? Were they in danger?"

"Then it's okay. The police will find out the truth, and Miss Martha didn't do it. You don't want me sticking my nose in. It'll only cause more trouble for them."

"What are you talking about? Help me to understand what happened."

"Nothing. Go away, *just* Addie." He buried his head in his knees and sobbed.

"Bill, did you hurt that man on the beach that night to keep Paige and Emma safe from something?"

His head shot up, and he fixed his blurry eyes on hers. "No, I told you I ain't hurt no one, nothing since the war. I couldn't ever again. Leave me be now."

"At least come back to the house. I can give you a warm meal and bed, and then we can talk again in the morning."

"No, ma'am." He began rocking again. "It's all good now. If Miss Paige and her little one are safe, I got nothing more to say."

Addie stood up and stared down at Bill, who was sniffling and rocking. It was no use to press him any further. He had shut down. She had seen him do this before. She glanced over at the stack of firewood he had collected and at the makeshift lean-to he'd built. The corner of some old blankets stuck out from the edge of it. At least, he would be warm and safe tonight. Whoever he was afraid of would hardly find him camped back here.

She started back to the house, his words about Paige and Emma being in danger playing over and over in her mind. The images of the clues she'd written on the board came back at her all jumbled and distorted. Nothing about any of this made sense. *What am I missing?* She stepped into the warmth of her kitchen and stopped short.

"Hi, Cuz." Kalea gave her a finger wave from the island. "Were you over at Serena's?"

"Nope, I wasn't." Addie kicked off her boots.

"You're probably surprised to see me sitting here,

drinking tea like our earlier disagreement never happened, aren't you?"

"I did say you had a week, so not really." Addie grabbed the kettle beside the stove, shook it, and plugged it in. "I am surprised, though, that you appear to be so chipper after the words we had this evening."

"I came back and waited up for you to tell you . . ."

"Tell me what? That you're leaving before the end of the week?"

"Not really." Kalea took a sip of her tea and studied Addie over the cup's rim. "To tell you that you were right."

Addie stared in disbelief.

"You know, what you said about honesty being the best policy."

"So, you finally came clean with Jared, and he's dumped you, and the business deal is off. You came back to beg me to forgive you for being such a deceitful little wit—"

Kalea took a sip. Her eyes danced with amusement. "No, exactly the opposite."

"What do you mean?"

"I mean that you were also right about Jared not being stupid enough to become involved in a business transaction without checking his client out."

"And?"

"And he's known all along that I wasn't the lady of the manor"—she waved her hand in the air—"and that the house and bookstore are actually yours, and I was penniless and living off your charity."

"I don't get it. If he knew, why was he willing to invest in your little charade? What did he expect to get out of it?"

"Duh, me obviously."

"In what way?" Addie's brow rose in concern.

"He was testing me to see how much integrity I had and when I would come clean with him. That's why he got so upset when he left tonight. You had given me the perfect opening to tell him the truth, and I didn't. He was disappointed, and he was ready to pull the plug on the dress shop deal, but I told him the whole truth. We talked about why I did it and how out of control it became. It was just a silly way to impress a man I liked, but I never thought it would go as far as it did. I was scared and didn't know how to get out of it." She sucked in a deep breath and grinned at Addie.

"And just like that"—Addie snapped her fingers— "all is forgiven?"

"Not exactly. He made it clear that he's not *giving* me the money. It's a loan, a business transaction, and he has set strict payment dates and everything, but yes, the shop is mine."

"Well, I'll be." Addie's jaw dropped. "You always do manage to come out on top, don't you? Even after you lie and—"

"Want to hear the best part?" Kalea said with a little giggle.

"There's more?"

"It seems I didn't only buy the dress shop on the main level, but the building it's in, and on the second floor, there's the cutest, to-die-for, one-bedroom apartment."

"You're kidding? Is it vacant, or are you going to be tossing some poor unsuspecting tenant out so you can move in?"

"That's part of the beauty. It's been empty for almost

a year. Mellissa and Keith got tired of being landlords when the last renter caused so much trouble with unreasonable demands."

"That means you can move in anytime?"

"Only if I want to pay rent until I take possession of the building, so . . ."

"So, you're asking me to give you an extension here. Is that what this is all about?"

"Yes," Kalea squeaked.

Addie stared at her cousin. On one hand, the woman had finally come clean and was attempting to clean up the mess she'd created. Though Addie could never approve of Kalea's tactics, she was still the only family Addie had. Her mind jumped back and forth between digging in her heels and giving in to the puppy-dog eyes staring back at her.

"Well, is it possible?"

"If Jared is so into you and is willing to forgive your charade, why isn't he helping you out with the accommodation issue?"

"He offered to book me a room at the hotel where he's staying, but I don't want to be indebted to him any more than I already am. I do have some morals believe it or not. I would prefer our relationship develops naturally and not because I owe him."

"Well, I guess that's progress for you."

"Addie!"

"Sorry, I shouldn't have said that. I just remember a past incident where you had no issue with being a kept woman."

Kalea's porcelain skin turned crimson.

"Okay, as long as you start buying your own food and

stop eating the food I have put away for special occasions for Simon and me."

"Does that mean I can also come back to work at the bookstore until the deal's done, too? I will need to make some money to buy my groceries."

"Don't push it. A roof over your head is all I'm offering."

"Okay, agreed. But what will I eat?"

"I'm sure Jared won't let you starve. After all, you're into him for a lot of money, and if you die of starvation, how would you ever pay him back?" Addie headed down the hall. She needed a good soak in the tub. There was just too much coming at her all at once, and her mind and body needed numbing.

Chapter Thirty

Addie trotted down the back stairs and across the yard toward Bill's campsite, a large thermos tucked tight under her arm. It was her hope that after a night's sleep, a steaming cup of her favorite brew might loosen Bill's tongue and persuade him to open up to her. His overt concern for Paige and Emma had wreaked havoc on her mind all night. She needed to know what kind of danger he thought her friend and her little girl were in.

When she got to the clearing along the cliff top, her hopes plummeted. His shelter was dismantled, and the rocks he'd used to ring the fire pit were scattered randomly over the area. Except for the mishmash of footprints in the blown snow, there was no sign that he'd even been there.

Addie plodded back to the house and halfheartedly prepared for work as her mind raced. The fact that Bill was on the run again scared her. He knew something other than who else was on the beach. He'd mentioned Paige had been or still was in danger, and her chest tightened recalling his words. How could she face her assistant this morning without letting something like that slip out and scaring her even more than she already was? No, she had to think of a way to flush Bill out, and on the drive to the bookstore, it hit her. Who, besides the stranger on the beach, was Bill most afraid of? It was the fire department that also kept him on the run, and they knew all his preferred hiding places.

She swung into her parking space in the alley and made a grab for the straw bag on the seat beside her. When nothing but air swept past her hand, she remembered the other reason she couldn't sleep last night. She missed the warm little body nestled close to her, and her heart ached now as though she had just lost her best friend forever. Fighting back tears, she marched to the front of the store.

"Good morning, Addie," Paige chirped, and looked up from a stack of books she was loading onto the book trolley. "It's a beautiful day, isn't it?"

Addie eyed her assistant warily. "Is everything okay with you?"

"It couldn't be better. I had a wonderful time last night. Logan sang me a love song." She swooned with a giggle. "Mom's lawyer called and wants to meet with her at eleven. Fingers crossed it's good news, and that whole thing about her not being able to reach the icicle means the charges against her are going to be dropped."

"Yes, fingers crossed," Addie said hesitantly.

She didn't have the heart to tell Paige that the call from the lawyer's office was no doubt about something else. He wouldn't have kept poor Martha in suspense and just outright told her the charges had been dropped, but then again, what did she know about legal matters? Perhaps he needed her to sign something for the courts. But it was clear that Addie wasn't going to be able to keep her mouth closed about Bill's comment much longer—her tongue wasn't going to be able to take all the chomping. She had to go by the firehouse to see if anyone there besides Logan could give her any other ideas about where she could look for Bill. If Paige was in danger, she needed to tell Marc, but until she knew what kind of danger, he'd say it was useless information and hearsay and to come back when she had more.

"Paige, it seems quiet this morning. Would you mind if I ran a quick errand?"

"Of course not, you're the boss. You can come and go as you like."

"I know, but I don't like to take advantage of that, so it's always nice to check. You might have an appointment or something, too."

"Nope, all's good. Oh, by the way, did you ever find Bill last night?"

Addie froze. She couldn't lie, but if she told Paige the truth, she would have to tell her what he said. "Actually, I'm just heading to talk to some people who might be able to tell me where I could possibly find him today."

"I sure hope they can help. Then the DA would have to drop the charges against Mom for sure if Bill can identify who he saw on Saturday."

"That's what I'm still hoping to find out because, to be honest, I'm at a complete loss with this. Because every suspect I have on the board has a police-confirmed alibi, and for the life of me, I can't think who should be on there that's not."

"Even that witch, Amber Carr, his latest girlfriend?"

Addie shook her head. "It's airtight. She was at the inn at the time of death, and there are witnesses. No, I'm pretty sure it had to have been someone I've already discarded as a possibility—" *Cliff? Could it be him?*

"Addie? You were saying?"

"Oh yeah, sorry, I just had a thought. Maybe it was a random attack. After all, there were a lot of people in town who answered the town council's call-out for volunteer drivers. Who knows"—Addie shrugged—"maybe Brett saw something, like a drug deal or a fight going down on the beach Saturday, and just happened to be in the wrong place at the wrong time."

"That's a possibility. But why was the body moved to the back of the bakery?"

"That's a good question and pretty much blows my random act out of the water, doesn't it? Whoever killed Brett knew the family history, or at least had witnessed the public arguments, and used his murder and the placement of the body as a direct hit on your mom. I've got to go. I need to find Bill before whoever is behind this finds him first. If that happens, we'll never discover the other person's identity."

Addie dashed out the back door. Paige's words rang in her mind. She had seen that in her chalkboard scribblings, but to hear the actual words made Addie realize there was no way Bill, as Simon had suggested, killed Brett. Aside from the fact that he had no way to move the body, his words the night before proved he cared deeply for Martha and the entire family. He would have never framed Martha for the murder. Bill was in more trouble than she had thought before. If the killer went to all the trouble of staging the scene, it proved this wasn't a random act, and he, or she, wanted Martha to pay for something.

Chapter Thirty-One

Addie pulled up along the curb in front of the fire station, checked her mirrors to make sure she was a legal distance from the hydrant, and headed toward the open, double-wide bay doors exposing the large but empty garage inside. The only vehicle in sight belonged to the fire chief, Keith Hubert, and was parked along the far side of the wide driveway. She peered around the door. Having never been in a fire station before, she had no idea what to expect, but the emptiness certainly hadn't been what she had pictured. On the television shows, groups of men and women sat around drinking coffee, shooting the breeze, or were cleaning equipment. The eerie silence bothered her.

"Hello, is anyone here?" No answer. She stepped inside the bay. "Hello?" Her voice echoed back at her.

Keith poked his head out from behind a shelf of canisters, a pen clamped between his right ear and ginger hair. "Addie? What a surprise." He tucked a clipboard under his arm and extended his hand in greeting. "What brings you by today?"

"Hi, I hope it's okay." She glanced around the empty

bay. "I've never been inside a firehouse before, and I must say it's nothing like I expected."

He tossed his head back with a chuckle. "Yeah, it's not quite as glamorous or romantic as you see in the movies, is it? It's pretty much a lot of grunt work and preparing for the next call."

"Is that where everyone is?"

"Not now. The day shift is refueling the two engines and the pumper. As you can see"—he waved the clipboard—"I'm doing inventory. It doesn't get much more glamorous than that," he said with a short laugh. "But what brings you in, or did you want a tour?"

"Actually, I was hoping to speak to a few of your crew."

"Is there a problem I should know about?"

"No, no, not at all. It's only that last night I was speaking with Logan Ashmore and—"

"Yes, Logan, a fine young recruit. He's going to do well here, and if I'm not mistaken, he's taken up with our little Paige. He can't do better than that, can he?"

"Well, you and I think so because we both think the world of her, but he told me that Old Bill—"

"The homeless guy who's always a pain in our butts?"

"How so?"

"He refused for years to go to the shelter and would set up camps anywhere and everywhere. Camps that were nothing but a pure fire hazard not only to himself but to everyone and every building in the vicinity."

"Well, yeah, aside from the fact that he is homeless and trying to keep warm, he does have some issues that have led him to that life."

"I agree, but we have to think about the community as

a whole and have to make every effort to put an end to his dangerous behavior."

Addie was taken aback at the force of Keith's voice. This sounded personal, and she wondered if Keith was aware that Bill still held a torch for Martha after all these years.

"Anyway, Logan mentioned that you had given orders for them to roust Bill from his camps whenever you come across them."

"Yeah, like I said, it's for the safety of the community, but I'm in desperate need of a coffee. Would you like one?"

"Sure, that would be great. I've kind of been on the run all morning and haven't had my fix yet."

"I have a fresh pot in my office, follow me."

Addie followed Keith past a couple of smaller offices, and on the right, there was a sign that said STAFF ONLY. "That's our bunk room for the night shift," he added as they passed. When they reached the end of the long hallway, he gestured toward another room. "And this is the common area. We eat, play, and watch television in here, and over here"—he turned to his left and walked past a small picture-windowed office to a larger one that looked out over the common room—"is where I call home." He sauntered over to a table and poured two cups of coffee. "Cream or sugar?"

"Just cream, thanks."

He handed Addie her steaming cup. "Now, where were we?"

"I was looking for suggestions from some of your crew as to where I might find Bill. Places they've chased him from in the past that maybe he's returned to."

"Why is it important for you to find Bill?" He peered at her over the rim of his cup.

"I'm not sure if you're aware," Addie said, leaning back against a desk, "but Bill was with me when I discovered that man's body behind the bakery last Sunday."

Keith took a sip. "I had heard something about that."

"And Bill mentioned that he saw Brett on the beach late Saturday night."

"He did, did he?"

"Yes, and then he told me there was someone else there."

"Did he say who that someone else was?"

"No, that's why I have to find Bill now. He seems to have disappeared, and I think whoever that other person was, is the killer. Finding that mystery person is the only way to prove Martha had nothing to do with the death."

"Look, as far as I'm concerned, Brett Palmer got what was coming to him." His cheek twitched. "The person who killed him should be congratulated not condemned. He did everyone a favor."

"You said *he*. Did you see who else was on the beach? Did you see the murderer?"

The dark-blue vein in his temple bulged and pulsated. He glanced away and took a swig of his coffee. The fine hairs on Addie's arms quivered. "You were there. Did you find out it was Brett who had stolen Paige's book'?"

He didn't answer.

"Keith . . . did you know about him stealing the book? Did you hear him on the phone with Amber talking about it?"

"That's not all that scumbag was going to steal."

"What do you mean?"

Keith spun toward her. Tiny beads of perspiration glistened on his brow, and he pinned Addie with a look of pure revulsion. Spittle sprayed from his mouth. "He planned on taking Emma and disappearing with her, him and that no-good woman of his."

"I don't understand." She pressed back hard against the edge of the desk. Pain shot across her hip.

"Like I said, whoever killed him did everyone a favor." Without taking his eyes off her, he clicked the top of his pen, propelling the ballpoint tip out of the pen casing. A distant glaze fell over his eyes as he toyed with it.

"Of course"—a knot twisted in Addie's gut—"why didn't I see it before? You're the other man Bill saw on the beach, aren't you? That's why he was so scared. You'd made his life difficult, and he was terrified that if he was the one to give you up to the police, everything would get worse, and you'd make sure he was hounded even more"—she searched Keith's unblinking eyes—"or worse . . . kill him for doing the right thing."

The fire burning behind his eyes reflected on his face as he took a step toward Addie and thrust the ballpoint pen tip in her throat. "Remember, I'm also a trained medic. I know exactly where to plunge this in order to silence you."

"That's . . . that's right. You're trained to save lives not take them." Addie winced with the pain of the edge of the desk in her hip. "That's why I didn't—no, couldn't—suspect you. You're not a killer."

"Don't test me," he said as he pressed the tip deeper into her flesh.

"Keith, you're not a murderer. You're the fire chief, a pillar of the community. A loving husband, and the father of two beautiful children who worship you, so don't do this." She stared down her cheek at the pen firmly clasped in his hand. The placement against her throat matched the wound on Brett's neck. Her gaze of comprehension met his equally fierce one mere inches from her face.

"Is this what happened with Brett, Keith? You overheard him on the phone, talking about his plan to kidnap Emma, and it made you so mad that you grabbed the first thing you could, an icicle, and went after him and stabbed him in the throat like you want to do with me?"

His glassy eyes wild, he studied her warily and dug the tip deeper. "I only wanted to scare him, but when I confronted him about what I'd heard, he told me I was crazy and said to mind my own business. He laughed at me, and accused me of having unnatural affection for Paige." Spittle sprayed across Addie's cheek, and she cringed when the fine tip of the pen chafed the skin on her throat.

"Then he ran off. I chased after him and caught him by the rocks. He told me he had the book and was going to sell it, and that's what he and his *new* family were going to live off until he could get another teaching job."

"I imagine that made you very angry because we all know that you thought of Paige as your daughter. You couldn't stand by and let this interloper take away the one thing you both loved—Emma. Could you?"

"That's right," he said, his hot breath searing her cheek. "It would have destroyed Paige. I begged him not to go through with it, but he laughed. I pressed the icicle to his neck just like this and—"

"Stop, Keith, you're not a killer." Addie's chest twisted as he pressed the tip deeper. "You killed Brett to protect

Paige and Emma, but if you kill me, that's different. If you turn yourself in, the courts might go easy on you because you did it to protect your family. Killing me to shut me up is something different." She sucked in a wobbly breath. "Think about your wife and children. Do you want them to live with knowing you killed two people, and the second was only to save yourself, not to save your family? If you go to the police now and tell them exactly what happened and why it happened, then I'm sure a judge will understand."

He snorted. "But I'd lose Mellissa and the kids for sure! No, I can't." His jaw set firm.

"You'll lose them if you kill me, too. So, please, put the pen down and let me drive you to the police station." For the first time, his eyes opened to her, and she knew he saw *her*. "Listen to me, it's Addie, you know me, and I *know* that you're not a murderer. You tried to stop a bad thing from happening, and it got out of control, right?"

His hand shook, and he nodded mutely. Then he and the pen dropped to the floor. His head in his hands he sat weeping. "What have I done . . . what have I done?" Rocking back and forth, he wailed. "Poor Martha, I never wanted to hurt her, too, only to make her experience some of the pain I felt when she told Mellissa to leave me and take the kids away." He flung his head back. "I'm so sorry. Will they ever be able to forgive me?" Tears streamed down his ruddy cheeks.

Addie bent over the sobbing man and helped him to his feet. As they staggered toward her car, it struck her that if he hadn't been on the beach at that exact time and happened to overhear the conversation between Brett and Amber . . . Addie shuddered to think of what might have been come Sunday morning when Brett was scheduled to pick Emma up for a supposed day visit—a day that would have concluded in an endless nightmare for Paige and her family. Although Keith didn't handle the overheard kidnapping plot in the way he should have, by taking it to the police and not trying to stop it himself, she couldn't help but feel some compassion for this man who loved his family so much that he killed to protect them.

Chapter Thirty-Two

Addie sat hunched over a cup of cold coffee. She glanced up at the clock above the front desk and cringed. Two hours since she'd given her statement and still not a word about what was going on now. All she had been told was to have a seat and wait until they were finished with Chief Hubert.

She pulled her cell phone out and shoved it back in her pocket. *Where is Simon?* Probably in surgery. When she'd sent out her text to tell him she was at the police station with the murderer, she expected a reply of some sort. Nothing but silence. Just like from Marc or Detective Brookes.

Marc's office door opened. Ryley came out, glanced fleetingly at Addie, and whispered something to Jerry behind the desk before going back into Marc's office. She left the door open. Jerry rose and went through the doorway behind the desk, and Addie edged forward in her seat, straining to hear what was being said in the office. But it was no use. She was too far away, and all she could make out were low mumblings. Jerry returned with three cups of steaming coffee in his large hands and took them into the office, came back out, and resumed his seat. He glanced up at Addie and returned to whatever it was he was working on behind the desk partition.

She sat back in her hard-plastic chair, took a swig of the coffee, and cringed. She rose and walked over to the desk. "Hey, Jerry, is there any chance I can get a cup of your coffee? The stuff from the machine is pretty foul."

Jerry eyed her. "Sure, as long as you stay put. I've had my orders." He chuckled as he disappeared through the door behind him.

Addie, ears pricked, edged down the long counter. She could hear Keith's voice as it rose in pitch, followed by a monotone mumbling. But the words were too muffled. Jerry returned and eyed her. Addie smiled innocently.

"Thanks, you're a lifesaver." She took the cup, and under the shadow of his suspicious gaze, retreated back to her seat.

Minutes ticked by and turned into another hour. She retrieved her texts from Paige, careful not to reveal what she was doing at the police station. How on earth could she tell her in a text that the brother-in-law she adored was guilty of murdering her child's father? No, that was something Paige and the rest of the family would have to hear in person. For now, she only said it had something to do with the investigation, and she'd be back as soon as Marc was done talking to her.

Addie jumped when a hand fell on her shoulder. "Simon!" she cried, and leapt to her feet. "Am I ever happy to see you."

"Sorry, I was in surgery when your text arrived and only just got it." He glanced at Jerry and nodded. "Why are you here, and what's this about bringing the murderer in?"

"Sit"—she pointed to a chair—"and I'll tell you all about it." Addie filled Simon in on the details of her morning adventure, and when she finished, she took a much-needed sip of her coffee.

"Who'd have thought?" He sat back and raked his hand through his thick black hair.

"I know, right? Keith wasn't even on my radar, but now that I think about it, he should have been. Right from the start, we knew he was at the beach late. I just don't know how I missed putting two and two together."

"I think it's more a matter of none of us wanting to believe it, not that we ever considered the possibility."

"Maybe you're right. He was so devoted to Paige and Emma. He's been part of their family most of his life as Mellissa and he began dating in middle school. Martha treated him like a son."

"Until he cheated on Mellissa."

"Yeah"—Addie sat back—"and then she turned on him."

The office door opened, and Detective Brookes led a solemn-faced Keith, his head drooping, out of the room in handcuffs and ushered him through the back door. The thud of his duty boots echoed on the staircase leading to the cells below.

Marc waved at Addie from the doorway. "Simon, you might as well come, too." He disappeared back inside his office.

Addie looked at Simon, a hesitant smile on her face. She'd spent many an hour sitting in Marc's office, discussing a case, but never in the company of his onetime rival for her affections.

Simon gave her a reassuring grin. "I am the coroner after all. I probably should hear what he has to say."

"Of course." She exhaled and headed through the door, and took the seat she had often thought of in the past as hers. Her hands stroked the smooth wooden arms. Memories came rushing back as she gazed across the desk at Marc's somber face.

"This is a tough one," he said, his voice cracking, "and one that's going to rock the entire community to the core. Many of the people we know and care about are going to have a hard time dealing with this." He shuffled the papers on the desk in front of him.

Addie was at a loss for words. His eyes were tearing up, and she could tell by the set of his jaw that he was fighting the urge to cry. Discovering that Keith, his life-long friend, had killed someone appeared to have shaken him badly.

Simon leaned forward. "I think by what Addie has told me about the circumstances, this wasn't premeditated, so I'm guessing he won't be charged with first-degree murder." His soft and even voice gave testament to the compassion he used with patients who were experiencing a life-changing diagnosis or trauma. Pride rushed through Addie. Trust Simon to find calm in a difficult situation and to help Marc save face in front of them.

Marc nodded and dropped the papers. "From what the chief said in his statement, it appears to be a case of voluntary manslaughter."

"Voluntary?" Addie sat upright and gripped the chair. "Shouldn't it be involuntary manslaughter? He didn't mean to do it. He was trying to protect Paige and Emma and prevent a kidnapping from occurring."

"That's true, and I'm sure the DA will take all that into consideration, but unfortunately"—his gaze dropped—"there was anger involved in his attack on Brett, which led to the death. It didn't occur by way of an accident—say, a slip and fall on the icicle. It's considered voluntary."

Simon placed his hand over Addie's and gave it a light squeeze. "He's right. Involuntary manslaughter is the *unintentional* killing of a person by someone who has no spite or anger, and who has no intent to kill the victim. It's generally a death that occurs due to an unforeseen accident."

"But Keith didn't intend to kill Brett. He just wanted to stop him from taking Emma."

"You're right, but he was angry, and Brett's death occurred because of Keith's actions toward him. The courts will see that as an act done with a reckless indifference for human life."

"However"—Marc cleared his throat—"the judge does have the right to take other factors into consideration. Any sentence handed down in a voluntary manslaughter case will depend on the facts particular to that case."

Simon shifted toward her. "Timing is one element of concern. If a judge feels that the person committed the murder in the heat of passion, as is the case with Keith, then he could be charged with voluntary manslaughter rather than murder. The sentence is generally lighter. Does it make sense?"

"What you're saying is the judge will consider the special circumstances leading to the incident and death? Is that right?" Addie asked.

Both men nodded.

"That's good because it's clear there was provocation on Brett's part leading up to his death," Addie said, shifting in her chair. "Will the judge go easier on him given the fact that he turned himself in?"

Marc held her inquisitive gaze. "It might have a bearing on his decision, and I must say, I am impressed that you managed to convince Keith to do that."

"Yes," Simon said, clearing his throat. "I've seen cases before when the courts were more lenient on a person who showed full remorse for their actions. So, I'm pretty sure, your convincing him to come in of his own accord will have a bearing on his verdict."

Addie's gaze darted from one man to the other. "What about the family? Who's going to tell Mellissa and Martha about what's happened?"

"Detective Brookes is taking an officer to Martha's now. According to Keith, Mellissa is there today, babysitting Emma."

"But Martha won't be there when she gets the news. She was meeting her lawyer today."

Marc shook his head. "Through the DA's office, her lawyer is aware of all this. He canceled the appointment."

"What about Paige? Somebody has to tell her. She thought of Keith like a father."

"I'm sure Martha will fill her in."

"But she's alone in the store. If she hears about this . . ."

"Go, be with her," Marc said.

Addie rose, and Marc's intercom beeped.

"What is it, Jerry?"

"The DA's on line one."

"Thanks." Marc clicked off the speaker. "Sorry, but I have to take this."

Addie nodded, and Simon placed his hand on her back as they headed toward the door.

"Are you going to be okay?" he whispered.

"Yes, I'm worried about Paige, though. This is going to hit her hard, and she can't be alone when she hears the news."

"I agree, come on. Let's get you back there fast."

"Will you stay? You're so good at helping people handle grief."

"Unfortunately, it goes with my job."

They stood in the doorway at the back of the shop. Paige was just finishing up with a customer. Addie leaned into Simon and whispered, "You check down the aisles to see if there's anyone else in the store. If there is, tell them we have to temporarily close." Addie straightened, held her head high, and made her way to the front, following the customer to the door. "Thank you for coming." Addie grinned. "I do hope you'll come back again."

"Oh yes, this is one of my favorite stops when I'm in town, and that girl who works here is such a cheery soul. Every time I come in, she really brightens this old woman's day."

"Yes, she is something special, isn't she?" Addie smiled and glanced over at Paige, whose radiant blue eyes twinkled with the woman's praise.

Simon gave Addie the all-clear nod, and she latched the deadbolt after the woman left and flipped the door sign to CLOSED.

Paige's eyes filled with questions. "What's going on? Why did you close?"

"Paige, we have to talk about something, and it's best you hear it from us rather than someone on the street."

Addie drew in a deep breath. She needed to breathe. *Just keep breathing.* "Have you talked to your mom recently?"

"Not since she called to tell me her lawyer canceled their appointment without giving her a reason. Why, have they taken my mom in again? Did they find more evidence against her? Are we going to have another witch hunt?"

"Paige"—Simon moved to her side—"I think you'd better sit down to hear what Addie has to say." He guided her onto a counter stool.

"Now you're both scaring me. Has something happened to Emma?" She rose to her feet. Her eyes filled with terror. "Where is she?"

"No, she's fine. Your mom and sister are with her."

"Then what is it? What's happened to make you both act this way?" Her voice teetered on hysteria.

Addie sat on the stool beside Paige, clasped both her hands, and relayed the events of the morning.

"That's impossible!" Paige leapt to her feet. "Keith isn't a killer. He couldn't hurt a fly. You must have gotten it all wrong."

"I'm sorry, Paige." Addie gently placed her hand on Paige's shoulder. "He confessed."

"Then he did it for a good reason. What did you say . . . that Brett was planning on kidnapping Emma?" Her eyes searched Simon's. "See, he did it to stop another crime. They can't find him guilty. He was helping us. He's a hero, not a murderer."

"That's for the courts to decide, not us." Addie didn't know what to say. Paige was right in one way. But was taking a life ever justified? At this point, she didn't know.

"Simon, tell me he won't be charged. As soon as Marc hears why he did it, they'll let him go."

"Marc knows, and Keith is in custody."

"No, not Keith!" she wailed. Her face went deathly white, and her knees buckled. Simon made a grab for her and settled with her on the floor. She clung to him like a rag doll and sobbed uncontrollably in his arms.

Chapter Thirty-Three

Simon shot Addie a side glance. "Have you ever been invited to have dinner at Martha's before?"

"No," Addie said with a chuckle. "I can't say as I have, and I'm curious to see what she's got planned."

"Why? She strikes me as a woman who is very capable in the kitchen."

"The bakery, yes . . . but a dinner party? Somehow, I don't think that's her style, do you?"

"Now that you mention it, no." Simon laughed and pulled his truck alongside the curb in front of the two-story Dutch Colonial. "Although, with five daughters, surely one of them is capable of cohosting a large event."

"The two that come to mind who would make sure it was an actual dinner party don't live in town. Ashley, who is an event planner, lives on the West Coast, and Jennifer, a mother of five, who I imagine is fairly good at whipping a dinner together, lives in Chicago. Of course, there's Mellissa, but after what she's been through recently with Keith, I doubt she's functioning on all cylinders right now." She opened her door and jumped out into a knee-high snowdrift. "Great place to park, Doc." She laughed and hobbled onto the sidewalk.

"Doesn't her other sister—what's her name?"

"Brianna."

"Yeah, doesn't she live around here?"

"She lives in Pen Harbor with husband, Darren. He's with the State Highway Patrol. She might be able to help put on a dinner party, but my best guess is . . . don't expect too much."

"As long as Martha has some of those amazing strawberry scones she makes, I'll be a happy camper."

Addie stood in the doorway and was struck by the scents that wafted past her nose. If she didn't know better, she'd have sworn she smelled roast chicken, a hint of cloves, and something delightfully cinnamony.

Paige let out a high-pitched squeal, dashed out of the living room into the hallway, and threw her arms around Addie's neck. "I'm so glad you came, both of you. We couldn't have made it through this ordeal without your help and support."

Martha stood sentry in the living room doorway and wiped her hands on a dish towel. "Come in, come in. Close the door. We're not heating up the whole darned neighborhood." She gestured toward the room behind her. "I think you know most everyone here."

Addie glanced around the corner into the large room at all the beaming faces and halted briefly when she got to Keith and Mellissa, his arm draped over his wife's shoulder. With her pixieish face, there was no mistaking her family resemblance to Martha and Paige. She also had the identical petite stature. Albeit, with maturity and having had two babies, she was a little more rounded like her mother than her youngest sibling. However, when Mellissa acknowledged Addie and Simon, she noted that behind the woman's eyes, which were etched in dark circles, Mellissa had the same endearing smile as her baby sister.

"Yes, hi everyone!" Addie gave a wave, took off her jacket, handed it to Paige, and stepped into the lively room. "It's so wonderful to be included in your family dinner."

Then words evaded her. Were her eyes deceiving her?

Addie blinked . . . twice . . . to be certain. There in the far corner of the living room was a somewhat familiar face, but Addie still couldn't believe what she was seeing. It was Old Bill, who at this moment didn't look old, or grizzled and world-worn, but more like a shy teenage boy. His mop of graying-blond hair was neatly trimmed to above his collar, and he was wearing a brand-new pair of well-fitting jeans and a blue dress shirt that made his once-faded blue eyes sparkle in the lights.

She grabbed Paige's arm and whispered, "Is that really Bill?"

Paige nodded with a grin. "Yes, Mom offered him one of the spare rooms but he refused, so Dad put an old heater and a bed out in the garage for him."

Addie's heart grew two sizes as she studied his beaming face. "At least he'll be safe and warm this winter," she said, returning his head nod.

"Thank you for inviting us," Simon said as he stepped into the living room behind Addie and shook Keith's outstretched hand when Keith crossed the room to greet them.

Addie returned Keith's genuine smile and ignored the

piercing glare that Martha fixed on the back of his head during his welcoming gesture. As wonderful as it was to see Bill being brought back into the fold with his high school friends after all these years, it appeared that not all was forgiven on all accounts, and having been on the receiving end of her old adversary's wrath in the past, Addie knew forgiveness for an indiscretion didn't come fast or easy for Martha. Never mind for someone who framed the cactus woman for murder.

Addie sensed that this might prove to be an interesting evening. Because it was clear by the venomous look in Martha's eyes when she glanced at Keith that not all was as perfect in this household as was being portrayed by this cozy gathering.

"Everyone, get your glasses. It's time to celebrate!" Ken called out as the cork popped off a champagne bottle. He made a round of the room, filling each crystal flute with some of the bubbly. "To the Stringer family, their significant others, and our dear friends." He nodded at Addie and Simon and then turned to Bill and raised his glass. "May we all live long and prosperous lives, *together*, as it should be." He drew Martha close to his side and planted a kiss on her flushed cheek.

Addie raised her glass in the toast. Out of the corner of her eye, she caught sight of Paige's beaming face.

"Dad's going to be staying around awhile," Paige whispered under the commotion of cheers and well wishes. "After being apart for twenty years he said he wants to try to work things out with Mom again." She laughed when her mother pulled away from Ken and swatted him with a kitchen towel. "Although, that might be a bit of a job because I'm not sure she can be that forgiving of him for up and leaving her to raise five little girls on her own."

Addie smiled warily at Ken. She couldn't shake the feeling that his words of reconciliation didn't ring entirely true. His sticking around probably had nothing to do with the family being reunited. Her gut told her it was more than likely because a book that was valued at twenty-five thousand dollars was still missing, and he was looking for an excuse to stay in town to try to find it. Then she looked at Paige's radiant face and hoped she was wrong. "Judging by how close Keith and Mellissa are tonight, it appears this tragedy did bring your family back together."

Paige took a sip. "Yes, it's too bad that we all learned a lesson about family the hard way. But in the end, I guess what Keith did, was . . ."

"Was what?"

"Nothing." Paige shook her head. "If I say it, you'll think me a horrible person."

"Never!" Addie placed her arm around Paige's shoulder and gave her a squeeze. "In my eyes, you're one of the best people I've ever met."

"Thank you. That means a lot since I think of you as a sister."

"You'll always be the sister I never had."

Paige's grin activated her dimples, and tears formed in her big, round blue eyes. She squeezed Addie's hand, and then wove her way across the room to her mother's side and whispered in her ear.

Martha bellowed over the high-spirited chorus of voices. "Paige has just reminded me that the chicken isn't going to eat itself. So, everyone into the dining room."

Addie and Simon filed in behind everyone else. She knew in her heart it was difficult for Marc to arrest Keith, and by law he had no choice. A life had been taken. But as she witnessed this family gathering, she couldn't help but pray that the courts would see the other side of their personal misfortunes before casting judgment. The tragedy that had occurred with Brett's death had definitely brought this family together again.

Keith slid up to her side. "I wanted to thank you personally for convincing me to turn myself in. I really don't know what I was thinking at the time."

"It was the right thing to do, Keith." She glanced at Mellissa, who placed a tray of steaming fresh-baked dinner rolls on the table. "Plus, it seemed to be the right thing to save your marriage by the look of it."

"It did that. We're finally talking, and we are even going to start another business together. Provided I'm not in prison too long."

"I thought after she sold the dress shop, she was going to take some time off."

"That was the plan but since I have to resign my position as fire chief, because the town can't have a murderer running the fire hall, right? We've decided to open a bed-and-breakfast—together."

"That's wonderful! Congratulations."

"Now, if I can only get Martha to forgive me for the things I've done, I'd feel much better about it all. She still won't even look at me."

"I'm sure all she needs is a little time, and then she'll come around."

"I hope so, because I have a feeling that she won't be happy until I'm locked up."

"You made bail, obviously. So I'm sure the courts can see that what you did was for family and show some leniency in your final verdict." She squeezed his arm. "I'm sure eventually Martha will, too."

"Yeah, I hope so, for the sake of Mellissa and the kids. Even though the charge is voluntary manslaughter and not murder because the death occurred in a fit of rage after I discovered what Brett planned to do with Emma, the fact still remains that I did take the time to move the body and stage the scene behind Martha's shop to punish her for disowning me." He ran his hand over his ginger hair. "That's the part of the case my lawyer is afraid the prosecutor will focus on, which means I could do some hefty prison time."

"Yes, but can't a doctor testify to your state of mind at the time? After all, you and your wife were separating. You weren't thinking clearly, and your anger with Martha, whom you thought of like a mother, when she rejected you after being so close for so long, you just snapped."

"You should be a defense lawyer."

"No thanks." Addie chuckled. "I think I'll stick to my books and solving the mysteries in them and leave the real-life work up to the professionals."

"Did I hear right?" Simon asked. "You're going to quit this amateur sleuthing business?"

"I'm going to have to as it appears. I'm not very good at it. I didn't solve the mystery of Paige's missing book, and when it comes to rare books, that's one I should have been able to figure out."

"So, the answer to my question is no? Because you can't stay away from a challenge, and we'll spend all our free time together hunting down this book, right?" He gave her a teasing smile as they took their seats at the long dining table.

She glanced across the table at Ken sharing a good-natured laugh with his son-in-law Darren, and whispered to Simon, "He's going to be the first one we investigate. He's hung around after he was cleared of the murder, and there must have been a reason for it."

"You're not buying the whole family together thing?"

"I'm having trouble with it, especially after all these years. I think it's more like twenty-five thousand reasons he's still hanging around."

"Peanut!" Paige yelled up the staircase. "Dinner's ready!"

"I'm coming," the little girl's small voice called back, and before long Emma thudded down the stairs into the dining room.

"You can sit beside Addie over there."

"Addie," she squealed. "Look at the book I got for my birthday." She grinned and held the duck book in front of Addie's face.

"I know, pumpkin. I gave it to you."

"Oh right." She giggled, climbed onto her chair, and looked at Addie with wide blue eyes. "You called me pumpkin?"

"Pumpkin is the name my grandmother used to call me, I guess—"

"Addie called you that because you're as yummy as the pumpkin pie we're having for dessert." Martha set a bowl of mashed potatoes in front of Emma.

"That's funny," giggled Emma. "Everybody has a different name for me."

"Oh, what else do people call you?" Paige tucked a napkin under Emma's chin.

"You and Grandma call me peanut. Addie calls me pumpkin. Uncle Keef calls me cupcake, and Daddy called me conductor."

"Conductor?" Paige's hand hesitated. "That's a funny name for a little girl, isn't it?"

"He said it was because I had the golden ticket."

"What on earth are you talking about?"

"Here, I'll show you." She hopped down from her chair and raced out the door and upstairs. A moment later, they could all hear a *thump, thump, thump* on the steps.

"What are you doing?" Paige called.

"Getting the ticket to show you." She dragged her pink-and-purple princess backpack behind her into the dining room and plopped down on the floor, legs crossed. She unzipped the top, and her two tiny hands reached inside and pulled out a book. "This is the golden ticket. Daddy told me to keep it to take on our Dora the Explorer adventure."

Martha snatched the book from Emma's fingers and gasped.

"When did Daddy give that to you?" Paige crouched on the floor in front of her.

"The last time he was here. He told me to hide this because it was a magic ticket, and we'd need it to go on our journey."

Paige rifled through the backpack and looked up at Martha. "It's filled with clothes, and her teddy bear that I haven't been able to find. Oh my God!" Paige gasped, and clasped her hand over her mouth. "Keith, he really was planning to take her away from me for good."

Addie glanced at the green and gold gilded cover of *The Secret Garden* in Martha's hand and then at Keith. He glanced at her, and their gazes locked. A slight smile tugged at the corners of his lips. Words her father used to say after a particularly difficult family case he had to investigate came rushing back at her. *"Sometimes good people do bad things for reasons they think are for good at the time."*

Simon clasped Addie's hand in his. "It's bittersweet, isn't it?"

"Mommy read me the part when the garden is beautiful again like the one we made for Addie's window."

"Oh, peanut!" Paige cried, wrapped Emma in her arms, and placed her on her knee hugging her tight.

Addie caught a glimpse of Paige's father's paling face. An unmistakable look of disappointment flashed in his eyes as he shifted uneasily, gaping at the recovered book. She glanced to the young mother reading to her child perched on her lap and at Bill, who gazed adoringly at Martha as she dabbed at her tear-filled eyes with the corner of her apron. Addie laid her head on Simon's shoulder. "You asked me if I was going to give up amateur sleuthing," she whispered.

"Yeah?"

"I've decided . . . I can't—I won't, as long as it involves people I care about."

"I know," he whispered, as he laid his head on hers. "That's just one of the many reasons why I love you as much as I do."

His words released a swarm of butterflies in her chest, and Addie gazed up at him. The look in his eyes clearly expressed all the love she was feeling, too. Her lips quivered, but still refused to repeat the words back to him. In her life, those three little words had led to grief and pain after they were uttered. She never wanted to feel that way again. His tender smile told her—he understood what the light in her eyes meant even though her voice remained silent—as he pulled her closer to his side and softly kissed her cheek.

Connect with Us

Visit us online at
KensingtonBooks.com
to read more from your favorite authors, see books
by series, view reading group guides, and more.

Join us on social media

for sneak peeks, chances to win books and prize packs,
and to share your thoughts with other readers.

facebook.com/kensingtonpublishing
twitter.com/kensingtonbooks

Tell us what you think!

To share your thoughts, submit a review,
or sign up for our eNewsletters, please visit:
KensingtonBooks.com/TellUs.